KRINGLE

BY **TONY ABBOTT**

ILLUSTRATED BY
GREG CALL

SCHOLASTIC PRESS ❋ NEW YORK

Library of Congress Cataloging-in-Publication Data
Abbott, Tony.
Kringle / by Tony Abbott ; illustrated by Greg Call.—1st ed.
p. cm.
Summary: In the fifth century A.D., as order retreats from Britain with the departing Roman Army,
orphaned, twelve-year-old Kringle determines to rescue his beloved guardian from the evil goblins who
terrorize the countryside by kidnapping and enslaving humans and, in the process, with the
help of elves and others along the way, discovers his true destiny.
ISBN 0-439-74942-5
Santa Claus—Juvenile fiction. [1. Santa Claus—Fiction. 2. Orphans—Fiction. 3. Goblins—Fiction.
4. Middle Ages—Fiction. 5. Coming of age—Fiction.] I. Call, Greg, ill. II. Title.
PZ7.A1587Kr 2005   [Fic]—dc22

12   11   10   9   8   7   6   5   4   3   2   1   5   6   7   8   9   10/0
Printed in the U.S.A.   23
First edition, October 2005
The text type was set in 12-point Caslon
Book design by Kristina Albertson

FOREVER FOR MY CHILDREN,
JANE AND LUCY
—T. A.

FOR RYAN AND AVERY,
SUN, MOON & STARS
—G. C.

C O N T

E N T S

FULL-PAGE ILLUSTRATIONS

KRINGLE

BOUT MYSTERY *of the boy, his early years, and how he came to be what he became, I suppose everyone everywhere has heard nearly every kind of story.*

Such mistruths and makings-up! Such fantasies!

Only a few remain who were with him from the start, and fewer still who could tell you the tale properly.

So many lies! And for so many years!

Finally, there was nothing left to do but take up the pen myself, which I had little expected to do at my age, and set down the facts from the very beginning.

That the boy had *a beginning, and that I was there for most of it, is all you need to know right now.*

So, gather around. Light the lamp. Settle yourselves into a comfortable place. Pity those who come in late, for once the story starts, it doesn't slow down much.

You might say it hasn't slowed down even now.

You might say it's still happening.

But never mind. There's time enough before we get to that. For now, shhh. Let me begin.

PART I

THE LITTLE HUT'S THATCHED ROOF, LOOSE AND CRACKED,
LET IT ALL IN: WIND AND ICE AND SNOW AND EVERYTHING. . . .

CHAPTER ONE

THE SPARROW

EEP IN THE LAND of ghosts and frost, back in the days of long ago, in the time before and a little to the left of the time we know now, when goblins roamed the land and rough tribes of men battled for this or that frozen inch of frozen earth, we might, if we turned our heads just so, peek through the eaves of a low-roofed hut, farther north than you or I would care to go, and see inside it a small boy crouched before a cold hearth.

"Tell me again," he said, his breath forming and fading in the frosty air.

Merwen bent over the hearth — yes, Merwen; that was the old woman's name. She would never let me forget her part in this story. She came from a place called Weary-All. That seems fitting. Merwen of Weary-All. She cracked some twigs and tossed them into the hearth.

"Tell you what, then?" she said. There was a little growl of

5

annoyance in her voice. And why not? It was night. Her fire was slow to light. Food was running short. The hut was freezing. Worse yet, the weather was turning more bitter by the half-minute, and the little hut's thatched roof, loose and cracked, let it all in: wind and ice and snow and everything.

"Tell me about the bird," he said.

The old woman heaved a sigh. She loved the boy. Of course she did. But how many times could she tell that tale over? Time and time again for, what, ten winters, not counting the two or so years before he could speak enough to ask for the story. Why had she ever told it to him in the first place?

"Well then, well then." She breathed out another long sigh and cast another long look into the hearth. She poked the logs around with a big stick she kept for just that purpose. One or two small flames started in the kindling and crawled up the logs like fingers — hesitant, wanting to escape.

"Merwen," he said. "The bird."

"Yes, yes!" She sank onto a low stool and turned to the boy. His long brown hair dangled on both sides of a pale little face. He *was* keeping his eyes on her, wasn't he? Those big brown eyes. He was small for his age, poor boy, and thin. But bright. Far brighter than me, she thought. Just look at his face. There's a twinkle in it! His mother told me he would *do* things. *Great* things! she said. The gods alone know what that means. But the boy does think about everything, doesn't he? Wonder about everything, say everything, *ask* everything! He always asks for this story on cold winter nights. So. It must be winter again!

The boy's eyes *were* fixed on hers. Why is she fussing so very long with her hands? he wondered. And why does she keep poking the fire with that stick and looking at me and not saying anything? Do I have to ask again? "Merwen —"

"Fine! Fine. But before the bird," she said finally, "before any bird at all, there was the storm, you know."

"A big storm, with lots of ice," said the boy, eager to get her talking. He did love the beginning of the story. "You said it was the worst storm —"

"It was! It was. For days and nights it came down, rain to begin, then snow, then ice pelting from the sky. The world was frozen through. The great wheel of the year had wound down to nothing. The days were short, and the nights longer and slower than ever before. It was midnight on the third day and the storm was raging still, the center of it getting closer, closer, when over it all you could hear the sound of a young woman, crying. . . ."

"My mother," he said.

"'Ohhh!' she moaned. 'Ohhh-ohhhh!' It was such a sound. It had gone on for hours. And now it was midnight and storming, and right in the middle of it all, *you* cry out! You, boy! Your little howling voice added to your mother's. And all of a sudden, there you were. In my hands and in the world!"

She paused, the whole weight of her nodding slightly on the stool.

The boy lowered his eyes, then raised them to her again. They glowed like pools of dark water in the firelight. "I was born in a storm."

"Mind," she went on, "the goblins were out there, too, filthy green creatures! Faces like mud! Ears like cabbage! I knew that well enough. They were out there. This was the Goblin Long Night, after all, the longest night and very end of the year, the night goblins like best! And this was no ordinary storm, for goblins *make* storms. We know that now. But we had never heard of that terrible wand back then, or how the goblins conjure wind and snow with it. And this storm, roaring for days, had wrapped around the village and all the houses nearby. Your good father was lost to a goblin not three days before, and here they were again —"

She stopped talking so suddenly that he knew she was listening. *Listening.* He'd seen her do it every time she got to the middle of the story and mentioned the goblins. Listening was something she did often, stopping whatever she was doing, turning her head up, and closing her eyes.

He listened now, too, above the crackle of the fire. He didn't breathe. He couldn't. He knew about the terrible black-eyed creatures. He knew about their storms. He knew they had killed his father —

Was that a sound?

Was it?

He had often thought their little house was too far away from everything else. It lay nearly hidden among the trees and rocks of a sharp drop called the Bottoms on the lower edge of the Black Woods, eight hundred thousand acres of the densest, most forbidding forest in the whole north country. From the Bottoms, the nearest town of Castrum was a full day's hard walk.

"No, no. It's nothing," she said.

There was no sound now except for the low wind-wail and whistle in the eaves and the near soundless fall of snow on snow. Everything else — if there *was* anything else — was silent. Nothing stirred. Good enough. Good.

"The poor woman takes you in her arms — your tiny self wailing like a stolen child — and she smiles with love for you —"

"And it comes!" said the boy.

"It comes! Out of the wind it comes! A sparrow! A *sparrow*, I tell you. Lost? Gone mad? Frighted by the goblins? Who knows! It was and is a mystery! But a sparrow it was, flying in the dead of night. Right through the open eaves and into the room it came in a sweep of snow, shivering and shaking, and then is gone again. Gone! The poor thing wasn't warm an instant but was lost again, poor sparrow. . . ."

She stopped, turned her face to the fire, and gave another long sigh.

The boy frowned. "But before it went —"

"Before it went —" she cried, leaping into her story again, "the tip of that sparrow's wing *struck* a bell hanging over the fire. I hear it still! Two little notes, more said than rung, more sung than said. In that moment, over all the wind's raging, your mother said — oh, how I never will forget it — *'That's his name, that sound is his name!'* And she spoke the word to me."

The boy stood now, his mouth open and his eyes wide and wet.

"The sparrow was gone in an instant." She sighed, exhausted by her own excitement. "What became of it in the wide world, I cannot tell. Your mother, poor soul, was gone then, too. With one single breath. *Hooo.* Like that.

"They heard the bell, too, of course. The goblins did. Don't ask me if it was him, their terrible king. I don't know. But whoever was out there heard the bell ringing out your name and they came and I wrapped you in a cloak and we fled from place to place until here we are. The two of us, you and me, alone together these twelve years."

She finally drifted off to silence, as she had done every time before.

A minute or two passed with neither of them speaking. Then, as he had done every time before, the boy crossed the room to a wooden box that lay on a shelf by the window. He took it down, set it on the table, opened it, carefully removed a red cloth, and unwrapped a tiny bell.

He shook it.

Kringle!

CHAPTER TWO

GOBLINS!

BEAUTIFUL BELL? Exquisite bell? Well-toned bell? It was nothing of the sort.

All Kringle knew, all anyone knew, was that when his mother, Elwyna, was a child, she had once found a lamb caught in a holly thicket. She had untangled the poor creature and freed it. The next morning she found the lamb's little bell in a shoe at her bedside. Where it came from, who put it there, no one knew.

When she grew up, Elwyna gave the bell to her husband, Halig, to wear. Halig was a woodcutter, and every night when Elwyna heard the bell, she knew he would soon be home from the Black Woods.

The bell had a tone so soft, it was almost a whisper. Yet when you jangled it, it clearly sounded as if someone were speaking a name. Someone like an angel, perhaps.

Kringle!

But the sound of the bell brings me back to our story.

For besides Kringle and Merwen, there was a third person who heard the bell ring that cold winter night. A person tramping through the Black Woods at the head of a snaking band of fellows. A person — if we can even call him that — with long, deep ears the color of boiled cabbage.

A goblin?

A goblin!

When Kringle's bell rang, those long green ears pricked up, and a dozen footsteps slapped to a halt in the woods outside.

"What did my mother do first?" Kringle asked, unaware. "Tell me everything that happened."

Merwen rose from her stool. Was it simply the wind swooshing through the branches outside? Through the eaves? Or was it something else? Her heart thumped.

"I put you . . . in her arms," she said softly, moving quickly across the room to him. "And she said . . . she said . . . oh, Kringle, hush. . . ."

Merwen closed her eyes and listened again.

"Merwen, no. You don't think . . ." His heart froze. "Goblins?" he asked. But he already knew. "Goblins!"

"Hush, Sparrow," she whispered. "Don't be afraid. *Don't be afraid!* Don't let them feel your fear. But . . . I think . . . they . . . are . . . here. . . ."

Goblins! Oh, but they were an evil, ruthless bunch: stingy, crabbed, ragged, thoughtless, menacing, murderous, and mean!

Nail biters and clipping spitters! Lurkers and slitherers! Ground dwellers and night attackers!

Without ever having seen one, Kringle knew as much about the spindle-legged, dirty beings as one could know. They had green skin from head to toe that looked like mottled leather smeared with mud. Their faces were very long, and their ears skinny and narrow. Tiny black eyes, cunning and shifty, were set wide on either side of noses that were no more than ridges of bone between sunken cheeks. Their green heads were pointed at the top and bald, except for a few sprouts of greasy, white hair. Goblins were nasty creatures of the night who fed on fear and stole, stole, stole!

Merwen quietly lowered two heavy planks across the door frame. Then she pulled something down from a shelf next to the hearth, wrapped it quickly in a cloth, and handed it to Kringle. "Put this in your father's cloak."

"What is it?" he asked.

She shook her head. "Bread."

"But —"

He started to move to the window, but Merwen pulled him down to the floor. "Don't let them see you! Filthy filchers and snatchers. They'll take you!"

Take you. Kringle crouched under the table, scraping his knees on the floor and banging his head. The goblins *were* thieves, he knew that. The worst kind of thieves. And the thing they most liked to steal was children.

No one knew why, but there was some terrible goblin secret that drove them to steal children. At first, they took those whose parents had died in the wars. Roman children. River children. Hill children. Heath children, like himself. Then they began kidnapping little ones right under their parents' noses. It made no difference.

It began, so Merwen had told him, soon after he was born. More and more children had vanished to the green horde. It was said they brought their little captives to the dreadful goblin palace, hidden in the Black Woods far from the sight of men. No one knew exactly where the palace was, of course, because if you found your way to it, you never returned to tell about it.

To help in their terrible deeds, the goblins had come into possession of a strange device. Ithgar, they called it. The Iron Wand. What a thing that was! A short staff made of black iron frozen at its tip into the shape of a claw, Ithgar held power over the wind and snow and ice, and no more so than on Long Night, the very end of the year, when night swallows up the day. Using Ithgar, the goblins had learned to conjure storms. The Iron Wand was Morgo's greatest weapon.

Morgo?

Our cast of characters grows.

Morgo was the Goblin King, if so grand a term as "king" can be used for such a base and sniveling creature. If all the bad smells of all the sewers in all the cities, and all the meanness of those who crave what isn't theirs, and all the foul thoughts of those who never see the sun could be massed in a single place, given form, and called a name, that name would be Morgo.

Oh, but Morgo's dark desire had no limits. He wanted everything. And if he didn't get something, Morgo was all the more ravenous, and vicious, and angry until he got it.

Was Morgo angry now? The little band of goblins at the edge of the Black Woods feared he might be. Already three hours into their nightly raid, they had not yet found a single object of worth, and empty-handed was not how they wanted to return to Morgo's palace. It was while scouring the edge of the woods for anything to make their light sacks heavier that the band's leader — an ugly creature with powerful arms and dark ears named Snegg — had suddenly halted.

Hadn't he just heard a tiny sound?

— *ingle!*

He had!

"Saaaaah!" Snegg hissed. "There is a house near!" His hand went up, and his five companions stared through the trees. "See it there? The light? The light always tells. . . ."

How strange it was, that in that single moment the three of them — Kringle and Merwen inside, and Snegg outside — mimicked one another's actions. They were all *listening*.

But while Kringle and Merwen heard nothing, hoping that if there were any goblins, they would pass by, Snegg knew that the hut's sudden silence meant that he and his band might have been found out. And when a goblin is found out, he attacks.

"Attackkkk!" cried Snegg.

In an instant, the green band leaped from the woods down to the Bottoms and began hurling themselves at the hut's door. *Whump-whump-whump!*

It was short work. The planks splintered, and the door swung inward wildly. Snegg and a fat goblin shrieked as they tumbled into the room. Two others followed.

"Child!" the fat one cried.

"No, no!" Kringle gasped, scrambling farther under the table. He reached for something to defend himself with, but found only the empty bell box — *where was the bell?* He threw the box at the goblins.

"Ha!" snarled Snegg. He caught it handily. The creature's eyes widened ravenously. "I take you, boy!"

"You'll have to cross me first!" Merwen snapped. She swung her fire stick, first one way, then the other, and caught Snegg and the fat goblin both in the side. They went down hard into their fellows, toppling back across the threshold.

"Kringle, get in the corner!" she yelled, and he crawled to the back of the hut.

"Geffo! Patcha!" Snegg cried, untangling himself from the heap of goblins.

Kringle heard the cracking of wood as the window shutter burst open and two more goblins dived into the room, their tiny eyes growing instantly as large and black as blocks of coal. All six of them were inside now. The latest two swept past Merwen and took hold of Kringle's ankles, binding them as tightly as bands of iron.

"Get off me!" the boy cried. He grabbed a pot from the edge of the hearth and swung it at the attackers. One fell back, but Kringle lost his pot to the other, who screeched with delight. The boy crawled free and held the stool in front of him. "You stay away!"

Snegg leaped to the top of the table now, and Merwen slapped her stick at his legs, knocking him onto his back. Yelling at the top of her lungs, she threw a cloak over Kringle's shoulders, snatched the stool from him, and with an arm more powerful than he had ever expected, thrust him right out the door and into the night.

"But — wait — no!" he cried, falling headlong into the snow. "Merwen, you need me —"

"Go, go, go —" she sputtered. "Run — to Castrum — now —"

At the word *Castrum*, Snegg shrieked suddenly. Merwen threw herself back against the door and slammed it shut from the inside. Kringle heard a wail, then a sudden crash of wood against the floor.

"Merwen!" he called out feebly. Grasping at the door from the outside, he pushed and pushed, desperately trying to get in. But the full weight of the woman was against it, and Kringle could not budge it. He stumbled to the window only to be thrown back to the ground: Snow was pouring out of it like a river!

"A storm!" he gasped, jumping back. "Ithgar!"

"Ith*garrrrr*!" Snegg howled as the storm exploded inside the little hut.

Kringle battered at the door again. But icicles were shooting out the eaves now, and the roof's thatch was blowing up and away, scattering straw in a great whirling circle of white around the house. The whole hut shuddered on its foundations.

"Go now, boy!" Merwen cried above the roar.

Kringle stared wide-eyed while two, three, four shapes lunged toward the window at him. Merwen's staff jutted into the frame, and the goblins were hurled back into their own storm.

"Run, Kringle!" she yelled. "Get away —"

He didn't want to leave, but his legs took over. He ran with all his might. He was a hundred yards into the woods before he knew what he was doing. Then he stopped and turned. Ice was flowing like thick water out of the window. It grew five feet high, then ten feet, joining with the swirling snow in a rising tower, completely surrounding the house with ever-faster winds.

"Merwen!" he shouted. "Merwen —"

All of a sudden, the hut exploded with a powerful blast. Kringle was thrown back into the trees. Through the whirling blizzard he saw green shapes rushing away into the night. There was a wail, but whether it was Merwen's or the goblins', he couldn't tell, and it soon joined in the general shriek of the wind.

It wasn't long before the storm ended, dying away in a coiling wisp of snow. Silence fell over the woods again. The Bottoms lay in a shambles of ice and splintered wood.

"Merwen!" he cried again, but there was no answer.

Kringle stumbled to the pile of wood that had been his home. Stunned, angry, he stared and stared, circling around it. He walked slowly at first, then more quickly, darkening the snow with his prints, wishing he could turn time back to the moment he'd rung that bell.

"Goblins, I hate you!" he said over and over. "I hate you. I wish I could . . . I wish . . ."

But Kringle didn't even know what he wished! Twelve years with Merwen hadn't given him the words to say what he really felt. Round and round the ruins he paced until he finally slumped to the ground under the nearest tree, staring fiercely at the wreckage of his home, and sobbed.

How long did he stay there? Hours, at least. Morning came. Morning went. Afternoon came. Evening went. Night fell over the woods a second time and another dawn rose after it, and not a single soul came anywhere near the house.

"No one," he said to himself. "No one. Of course, no one. No one ever comes to the Bottoms!"

By now the goblin storm was long over, but snow had begun to fall from the sky, covering everything in a veil of white powder. On the pale morning of the third day, frozen, hungry, empty of will and full of sorrow, Kringle rose and searched the remains of the hut one last time.

The bell was not there. Nearly nothing usable was left. He took only one thing from the storm-wrecked house: Merwen's fire stick. It towered over his head, more a staff than a stick. He gripped it in his hand. It was a heavy, six-foot length of oak, blackened from fire and forked at its upper end like two stout fingers pointing skyward. Everything about the stick reminded him of Merwen. The whorls in its grain and the nicks in its curves were like the wrinkles and dimples in her old face. Its curved midpoint was burnished almost black by the oils from her hand.

"So," he said, trembling. "This is mine now." Catching himself, he added, "Until I give it to you again. That's right.

I'll keep it for you, Merwen. I'll give it to you when I find you."

And finding her was all that he thought of now. He wiped his mind clean of anything else, just as he wiped his cheeks of tears. When he closed his eyes he imagined her alive. He had to believe that she was. Whatever else happened, wherever his search took him, he would find her.

"I will, Merwen. I will. And then we'll find a place to hide again, and we'll live . . . and . . . well . . . we'll just live!"

Shaking the snow from his father's cloak, Kringle pulled it tight around his small shoulders and tucked it up over his belt so it wouldn't drag behind him on the frozen ground. Then he planted the big staff in the snow and pushed away from the wreckage of the Bottoms, not looking back from that moment on.

Three hours later, he found the road.

CHAPTER THREE

A KINGLY THING

THE ROAD. Even buried under days of new snow, it was easy enough for Kringle to find the road. He came hobbling over a low, windswept rise in the land, squinting through the driving flakes, muttering all the while — "Where is it, Merwen? You said it was nearby. Three miles, not more. So where is it? Wait . . . you were right . . . there it is, there it is!" — and there it was.

Merwen had told him all about the road (hadn't he constantly asked her what life was like outside the Bottoms?). And it was just as she had said.

The road ran higher than the surrounding ground and was flat and straight and bordered on both sides by shallow ditches. It stretched boldly up the western side of the Black Woods and straight north across the white land.

"Good road," he said aloud. "Straight road. Fast road."

Stepping over its eastern ditch, he set his boots firmly on it and stamped on the stones. "If I take this road, it'll keep me away from the goblin woods and bring me all the way to Castrum. I'll get help there. And I'll find you, Merwen. Don't ever think I won't."

The old woman was right: Kringle said *everything*. When a thing was on his mind to say, he said it, whether someone was there to hear it or not. What did he care? He had words and he would use them. He had rarely been quiet about anything and he wasn't going to start now.

"So, to Castrum," he said.

Where Kringle's staff sank to the roadbed, it struck gravel in some places and pieces of flint and shale in others. The road was as wide as six broad-shouldered men standing abreast. Or rather, *marching* abreast.

"Warriors from beyond the sea came here centuries ago," Merwen had told him. "They cut up the land and laid the road for their armies to travel on."

"Romans," Kringle had said then. He said it again now as he strode along. "Romans built this road."

Romans *had* built that road. They were towering conquerors from the warm south who had swept into the country long, long ago. Some stories said they sailed in three hundred ships with ten thousand men, and then more came and more, until they beat down the native tribes with their unquenchable might. They needed sturdy, flat roads to get their foot legions and horse soldiers and wagons and carts quickly from one place to another. They had built the town he was on his way to. In fact, they had built many roads and many towns and cities all over the country. The Romans were like that. They had already been building things in the country for over four hundred years: walls, forts, bridges, cities. It was the way they did things. They saw a country they liked and went there and settled their legions in and built things and told the native people what to do.

"Until now," Kringle muttered, huddling in his cloak and pushing forward into the slanting snow. "Merwen told me that."

True. Until now.

Because now the Romans were using those same flat roads to leave the country and return to their home in the south. First, they pulled up from the lowlands hundreds of miles south of the Black Woods. Then they abandoned towns and forts here and there in the other parts of the country. Pretty soon they were leaving all over. It was only a matter of time before they left the north, too.

"The Roman king in his castle far away told the soldiers they must return home," Merwen had said. "There are plenty of enemies at their own doorstep for them to fight."

"Goblins?" Kringle had asked.

"No, no, goblins only like the north!" she had said. "Goblins like the snow and ice and darkness. The south is full of sun and warm skies. Other tribes are attacking Rome. The soldiers are needed there more than here."

"So they're leaving us?"

"They are," she had said. "'Home,' they were told, and home they are going!"

And home they went. They left in the night and took the light with them. If you had been a bird you might have seen the fires going out one by one by one all across the land when the Romans picked up and left. And what did they leave behind? Just what they found when they got there. Tribes of poor heath folk and peak dwellers, forest people and midlanders.

Did the goblins know the legions were leaving? Of course they did. They had been waiting for it. No sooner was a city or an outpost abandoned than goblin raiders began to emerge from their earthen kingdom more audaciously. They came out in the waning hours of daylight and stayed abroad until the very first fingers of dawn streaked the sky. And they used every hour to commit their devilish acts of thievery!

Of course, goblins weren't the only ones who came. Once word spread that the Roman armies were on their way out, others came, too.

"Invaders!" Merwen had said. "And pirates!"

Greedy tribes from across the sea came in dozens of ships with hundreds of warriors. Emboldened by the departing legions, they preyed on the native folk. They wanted whatever they could put their hands on and sail away with.

"Pirates! Invaders!" snarled Kringle, as he trekked north over the snowy road. "Why don't they leave us in peace?" Yet even as he said this he wondered if peace, like Merwen herself, was one more thing lost at the Bottoms.

He pressed on, fighting the snow and wind, muttering to himself and pausing only to wrap and rewrap his father's giant cloak around him.

Now about that cloak. It was the deep reddish-brown color of crushed berries, and it was rather a mystery how his father, Halig, had come by it. Merwen told Kringle some hundred or so times that his father happened to be wearing it when Kringle's mother found him alone and dead at the foot of a half-chopped tree in the Black Woods.

Kringle stopped and turned toward the forest now. He imagined his mother, Elwyna, already carrying him in her womb, listening that long-ago night for the sound of the bell. Listening, but not hearing. How she ran through the forest! How she stopped, aghast, when she saw her fallen husband! All around him in the snow were strange little tracks. She guessed right away that goblins were to blame. She knelt by Halig and kissed him, but he had already given up his spirit.

The darkest part of the story came next. For when Elwyna heard noises all around her in the woods, she quickly draped herself in Halig's cloak, loosened the lamb's little bell from around his neck, and hurried for home.

"But the woods tricked her," Merwen had told Kringle. "She was lost for a day and a night in the storm before she stumbled onto my doorstep. For a second day she lay in a fever, telling me everything. On midnight of the third day, you were born, small and pale and as noisy as a flock of sheep at suppertime."

Last winter was the first year he could stand up in the cloak without tripping. Its bottom edge still scraped along the ground, but you wouldn't have been able to get it off him if you tried. Being inside it was like being wrapped in his parents' embrace. He felt their presence in its strange, dark weave. To Kringle, wearing the cloak was like being home.

"And since now I have no home . . . ," he said. "And no one . . ."

Well, that was true, too. He was alone. Completely alone, in fact. He had not seen a single soul since the goblin attack four days before.

Now, finally, on the morning of the fifth day, as he came over a slight rise in the land, he spied a thin coil of smoke drifting up over the horizon. "Castrum! Merwen, the town! You were right!" His heart leaped. He ran toward the smoke as quickly as his tired legs would carry him.

Long before anyone within the city walls could possibly hear him, he began calling out, "Hello, there! Hey, hello!"

After running a mile or so, he saw the stone wall rising into view below the smoky sky. The road ran straight up to a gate flanked by two tall watchtowers.

"Hey!" he bellowed. "I need help! Hello! Hello —"

Kringle ran and ran until he couldn't run anymore and had to slow down to catch his breath. The Romans had long been friendly to the native peoples — "the heath and forest dwellers," they called them — and after all, wasn't Castrum where his father had sold much of his wood a dozen years ago? But as he approached, he realized that there had been no answer from inside the walls nor any kind of movement on top of them. Looking down the length of the wall in both directions for some minutes longer, he still saw nothing.

One of the gates stood slightly ajar. Kringle felt his neck bristle. "I don't like this."

"Not at all. Why isn't there any movement?"

"Or any sound?"

"This is Castrum, after all. Lots of people live here."

Merwen had told him Castrum was "a kingly thing," a city of large walls and houses and towers. "The work of giants," she had said.

He noticed now that the smoke billowing up from behind the wall was coming, thick and black, from many places at once, as if from open fires, not from chimneys. Trembling, fearing the worst, Kringle moved carefully up to the gate and peered around it. He didn't see much. A guardhouse inside the gate. The corner of a block of stables. Gripping his staff tightly, he stepped in.

"Oh! No, no, no!"

A large hall in the center of the town was smoldering. Its tower was cracked in half and leaning sideways across its foundation. The big, gabled roof had an enormous gash in it, and he saw snow pouring down into the hole while flames leaped up from inside. Several buildings in the distance were completely blasted to the ground, their timbers and stones scattered everywhere amid snowdrifts as high as a man.

"Goblin storm!" he hissed. "Goblin fire!"

He tensed suddenly. Were the creatures still there? He didn't smell them. Were they the same goblins that had stolen Merwen? Perhaps they were. . . .

As he moved silently through the streets, he saw hundreds of webbed goblin tracks crisscrossing the muddy snow. He passed house after house either iced over or burned or both. A stone shrine to several Roman gods stood open and roofless, its statues shattered and torched. A second altar was ravaged, all its gift offerings dashed to the ground.

When he heard the faint creak of wood on wood, he stopped, breathless. He closed his eyes and listened. He *listened*. There it was again. His heart pounded in his chest. He glanced back at the gate. No, it was too far away now.

Merwen had told him not to be afraid. "Don't let them feel your fear," she had said.

"Easier said than done," he told himself.

"I'll have to fight."

"Of course I'll fight. Wait. Me? Fight? I'm just a boy!"

"Still . . ."

Clutching his staff even more tightly, Kringle moved around the side of a house to the alley behind it. Standing nearly empty was a large wagon with an old, saggy-backed horse tied to it. Wind howled down the alley, the horse shifted, and the wheels creaked again.

He let his breath out slowly. "So, all right. Nothing —"

Suddenly, two shapes — not goblins — hustled down the alley toward him. One of them looked up.

"Oh, my dear boy!" It was a woman. She had her arms around an old man who hurried next to her with his eyes closed. "Why are you still in Castrum?" she asked.

"I just got here," he said. "What happened? Was it . . . goblins?"

The woman nodded, hurrying the old man to the wagon. "First came the storms, then the fires," she said. "They burst upon us in the dead of night. They came for the children, then they took everything else. Swords, armor, wagons, pots and pans, they drove all but a few of the horses off —"

"The goblins took my friend, Merwen!" Kringle blurted

out. "They tried to get me, but she fought them off. She saved me."

"You were lucky," said the woman. "They stole the poor children, innocent souls. All taken."

Taken. The children all taken by those terrible creatures? He couldn't imagine the horror of it. He felt an ache in his chest, but held back a sob. "Did the soldiers fight back?"

"The legion left two weeks ago!" the woman said, helping the old man up to the wagon's seat, then pulling herself up next to him. "We were defenseless. We stayed too long."

"Everyone's gone?" said Kringle. "But I came here for help."

"We would have been gone, too," said the woman, "but my father was too sick. We hid during the attack. . . ." She paused. "Boy, come with us. We're going to Corbridge. You can't stay here." She reached down from the wagon, opening her hand to him.

Go with her? Leave? But he couldn't. He couldn't.

Kringle shook his head. "I have to stay. Merwen is out there. The goblins took her instead of me. I was hoping to get help here. But I still have to find her."

The old man looked blankly at him. The woman sighed. "It's foolish — foolish, boy. The goblins are everywhere now. But you know best. May you find your friend safe. Be careful."

With a snap of the reins, the woman guided the horse

down the alley, around to the gate towers, and quickly out between them. He ran after her, but stopped at the gate. The wagon made its way slowly up the snow-covered road, skirting the edge of the woods and heading north, then east, along the road. Kringle ran up the inside stairs to the ramparts and watched the wagon fade into the whirling snow until it was gone.

Exhausted, he slumped down on the wall. "Now what, Merwen? There's no Castrum anymore, no one here, no one to help me. Now what? I've got to find you. But how?"

The morning wore on, gray and cold. His shoulders ached, his stomach burned with emptiness, and his feet were frozen. Long after the wagon was gone, he found himself staring at the spot where it had disappeared, wondering whether letting the woman go without him had been a mistake.

But how could he be expected to know what to do? Every moment was new to him now. Hadn't Merwen taken him in twelve years before and rarely let him out of her sight? Hadn't they hidden in one hut after another after another until she felt they were finally safe at the Bottoms? The Bottoms! That little house was a part of his life he had no hope of recovering. He was alone. He didn't know what to do. And he was hungry.

"Very hungry," he grumbled. He peered into the pocket of his cloak. No matter how little he had eaten over the last few days, pinching ever-smaller bites of bread from the tiny bits Merwen had made him stuff in there, his stomach hadn't been full since he'd left the Bottoms. So, was there anything more in there? He dug his frozen fingers in to try to feel something his eyes hadn't seen. But no. There was nothing else. The five crusts had finally run out.

"Fine," he said to himself, and, "all right, then," and "oh, well." He might have cursed. He certainly thought about cursing; there were some quite bad curses he was beginning to think of and might have spoken. But it wouldn't have changed things. It was all the same, either way. He was hungry, alone, and without a single idea of what to do next.

It was a good thing, then, that a movement near the edge of the woods happened to catch his eye. When he looked he saw a tiny thing of white and brown and black swoop down from the gray sky and drop to the ground between the wall and the forest. It was a bird, and it was pushing the snow aside with its little beak — *flick, flick, flick!* Kringle jumped up on the wall.

"What?" he said. And again, "What!"

Was it . . . a sparrow? It was a sparrow!

"Oh, wait!" He ran down the stairs two at a time, tore through the gate, and raced across the snow toward the forest. "Wait . . . wait . . ."

Flick, flick! The bird dug at the icy crust and into the snow, probing, flicking, bobbing, until it stilled and dipped its head into a hole. Kringle ran to the bird, watching its tiny beak clamp on to something hard and small. In a flash, the sparrow was back in the air, winging into the sky.

"No, wait, wait, wait —"

But the bird looped up and away so quickly into the gray clouds that it was gone before he knew it. He watched and watched the skies, but it did not reappear. Gone! Gone. All the way gone. Then, just as he was about to turn away, he heard — Oh, glory that he heard it at all — he heard the sound of his name being spoken from beyond the clouds. It was a sound more said than rung, more sung than said. It was the sound of his bell.

Kringle!

He jumped in the snow and roared with joy. "The bell! Merwen! Merwen! The sparrow found the bell!"

CHAPTER FOUR

WINTER GIFTS

RINGLE WAS AMAZED at how quickly he understood what must have happened. The only way his bell could ever have gotten to that particular spot in the snow, he reasoned, was if Merwen had had it with her when the goblins kidnapped her from the Bottoms!

"She had it," he said, gazing at the hole in the snow, then at the woods beyond, "and at the first chance the goblins weren't watching her, she must have thrown it here, hoping I would somehow see it. Well, I didn't see it, Merwen. But the sparrow did, and it shook the bell, and I heard it, and that's just as good!"

His heart racing, he stepped toward the Black Woods. He wanted to rush right in — the first trees were no more than a hundred feet from where he stood — but he knew it would be foolish beyond belief. "We're talking about goblins, after all. Be careful. Be careful."

And he was careful. Leaving the abandoned city behind him, he moved slowly across the snow to the edge of the forest and stopped. He listened. He heard no sound of goblins — "Wretched creatures!" he said. "Nasty beings!" — but, sure enough, just inside the cover of the trees he saw signs of their trail, a slithering line of webbed tracks in the midst of which were Merwen's tramping boot prints. "Yes, yes — oh, yes!" he said, his heart thundering. "I found you!"

It was now going on midday. Since the goblins moved only under cover of darkness (they hated sunlight, Merwen had told him, and never traveled in it), he reasoned that the trail might have been made as recently as five or six hours ago.

"Well, all right," he said. "There's no question of what I have to do now, is there? If I hope to find Merwen again — and I do! — I have to enter the woods."

"What? Enter the Black Woods?"

"Well, there's no help to be had in the town."

"No, none."

"No help to be had anywhere."

"I suppose."

"So, I have to go into the woods, and that's that!"

And that was that. Kringle left the open ground and stepped in among the trees. Carefully, his senses as alert as they had been on his last night in the Bottoms, he followed the goblin tracks, weaving just inside the forest's edge. He did this for one hour. Two hours. He imagined the goblins staying always in the shelter of the woods, but peering out beyond the trees, ever within striking distance of any light they chanced to see. Up along the fringe of the forest, then deeper into the darkness he went. All the while, snow continued to fall, slanting into the trees from the west and making the trail harder and harder to follow.

To make matters more confusing, when he entered the thicker woods, he became aware of noises all around him. There was pattering and whispering and snapping and splashing and crackling. Not goblin sounds, he knew. Goblins were near silent when they moved and besides, it was still day. These were the noises of the woodland creatures. Weasels were slithering in and out of the underbrush, and stoats were there, too, as well as squirrels in the trees and badgers and moles on the ground and otters in the streams. And they were all moving as he moved, and he knew they knew he was there, and that they were watching him.

Another hour, and another. Finally, night was coming on, and he began losing the tracks, picking them up, and losing them again.

Now a thought was beginning to form in his head.

"To follow goblins at nighttime would be foolish. Nighttime is *their* time."

Besides, wasn't he out of food and rather lost?

Completely lost, I should say. Kringle looked around at the darkening woods, and the snow fell on him and fell and fell and fell. Soon he couldn't see more than a few feet in any direction.

But Kringle was, well, Kringle. Which meant that he would not look back and would go on, anyway. This was probably something he learned his first day on this earth. He had to get going that day or be kidnapped by goblins, and he had been going ever since. Hadn't he and Merwen lived at five places before they came to the Bottoms, staying each time one step ahead of the goblins? Besides all that, he had a hope that now he was going somewhere rather than nowhere, and so he would go on.

But he was so dead on his feet. His legs felt as heavy as logs. He needed to rest or he would fall in the snow and stay there and freeze and, well, that wouldn't be good. Heaving a very big sigh near the foot of a pine tree with broad boughs that drooped nearly to the ground, he said, "So, here, then?"

He looked both right and left. "Yes, here. It's as good as anyplace, I think."

"It's settled, then. Just a very short little sleep. Just the night and no more. All right?"

"All right. Then, when morning comes, I'll go even deeper into the woods, where the tree cover is thicker and the snow not so deep" — he yawned then — "and I'll pick up the goblin trail again."

"And, of course, stay clear of goblins the whole time. That way, I'll find her."

He yawned again. "Good plan."

With that, he squirreled himself into a small space under the branches, wrapped his giant cloak around himself nearly twice, laid his staff across his lap, and closed his eyes. The last thing he saw was the snow falling more lightly now. "Good," he murmured. "Good."

Now, I like to believe that everything happens for a reason. *Whose* reason, well, that's quite another question. But I believe that there is always some sense in what happens, no matter how silly or harsh or wonderful or unimportant it might seem.

And that goes for the hat and the apple. If you stretch the idea, you could say it went for the tree, too.

When Kringle slept, what did he dream about but his old house at the Bottoms? The Bottoms. Merwen was talking softly to him from her stool by the hearth. She was telling him about the Romans and pirates and goblins, his mother and father and everything. He asked and he asked and she told and she told. This went on for a long time, until she finally got around to the bell. But when he took it from its box as usual and shook it, the sound rang in his ears so loudly that he woke up on the instant.

Kringle!

He woke with a start, I tell you, and had the immediate and terrifying sense of an animal gripping his head with two large paws.

"Get off! Ahhh! Get off!" he shouted, jerking himself up from the ground and wrestling the creature off his head. When he had finally swatted it away, he tripped over the folds of his own cloak, tumbled into the snow, and found himself face-to-face with something small and red.

"What are you?" he cried, his heart beating wildly.

The thing didn't answer him. It didn't move, either.

Kringle crawled away from it, then reached back with his staff and prodded it. It didn't run or jump or growl or do anything. He slid the staff under it and lifted, carefully pulling the thing closer (very close, in fact, because it was still dark) until he finally dropped it to the ground next to him and found it to be nothing more or less than a cone of fabric with a woolly ring of fleece around the edge.

"A hat?" he said.

It was a hat. It was a hat, he decided, that had somehow gotten onto his head while he slept.

"Wh-wh-who's there?" Kringle stammered, glancing around. He immediately hushed himself. It was still night. "Goblins?"

But he saw no one and heard nothing. He sniffed the hat in his hands. It had a vaguely sheepy smell, which was not a goblin smell, and was still warm from being on his head. He shook the snow off it and pulled it low over his head again.

"It *is* warm."

That's when he noticed something else. All mixed up

with his own helter-skelter prints on the ground were some that looked as if they had been made by a child wearing small boots. The footprints meandered off in a direction he had not walked. There they met some dozen similar prints and a set of parallel tracks that appeared to have been made by a very small wagon.

His heart quickened. "I've been seen. I've been seen by . . . several creatures with small feet. And I've been given a hat by one of them. But not goblins, I think . . ."

"No, no. Goblins wouldn't do that. They don't give you things. Except chains. They give you those. I'd be wearing chains right now and not a hat if there were goblins about —"

He stopped. On a flat tree stump not very far away sat a bright red apple. The tree itself was gone. It had been cut clean, which made him think about his father chopping wood in the forest the day the goblins attacked him. But he pushed that thought away. Or rather, his stomach pushed that thought away. "An apple!" he said.

He waited in silence, glancing around. Nothing happened. When, finally, his stomach got the better of him, he darted to the stump and snatched the apple off it. When nothing happened then, Kringle decided that the apple on the stump was just an apple on a stump, and he ate it right then and there. It tasted *so* good as it gurgled and rumbled around his empty stomach.

"Thank you!" he said to whoever might be listening. "That was very good!"

Fortified and warmer than he had been for days, he looked once more for the goblin tracks, but found that as light as the snow was, it had managed to cover the trail pretty well. And as it was still night, it wouldn't do to follow a goblin trail too far, anyway. All he did see were the little boot and wagon tracks, curving away from the stump and sliding off into the forest. Maybe, he thought, whoever belonged to those tracks could lead him to Merwen, after all.

"And what choice do I have?"

"None, I think."

Besides, he rather liked following hat- and apple-givers rather than goblins, at least at night. So he started after them.

Now, with his new hat pulled low, his eyes turned down, and hurrying along after the new tracks, Kringle never even saw the tree. Nor did he hear the sound of himself hitting the ground after he ran straight into it. But, as you might have guessed, someone else did hear.

When Kringle opened his eyes some half an hour later, he saw trees and sky rolling *down* in front of him. Bringing all his mind to bear on the situation, he decided he must have been lying flat on his back in something moving.

"A wagon?" he thought. "Yes, a wagon."

What he didn't know just yet was *whose* wagon.

On both sides of him and under his head were large brown sacks bulging with he couldn't tell what. Tensing his arms and legs for a moment to discover whether they moved freely, he found they did. He felt his staff resting across his legs, grasped it, and slowly pulled it close. Turning ever so slightly to his right, he glimpsed the moving spokes of a large wheel and through them the bright young face of someone walking beside the wagon. The face bobbed up and down, not three feet above the ground.

Kringle blinked. The face did not belong to a goblin, but it was not a human face, either. It was as pink and round as a small pie and had a faint V-shaped chin. On either side of a slender, intelligent nose were bright hazel eyes. Long chestnut hair was parted in front of and behind ears that were slightly pointed and standing upright like a fox's. The creature turned to him and nodded affably, its whole face lighting up in a smile. "Hello, boy," it said.

Kringle nodded. "Uh, hello . . ." Raising himself on his elbows, he looked over the side of the wagon at the creature from head to toe. It sprang along on slender legs covered in baggy woolen trousers that were tucked inside small brown boots. Everything it wore, from its fleecy hat to its tight-fitting tunic, was the same berry-brown color.

"Who are you?" Kringle whispered, wondering immediately if he should have asked *what* it was.

"Gussi," said the creature brightly. Then, as if he had heard Kringle's unspoken thought, he added, "I'm an elf. We're all elves. And we found you!"

"Elves," Kringle repeated blankly.

"Sorry 'bout the hat," said a voice from the other side of the wagon. Kringle turned to see a hatless elf whose ears were turning rosy red. "I got elected because of my head's big. It's even prolly a bit loose on ya."

"No, no," said Kringle. "Well, maybe a bit. Thanks."

"We'll make you another, then!" boomed an older voice. Kringle looked up over his knees to see an elf with a bushy beard who was almost a foot taller and wider than the others and who tramped just after the wagon. He had a pair of big wooden clubs hanging from his belt, and his voice was very low and growly. "I'm Vindalf, young sir. I'm the elder elf but one from the tribe of elves of Elvenwald! Torgi's best for making hats, aren't you, Torgi?"

A high laugh came from somewhere ahead of the wagon. The laugh was so sweet that Kringle thought its owner must be female. "Aw, my pleasure, young sir . . . sir . . ."

"Kringle," he said to the elf.

"Sir Kringle!" she said.

"Not sir," he said. "Just Kringle."

"Well, that's that, then," said Vindalf. "A new hat for Just Kringle!"

The wagon began a mild descent into what Kringle felt

must have been a sort of valley in the forest. He turned his head and saw now that the wagon was being drawn by a pair of extremely stout white sheep.

"We're comin' from Penrith," said the hatless elf. "We found you almos' frozen under the tree back there. We couldn't just leave ya —"

"No," said another from the front, "because of the cloak —"

"'Cause of everythin', and that's that!" snorted the hatless one. "I'm Ifrid, by the by, Just Sir Kringle."

"Ifrid," repeated the boy.

A fifth elf took up the story. "Going to Elvenwald now, of course. Forward, Blendl . . . pull, pull!" he grunted in a low voice, prodding the lead sheep this way and that. "Couldn't bring you back to your home, wherever that is."

"But I have to find Merwen," said Kringle, on his elbows again. "The goblins took her —"

"Find nothing with a knob like that on your head," the sheepherding elf said. "Besides, goblins coming. Would have found you. Also besides, no time. There's the Work. Must do the Work, then get back to Penrith before dawn!"

"That's Holf," whispered the one named Gussi, leaning in. "Holf never says *I* or *we* or anything!"

Kringle nodded, and when he did, his head ached again. All this elven talk was mysterious to him, and he thought he might still be dreaming. That would explain why nothing made much sense to him. Except for the bit about Penrith, he thought. Merwen had told him about the Roman fort southwest of the Black Woods. That, at least, was real.

"In the morning we'll bring you back to where we found you, if you like," added Gussi. "It's far too dangerous tonight!"

"Yes," said Kringle, rubbing his head. "Dangerous."

"Goblins about," said a sixth elf, another bright-faced female whose golden hair curled down on either side of the one ear that Kringle could see. "Close by. Close."

Elves. Penrith. Vindalf. Gussi. Goblins. Ifrid. Elves!

It occurred to Kringle to ask a thousand questions, but the night was late and the wagon rocked him back and forth and his head ached and ached and his journey had been such a long one that he felt himself sinking back and back and back until he fell asleep again. And that was that.

PART
II

KRINGLE WATCHED AS LIGHTS SUDDENLY APPEARED EVERYWHERE AMONG THE HIGH TREES.

CHAPTER FIVE

ELVENWALD

K RINGLE HADN'T SLEPT more than an hour before the wagon began to slow. When he sat up, he had a very bad ache in his head from where it had struck the tree. It was bitterly cold, and he found himself hungry again, but soon enough the questions began.

"How long have I been sleeping? What's happening now? Just where exactly are we?"

"About an hour," said the one named Vindalf, "going to Elvenwald, and not far from home!"

Looking around, Kringle saw that the elves had brought him deeper into the forest than he had ever been. It was still night, but the moon was shining higher now through disappearing clouds, and the woods shone completely white, with only the lightest, laziest snow falling through the treetops.

"Ah! And so!" sighed Gussi as the wagon pulled to a stop

between two giant fir trees. Beyond the firs were pines and other evergreens leaning together with great fat leafless oaks and tall alders and bare ash trees. They formed a natural fence that surrounded a broad, white clearing. Icicles dripped down from the high trees in coils and swirls and playful fingers, mimicking the long vines of ivy that looped brightly between the branches.

"Why did we stop here?" Kringle asked.

Now, to you or me, asking such a question, or any question, of an elf, instead of asking, say, "*Are you really really, REALLY an ELF?*" might seem silly. But Kringle was a smart boy, as you knew from the beginning, and a smart boy really does have to get on with it.

"Because, Just Kringle," said Vindalf, "we're home!"

Then, as if the forest itself took the old elf's word for a magical command, everything in the clearing began to move.

Kringle watched as lights suddenly appeared everywhere among the high trees. He heard pleasant-sounding calls and shouts begin. And finally, a small creature in a berry-brown tunic and boots began to *walk down the air* in front of them. Another followed a few steps behind that one. And then another and another. They walked down the air, I tell you, as if they were stepping down a set of stairs! More than a dozen elves now — all in berry-colored tunics, some wearing hats with balls of white fleece bouncing on top, some wearing capes — came stepping slowly down the air toward Kringle!

Vindalf laughed. "Ah!" he said. And, "Ho, ho!"

Only after he stared and stared, astonished, and stood up in the wagon and stared some more, did Kringle see what an instant before had been invisible: that there actually *were* stairs coming from a high, many-armed oak in the back of the clearing. There were branches and logs and planks twisting and twining down from the great old tree to form a slender stairway all the way to the ground.

Kringle couldn't believe his eyes. "This is where you live?"

There was a whisper behind him, and Gussi and Torgi together sang, "Welcome to Elvenwald!"

At once, doors began to open among the snowy limbs, and Kringle saw that the trees were actually crowded with little houses — houses! — made of logs, planks, and living branches. Some were tiny boxes, while others had porches and decks and galleries and gardens. Bridges swooped gently from one house to the next and the next, forming a single, long, looping walkway from tree to tree in a complete circle around the clearing.

"This is beautiful. It's amazing!" said Kringle, jumping down from the wagon.

"Thankee!" said Vindalf. "We like it."

"Baaa!" A rush of sheep scampered past the sack-filled

wagon, and the two that had pulled it followed them, rolling the wagon away as if they knew just where to go.

"We raise sheep, Kringle," said Torgi. "Well, Holf does mostly."

"Do!" said Holf, hustling after them. "Blendl! Sempa! Steady there!"

"Now then," said Gussi, clapping his hands together. "After such a journey, I'll bet you are hungry, eh? An apple couldn't possibly —"

"Soup!" boomed Vindalf. "Give Just Kringle some soup!"

The boy's stomach grumbled loudly.

"I'll take that as an 'aye!'" said Ifrid, waving the boy up the stairs. "Right this way!" Laughing, he and Gussi and Vindalf and Torgi hooked their arms around Kringle and brought him right up the stairway and into the main house.

Oh, the main house! You have never seen such a great big hall built in the air! It hung between two giant oaks that flanked the very far end of the clearing, and it was magnificent. If the elves had had a king and queen (which they did not), this certainly would have been their palace.

The outside walls of the great house were fashioned mainly of stout logs set lengthways, interlaced with narrow planks in a zigzagging crossways pattern.

Even in his astonishment, Kringle tried to take in everything and, being himself, tried to find words for it all. "Invisible stairs! Giant house! Nice designs!"

He noticed as he approached the house that a kind of mulchy earth was daubed into all the spaces between the logs. It made the house appear as dark as night. So he was even more surprised when brilliant light beamed out from inside when the low front door was opened.

"Oh, my, my!"

"Indeed so!" agreed Vindalf. "Watch your head, boy. It wouldn't do to bump it twice on the same night. In, then, in!"

Crouching to fit through the door, Kringle entered a large, long room that was magnificent in its simplicity. This was the elvish way. Simple things everywhere. An unbroken row of long tables sat against each of the lengthwise walls, with a third row filling the center. All except the head table were crowded with dozens of elves chattering away.

"More elves!" said Kringle, astonished.

Gussi smiled from ear to ear. "More elves."

Elves, yes, and every one of them was busy. They were pounding with hammers or sewing with needles or gluing with glue or polishing with polish! Seeing Kringle gaping at them, they paused to look up. Some nodded pleasantly, some waved, but they all went back to work in an instant.

"There are nearly a hundred of us, to be exact," said Vindalf, beaming proudly at the elves. "Some of us came from Morpeck. Others from Timtamblybush. Or Frippenith or Pernbury. But Elvenwald is home for us all now."

"Sit, please," said Torgi. "You are our guest!"

At a nudge and a word from Ifrid, the elves at the table closest to Kringle told him their names.

In addition to Ifrid and Torgi and Vindalf and Gussi, whom he knew, there was Elni and Penda and Yffli and Horsa and Nar.

"Holf and Vindalf and me are brothers!" said Nar, who, while Vindalf and Holf were much older, had the appearance of being one of the youngest elves.

Kringle tried to take it all in, but felt the space behind his eyes begin to throb. "I won't be able to remember all your names," he said.

"We tell you again!" said one of them. "We love to speak the names of us!" Then the elf — Kringle thought at first it was the one named Horsa, or possibly Yffli — went around the table once more, naming every last one of them, pointing a stubby finger at each, who then stood and bowed and laughed and plopped back down again. The elf ended with, "Elni and Ifrid and Penda and Torgi and Gussi and Yffli and Horsa and Vindalf and Nar!"

After a long round of laughter and chatter came the drink. Many tankards later (Kringle guessed the drink was a kind of apple cider), the food arrived, but it came in the strangest manner. Platters of fruit and nuts clattered onto the long tables in jerks and starts, as if appearing from nowhere and landing abruptly.

"What's happening?" Kringle asked. "Is this some kind of elvish magic?"

Vindalf laughed. "Ho, ho! Not much! Only the elder is truly magical. This, well . . ."

Torgi smiled. "It's how elves move when they want to. It helps us remain unseen by people."

"It's so . . . fast!" said Kringle.

"Fast it is!" agreed Ifrid, peering longingly toward the end of the hall. "Hey, there! Is first dessert ready, by any chance?"

More platters suddenly appeared. On them, mostly, were yellow elf cakes, three inches round, two inches high, and flat on the top. The cakes were dense but surprisingly light, and were either topped with mint leaves and candied red buds and syrup, or they were plain. Kringle took one off each platter as it passed and stuffed them into his mouth.

"I love elf cakes," said Penda, leaning forward. "So does Holf. He's grumpy, but that's the way to his smile!"

"Hmmf!" said Holf, who had come in after tending to the sheep. He was now licking the syrup from one cake. "Like them. Don't pretend not to. Smile? Sometimes. When something is funny!"

"Like you!" Vindalf laughed, jingling his chest full of medals (he had quite a few) and slapping the table as Kringle lunged for a soup bowl, which had just been delivered, and devoured it. "If he had two spoons, this boy, he'd eat twice as much!"

The supper (or breakfast; Kringle wasn't sure), which started with nuts and fruit and was followed by dessert and soup and ended with meat and apples and a second dessert, did not stop coming for a full hour. During that time, Holf and some of the other elves left the main hall, and Kringle was pulled around the tables by Nar. At each he was flooded with still more names, including Neol and Loki and Thrymni and Rindur and Sifl.

Finally, Gussi got up from the table, looked around, and rapped on it firmly. "There, there, I should think it's time to get back to work —"

"Call it *the Work*!" said Vindalf, imitating Holf.

The tables were cleared as quickly as they had been filled. Then Torgi went to the door, swung it open, and glanced down the stairs. "Holf?"

"Coming through!" the grumbly elf said, pushing through the door with two sacks from the cart over his shoulders. Ifrid and five others followed with the rest of the night's booty.

Or rather, I should say, the night's *boots.*

For when Holf grunted and pointed, the elves emptied the sacks onto the first few tables, and dozens and dozens of large shoes and boots fell out. At once, troops of elves charged up and began to sift through them, each taking two or three pairs back to their tables. Right away, the clatter of tapping and hammering began again.

If Kringle was amazed by the strange elven meal, he was more amazed by what he was seeing now. "Wait. Are those the sacks from the wagon?"

"They are," said Gussi, squinting inside a large boot.

"Whose shoes are they?"

"Belong to the people of Penrith," Holf said.

"Well, did you, I mean, did you . . . steal them?"

Holf's face fell. "Steal them! Borrowed them! And not for very long, either! Elves repair shoes, boy!"

"You repair shoes," he said. "The Romans let you take their shoes?"

The elves laughed.

"They don't even know who we are!" said Gussi. "We sneak the shoes away, work all night, and sneak them back, fully mended and cleaned by morning, and all in secret."

Kringle didn't understand this. "But . . . why? The woods are dangerous at night. You said so yourselves."

Vindalf blinked. "Why? Because it helps them!"

It helps them? Kringle knew about being secret. He knew about hiding. He had been hiding with Merwen for twelve years. But to venture out at night in the Black Woods? Simply to help?

"It's a little something we can do in man's big world," said Torgi. "With all their warring and marching and doing, they have little time for such things."

"Of course, we've lost brothers and sisters to the goblins," said Vindalf sadly. "It's not safe work. No, no. But it's elf work."

Elf work. If the noisy bustle of the elves in their desire to help amazed Kringle, it also strangely calmed him. There was something comforting about a big room of workers, all chattering and humming away for a common purpose. It was not something he had ever experienced before, but it felt right. Nor could he take his eyes off of the little people. They hammered and poked and unstitched and stitched without stop. Each elf seemed to have his or her own specialty. Vindalf ripped away the old soles, while Ifrid sliced off ratty laces and broken leather straps. When Torgi held up one giant boot, then wiggled her fingers through a hole in its toe, all the elves around her whooped with laughter.

Drums began to be thumped now, and little harps plucked by a small group in the corner. The music was soft enough not to disturb the elves, but kept them all the more busy at their work. Finally, during a cider and cake break, several of the elves gathered and sang a strange little song.

> *"Remove, replace, repair, rejoice!*
> *Shoes shall shine*
> *By breakfast time!*
> *Hammers hammer.*
> *Groovers groove.*
> *Rejoice, repair, replace, remove!"*

Songs like this, and the elves' busy business, went on long into the night, and Kringle was so very tired as the hours pressed on toward morning that more than once his head dropped onto the table with a soft *thud*.

Finally, though, the shoes were finished and marked. A fresh batch of elves came and loaded the sacks into a new wagon hitched to a fresh pair of sheep, and headed off to Penrith.

When Vindalf said, in a rather official-sounding voice, "A good night's work is now well done," Gussi and Nar took Kringle by the hand and led him to the gallery outside the big house. The woods were dark except for the tiny golden lights shining from a couple of elf houses way up in the highest trees.

"Now," said Gussi, "we sleep."

"That sounds very good," said Kringle, yawning.

Together, the three traveled along the walkway to the next tree and the next, where two small huts were clustered in the crook of four thick limbs. Stopping at the first one, Nar nodded without saying a word, then opened a small door.

Kringle peeked in. By the light of a little candle, he could make out a small girl of two or so years old covered in a thick woolen blanket. She was asleep in a tiny bed. Her hair shone golden in the firelight. Sitting on the floor by her side was an old hunchbacked elf in the style of cape and hood Kringle had noticed was usually worn by female elves. The elf, whose name Kringle later learned was Retta, turned and smiled up at them. Putting a finger to her lips, Retta whispered, "She sleep, little Mari, now."

"Mari," said Kringle softly.

"She stay with," the old elf said. "No mama or papa. Goblin try to took her. We find . . ."

"She's an orphan?" said Kringle.

Gussi nodded. "The wars make orphans so quickly and easily. Some children, even ones whose shoes we fixed tonight, are orphans. Or orphans-soon-to-be."

Orphans-soon-to-be. Kringle felt a lump growing in his throat. The old elf beside the bed reminded him of Merwen. "So you take care of her?" he asked.

"We," said Retta, pulling another cover up to Mari's chin. The girl's little face was so calm. "We all."

Kringle gazed upon the girl another moment, then turned and followed the elves up the walkway to the second hut, where two beds were set head-to-head along one wall. Gussi squeaked and jumped into the closer one. Nar swept his hand toward the second. "For you."

"For me?" asked Kringle.

"For no one else!" said Nar. He shook Kringle's hand officially, then marched back down the bridge to the big house, leaving Kringle and Gussi alone together.

The little tree house reminded Kringle of the home he had loved so much. After all his journeying, and the bitter cold, and the sight of little Mari, he felt his eyes growing wet. He slumped down on the bed and began to cry.

Gussi was quiet. "Tell me about your house."

"It was called the Bottoms," he sobbed. "Whenever I smell wood burning, I remember our little house hidden away from the world, and the hearth where Merwen and I spent so many hours together. Every now and then I close my eyes and think I see her."

"You had your own bed, did you?"

Kringle sniffled. "I did."

"And your parents?"

He shook his head. "I didn't really know them. Or what they were like. Except that my father was a woodcutter. My mother told Merwen that he was so fast, his ax must have been magic. My mother's name was Elwyna. . . ."

Gussi's eyes widened. "Interesting name."

"What about it?"

"Elwyna means 'friend of the elves.'"

Kringle wiped his cheeks. "Really? She found a bell in her shoe once."

"Ah. Her shoe. Hmm."

Kringle told Gussi everything he could remember about the goblin attack and how they stole Merwen away in the stormy night. He told him of his journey to Castrum and about the Roman woman and everything that had happened since he had left the Bottoms.

Gussi nodded and nodded, then finally said, "The goblins are horrible beings, Kringle. Kidnappers and worse. But they do know one thing. They know they aren't fit to watch over the children they steal. I think that your Merwen was taken to care for them. With her there, they must be happier. Like you were happy with her. They must have hope. You must have hope, too. People have escaped the goblins, you know. Sometimes."

"Really?"

Gussi nodded. "Every day and every night we'll be on the search for your Merwen. We see things all over. If there is any news, you'll know it."

"Thank you."

Neither of them spoke for a little while, until Gussi said, "Kringle, it's like when you look around the woods in Elvenwald. You see the trees. Trees lean on other trees. Elves lean on elves."

Kringle's head felt so heavy now. All he could think of was how he had fallen asleep in the snow not knowing what to do, but that now he had been found by the elves, and he already felt a part of their little forest family.

Gussi's eyes were moist now, too. "You lean on Gussi." The elf's face grew a deeper shade of pink when he said this. He nodded once, pulled a blanket up to his chin and, as Kringle watched, his little face grew even smoother, and he began to snore.

CHAPTER SIX

THE GRAY STONES

HE NEXT MORNING, Kringle bolted upright in his bed to the strains of another elven song, this one about the snow and cold.

"White world! White winter! White winter world!
Soon snow snows so, sweet splendid snow!
Cold comes, cold claims, cold cares, cold curls!
Din-dingle! Dan-dangle! Don-dongely-dough!"

"Gussi, what are they up to?" he asked. But the elf's bed was empty and already made. "What a layabout I am. He's gone down without me!"

Jumping to the shutter, Kringle pulled it open and was nearly struck on the nose with a snowball. "What! Hey!"

Looking down on the rooftop of the main house, he saw, what, twenty elves? — it might have been twice that many! — busily sweeping and shoveling several inches of new snow from the thatching and singing at the top of their lungs.

"Sin-single! San-sangle! Son-songely-snow!"

Miniature snowstorms whirled up from the shovels and brooms and plopped down to the forest floor. This sent half the elves on the ground racing for cover, while the other half stood firm and snowballed back at the ones on the roof. All of them were laughing.

Kringle laughed, too, until a second snowball struck his window frame and exploded over his face.

"Oh, you think so?" he shouted down at Ifrid.

"I do!" the elf roared with delight; but before he could fire again, Kringle had scooped a handful of snow from the sill and sent his own missile hurtling back in reply.

Ifrid dodged out of the way, and the snowball struck Nar, who was crouching behind him. The young elf fell on his back, roaring, "I'm hit! I'm hit!"

Snow shot up and down for the next ten minutes until there came the quick, bright pluck of harp strings from the main house, and everyone — Kringle, too — stopped their play and hustled down from the roof and up from the ground and, shaking the snow off of themselves, entered the great room.

There, perched on a high stool at one of the long tables, was a very tiny old elf dressed in a pale tunic of white embroidered on white. Kringle guessed that if Vindalf was the second-oldest elder of the Elvenwald tribe, this elf must be the eldest.

He was thin and extremely old and very pale, almost completely white himself, and his tunic was as loose on him as if it were a sack hung on a broom handle. And yet when he saw Kringle enter, his eyes glimmered as happily as a child's.

"Our newest guest!" he said in a frail voice. "Come, sit by me. Come, you, whom everyone calls Kringle."

"And I call Just Kringle!" snorted Vindalf, taking a seat on the far side of the old elf. The old one didn't rise, but motioned to the stool on the right side of him, and Kringle sat down.

"I am Hrothr," said the tiny elf. "As you can see, I am the oldest living thing in this forest — aside from some of the trees, of course. May I offer you my own welcome to Elvenwald?"

"Thank you," said Kringle. "I owe my life to the elves. They saved me from being captured by the goblins and from dying of hunger and cold."

Hrothr smiled at the others at the table. "I expected no less from my brothers and sisters."

When everyone was finally seated, Hrothr looked up and down the tables with a sly smile on his face and a twinkle in his eye. "Now, then, elves. To new business?" He glanced at each table, raised his hand ever so slightly, then let it fall.

Oh! You should have heard the *rat-a-tat* of fine little

hammers then! The elves drove tiny nails into pine and fir and oak and leather. There was the smell of flamed tin and copper — gotten who-knows-where in this frigid land — beaten into tender shapes by little hands. More shoes and boots were coming together!

"What are these?" asked Kringle. "New shoes? Who are they for?"

Hrothr smiled. "Ah, an elder long before me thought of this. You see, sometimes no matter how often you repair them, shoes simply wear out. Wouldn't it be nice every once in a while to receive new shoes to replace the old ones? So we spend every seventh day making new shoes to leave on our next nightly visit."

"Elves have been cobblers forever, Kringle," said Vindalf. "It seems we do nothing quite as well."

Kringle looked among the tables of busy elves and was puzzled. Ever since he had seen their mad scramble for shoes the night before, something had bothered him. "But you must work on hundreds of shoes. Thousands. How do you keep from making mistakes? How do you ever get the right shoe to the right person?"

Hrothr laughed softly. "Gussi, if you please. The red book!"

Gussi stopped tapping a new heel onto a child's left boot and went to a high square table in the corner. "It's all in here," he said, holding up a very big red leather book that

Kringle had noticed when he walked in. "Everything we need to know is written on these pages."

He set the book down in front of Kringle with a *thud*. The book was nearly a foot thick from cover to cover. When Kringle opened it he saw many thousands of names like Faran and Arthr and Maurelle and Gallus and Cassia and Alban written in tiny columns under headings like "Netherbliss" and "Corbridge" and "Ravenbuck" and "Barrowfoot." Next to each name was a carefully drawn sketch of a shoe or sandal or boot, with tiny measurements and size numbers written next to it.

"This is, well, amazing!" said Kringle.

"It's a book about people and their feet!" Nar said with a laugh.

"All the names and places of every shoe owner are here so we don't make mistakes," said Gussi. "This one likes straps. That one prefers a taller heel. This one has a wide foot. That one gets bunions and corns, so the leather must be soft. This one sleeps against the wall, that one by the door, the other in the room over the stable."

"But how we get their shoes in the first place!" said Nar, giggling. "At the beginning of the night the elves steal into a house," he said, pawing his little hands in the air as if he were an animal creeping along the ground. "Then, sneaking around, we spirit away the old shoes from under beds and from all their little places by the fire."

"And," Penda went on, "we bring them here, and tap-tap and sew-sew, and work-work all through the dark hours until nearly dawn to fix them!"

"Better than new, I say!" added Vindalf.

"Finally," said Ifrid, "we take the shoes and — *sprit-sprit!* — put 'em right back where we found 'em, along with any new ones we've made!"

"Now that's good work well done," said Vindalf brightly. "And the best part is — no one's the wiser. Ho, ho!" His whole body shook when he laughed.

"Kringle," said Hrothr, "as you well know, we leave Elvenwald only at night. We travel quickly when we need to, but nighttime is also the goblin time. And since goblins no longer keep to the forest, our work has become very dangerous indeed."

"Dangerous?" said Holf. "Hmmf! Live by danger. Drive the wagon, don't you know. Keep the sheep in line!"

Danger. Kringle didn't know why, but the idea of being on a mission with the elves stirred something in him. It may simply have been because he was a boy, I suppose, or because his life had begun with a goblin attack. Or maybe it was because even though he had been in Elvenwald but a day and a half, he already felt a kinship with the elves, and perhaps a love for them. Or it may have been the thought that he might learn something of Merwen. But whatever it was, the desire began to grow in him that he could go on a mission with the elves and that he *should* go with them the first chance he got.

Kringle's days passed quickly into weeks at Elvenwald. With one ear trained on every report that came in from the outside world, he learned that Merwen had been sighted not once, but twice — "She's free! She escaped the goblins!" — but neither time did anything come of it, for she was always on the move. The first time, a talkative child whom Ifrid had discovered on a mission had said he saw a woman who sounded like Merwen, but she was passing through on her way to the coast. The second time, Kringle heard she was heading north toward the fringes of the Roman territory, past the town of Netherbliss.

"North," he said. "To the land of the snows."

He was overjoyed that she was free, but sad that he could seem to get no closer to her.

But if he learned little definite about her, he learned more than he wanted to about the goblins. They were growing bolder. Three heath children had been taken in the last week, and two more from the forest dwellers in the eastern woods.

Once or twice, the elves had managed to rescue a child fleeing from a goblin raid, or — though this was rarer — one who had escaped their cruel captivity. Sometimes, Ifrid told him, children turned up mumbling of goblin horrors going on deep under the earth.

"'The Fires of the North,' I heard 'em say," said Ifrid. "And oh, the fear you can see in the children's eyes then!"

The fear in their eyes. This reminded Kringle of how Snegg's own eyes had swelled when he felt the boy's fear in the Bottoms.

The first thing the elves did when children were brought into Elvenwald was feed them and tend to any wounds. Then they gave the children new clothes. The elves were such extraordinary stitchers and weavers and knitters with those little hands, and the clothes they made so much brighter and warmer and happier than the old rags the children had been found in, that color — real color — soon returned to the pale little faces.

Such children didn't remain long in Elvenwald, however. "We find good families for them," said Torgi. "They are so innocent and weak and small. But they can't stay here. They are not elves, after all."

"Only Mari and you are without homes now," said Gussi. "And we'll soon find good ones for you, too."

As time went on, Kringle spent more and more of his time learning how to repair shoes. His tasks were simple at first — preparing the tools and materials for the elves, sorting and tagging shoes according to the red book. After a suitable training period, however, he was allowed to trim leather, hand-form a toe, and tap on a sole until he finally repaired his first pair of boots.

Vindalf declared the result, "A good effort. A fine pair of footwear!"

One night, Kringle was in the great hall at the very end of the evening, waiting for the wagons to bring a new batch of shoes and watching Mari play with scraps of wool and bootlaces. The girl loved the elves' workshop and was never happier than when she was playing there with the ball Gussi had made for her out of leather sewn tightly around a round wooden heel-shaper. She tossed and rolled the ball and followed it and kicked it, running barefoot under the elves' tables, giggling the whole time. Torgi and Penda chased her under the tables, laughing and making a splendid game.

When Kringle tried to join in, he found he was too large to fit under the tables, so he was happy when Gussi called for a new game. "We can all play this one!" the elf said.

The new game involved tossing the ball and trying not to drop it for a hundred throws. This proved impossible, as Mari was not a good catcher. She laughed with each catch and laughed even louder when she dropped the ball, and they had to begin the game again.

"Fun!" Mari cried when they finally reached twenty catches. Torgi then got the idea to make the game a little more challenging by stepping back once with each successful catch. They had reached twenty-six catches and Kringle was just tossing the ball to Gussi, when the door flew open between them and Holf charged in with three heavy sacks over his shoulders. The ball smacked him in the nose, rolled over his shoulder, and fell down his back.

"Owww!" he wailed, dropping the sacks and clutching his face. "Doesn't do to kill the worker, you know!" he growled. Then he turned and looked directly at Kringle. "Your Merwen," he said.

Kringle shivered. "Yes?"

"Little boy saw her," he said. "Told about it. Saw her not two weeks ago in Barrowfoot, where these shoes came from. Had just escaped from the goblins with ten Roman children —"

"Oh!" Kringle whispered.

"Was going in search of you," Holf said. "Boy got sick, though, was sent to bed, didn't know if she was still there. These shoes going back before dawn. Maybe you —"

"Can I go?" cried Kringle, looking at all the elves. "Oh, can I go with you? I have to! Merwen could still be in Barrowfoot!"

"Ahhhh," came a small voice behind him. "I was wondering when you would ask to go!"

When Kringle turned, he saw Hrothr walking slowly toward him. The old elf's lips were curled in a curious half smile, and his eyes beamed.

"So, you want to go on a mission, do you?" he asked.

Kringle flushed. "Well, that is, I've been thinking about it. I want to help. Maybe I can — I don't know — protect the elves while they put the shoes back. And maybe I can find out something about Merwen."

"Oh?" the old elf whispered. His eyes twinkled and shone in the room's candlelight. "Perhaps so. But first, I think you should come with me. There is something you must see." He glanced around, looked at Gussi, and nodded.

The young elf smiled. "Follow us, Kringle!"

Together, the three of them left the main hall to the sound of strumming and chattering and tapping. They hurried down the curving steps to the ground. Kringle thought he sensed a third elf following them, but looking back, he neither saw nor heard anyone.

"Hrothr, what do you want to show me?" he asked.

The old elf was silent as they made their way across the snowy clearing. Then, slowing his steps, he turned. "Kringle, you said *help*. You said *protect*. Let me tell you a story. Not so very long ago, when I was a bit younger than now and could do such things, I was running through the Black Woods, trying to get safely back here. It was near Long Night, after all. The most dangerous goblin time. And sure enough, a goblin was after me! After *us*, I should say, for with me was Freya, the elder elf before me. She was some three hundred and ninety then. She has passed now. But then she was still a good runner.

"Kringle, goblins do not like very many things, but the thing they dislike most of all, I think, is an elf."

They reached the edge of the clearing and passed under the twin fir trees. "Why don't they like elves?" asked Kringle.

"Well you may ask!" said Hrothr. "We have some bit of magic that they have been after for ages. There have been, well, prophecies about the end of the goblins. But mainly, I think it is because we will do anything to help people, Kringle. Long ago the elves dedicated themselves to giving. They 'gave' themselves to helping."

"Just like you helped me and Mari."

"You, among others," said the old elf as they walked on. "Well, then, as Freya and I ran through a clearing in the Black Woods, we came upon a man."

Hrothr paused to look Kringle up and down, smiled, and went on. "'Hide!' we told him. 'Run! A goblin is after us!' But no. This man knew we were in danger and immediately stood to defend us. 'Elves,' he said stoutly, 'get behind me. And *you* run!' Kringle, this man let us escape, and when Morgo — yes, it was he — when Morgo came bounding into the clearing, this man fought the goblin himself. Freya and I fled to safety while he drove the Goblin King off. He drove him off, I tell you, with the single weapon he had."

Kringle stared at Hrothr. "What weapon was that?"

"An ax."

The boy trembled. "No, no . . . you don't mean . . ."

"Yes, Kringle, it was your father. When we came back

later to thank him, we found his wound was mortal. Soon, he would die."

"Poor man," said Gussi, his eyes wet.

"Ah, yes," said the old elf. "But rich in honor and goodness and courage. Together, Freya and I gave him whatever food we had. I treated his wound. I covered him to keep him warm. I saw the little bell he wore around his neck —"

"My mother gave that to him," said Kringle.

Hrothr nodded. "Then, Freya proclaimed what to this day is the greatest mystery!"

Kringle could barely breathe. "What did she say?"

"She said, *The child shall know.*'"

The boy frowned. "What child?"

"I don't know, but I can guess," said Hrothr.

"What will the child know?"

The old elf smiled. "I think only the child who knows shall know *what* he knows! But Morgo heard it and took it as a prophecy of the worst kind: that the child shall know how to rid our world of goblins!"

Kringle felt his head begin to throb. "But why did she even say it? And what made her say it to my father?"

"For the answer to the first question, you must follow us!"

The deeper they headed into the wild forest, the more Kringle began to think. Thinking led to wondering, and wondering finally led to asking. "Did the elves ever fight the goblins? Vindalf has a great lot of medals and carries those big clubs."

"In the old days, we fought them," said Hrothr, stopping in front of a boulder that looked as if it had grown up out of the ground. "We did not win. And in the dozen years since Morgo discovered the storm-making wand, Ithgar, the goblins have become more powerful. Even though we continue to help the world of men, we must ever be more careful. As you know, Elvenwald can seem quite invisible when it wants to. Gussi?"

Fwish! The young elf lit a candle and held it up. Then he moved slowly behind the boulder and vanished inside it!

"Where did he go?" asked Kringle.

"Follow the light!" said Hrothr. He waved Kringle foward, and the boy stepped around the great rock. There he saw a narrow cleft outlined in dim candlelight. It led inside the rock.

"There's a cave inside?" he asked.

"A cave, Kringle. Enter."

The boy slipped into the darkness of a slender passage, with Hrothr following behind him. In a moment, they found themselves in a small chamber in the center of the boulder. All that was in the room was a flat rock about a foot high and two feet across. It was nearly perfectly round. Some twenty-odd small gray stones lay in a circle around the top of the rock. Carved on each stone were simple markings.

"Rune stones," said Hrothr. "Some people think they bring good luck. More than that, Kringle, these stones tell mysteries, secrets, truths. The runes are the letters of a very old language, far older than me, if you can believe anything might be that old. But together these runes form much more than simple words. Kringle, there is magic in them. There is power."

The boy wasn't sure how there could be magic or power in these few small stones. "Vindalf said that of all the elves, you had the most magic."

Hrothr laughed. "No, no, no. Once, I was blessed with future-sight. But I am old now, and that sight is dimming. I can see ahead but a few hours only!"

Whether the stones were magical or not, Kringle liked their markings. They were all made up of straight lines only and were somehow both strange and beautiful.

"There are twenty-four stones, Kringle," said the old elf. "A kind of family. It is said that if ever they are apart, they will call to one another to be reunited, for only by working together can they summon the real magic of the ancient days. A legend says that while the great god of the north whom we call Odin was hung on a tree to die, he learned the meaning of the runes. Through his suffering, he passed on this knowledge to men and to elves."

"But the men have all forgotten!" said Gussi.

"True," said Hrothr. "But the goblins have not forgotten.

They are driven to possess this power. They sense the runes, as a hungry wolf senses food. It was for these stones that Morgo chased Freya and me through the woods twelve years ago.

"Kringle, we have entered a dark time. I fear for the world. I show these stones to you because knowledge of the great truths may be the only thing to stop Morgo. Go ahead," he said, "take them up. You may."

Kringle thought he heard sounds coming from the forest outside.

"Cast the stones, Kringle. I shall read the words."

"I love this part," said Gussi softly. "Even though I don't know what it means."

Hrothr smiled. "Runes do not speak to everyone, dear Gussi. Kringle?"

The boy knelt to the round rock. The small stones were cold when he first handled them, and they reminded him of everything about the north country: gray, hard, spare. Within moments, however, they began to warm in his fingers. Soon Kringle felt as if he were holding not simple stones but the hands of a close friend.

He tossed the runes. They clattered and stopped.

"Ah . . . ah . . . ," Hrothr murmured.

"What do they say?" asked Gussi eagerly.

Hrothr spoke the letters. "Kenaz . . . Raidho . . . Isa . . . Ingwaz. Together, they say . . . 'From the warmth of hearthfire a journey is begun, through stillness, darkness, and the coldness of ice . . . and yet the greater journey is within. . . .'"

Still kneeling, Kringle gazed at the stones one by one. "'From the warmth of hearthfire.' So, I've begun a journey?"

"We're all on journeys, Kringle," said the old elf.

"How exciting!" whispered Gussi.

"Only time will tell where your journey takes you."

The old elf touched a single rune whose design was two interlocking angles. "Look here. This is my favorite rune. Jera. It speaks of the changes that happen yearly in nature." He turned from the stones. "Kringle, it was from these runes that Freya learned 'the child shall know.' From the first time you set foot in our hall I knew that you were that child. I knew because . . ." He laid his hand on Kringle's arm. "This is the cloak I gave to your father. It was my *elvencloak*."

Kringle trembled. "*Your* cloak?"

Hrothr smiled. "Its magic is that it assumes the size of the person wearing it. That's why though I am short, it became as tall as your father was."

Gussi blinked. "But it's far too big for Kringle!"

Hrothr studied the boy closely. "Perhaps it's waiting for you to grow into it."

Kringle wrapped his arms around himself and stared into the old elf's deep eyes. His throat caught in a sob. "I can't believe that you were there . . . with him."

"Now he is here with you," Hrothr said. "The elves are givers, Kringle. We all have a choice, you know. To give or take or do nothing. Your father was a giver. He gave his life for the elves. He gave when he could have done nothing. He helped when he could have hidden away. Now you know what kind of man your father was."

Kringle's tears came freely now. For a long moment, he stared down at the stones. Finally he said, "He loved my mother, and she loved him."

The wrinkles on Hrothr's face seemed to smooth away suddenly. "I found, when Freya left this life — which is when elven elders pass on their secrets, you know — that seeing your father in the woods was not the first time she had ever laid eyes on the bell around his neck."

Kringle looked up at him. "It wasn't?"

"Some twenty years before, her favorite lamb was caught in a thicket."

"My mother found that lamb!" cried Kringle.

The old elf nodded. "The bell she found in her shoe was Freya's. You see, all things connect, Kringle."

The boy felt more tears coming when, suddenly, there was a sound from outside the chamber.

"Someone's coming," said Gussi, blowing out the light.

"Not goblins?" whispered Kringle.

No. Not goblins. It was only Nar, running along the forest

floor toward the boulder. The little elf was wide-eyed as they emerged from behind it.

"Yes, my boy?" said Hrothr, stepping up to him.

The little elf blurted out, "The shoes! They're ready! We're going to Barrowfoot!"

CHAPTER SEVEN

TO
BARROWFOOT!

HEN KRINGLE AND THE ELVES returned to the clearing, six stout sheep and three small wagons were standing in a row near the entrance. Each was piled high with sacks of shoes and boots, and the cold air was filled with the aroma of new leather and polish and fleece.

"You shall go, Kringle, shall you not?" said Vindalf, glancing at Hrothr, a broad smile visible under his beard. "You have wanted to for very long, I think."

"I have!" said Kringle. "Will you let me go?"

"We shall," boomed the elf, slapping the boy on the back. "You shall join our mission to Barrowfoot."

"It's a small fort on the coast of the western sea," said Gussi. "The Romans haven't abandoned it yet."

His first mission! Kringle remembered what Merwen had told him once about Barrowfoot. The Roman fort was built on the slope of a large round hill called the Barrow. It was on

84

the western coast some thirty miles from Elvenwald and the Black Woods.

"Besides, what would the big Romans stomp-stomp in without good shoes and boots, eh?" asked Ifrid. "Feetsies and toesies? I don't think so, no!"

"Most like they'll use them to march home," grumbled Holf. "The faster to leave. Leave the goblins free to roam."

"We'll stuff the shoes back under their beds," said Torgi. "And by their fires, and then sneak out as if we'd never set foot in Barrowfoot."

"And I'm going, too. My first raid!" shouted Nar, appearing suddenly behind them. "Yay for Nar!"

The excited elves were trying to make light of it, but Kringle knew their mission would be dangerous. Morning wouldn't come for four hours, and even though they might travel very quickly, there was still plenty of time to run into goblins.

"Now, now, everyone!" Hrothr said, calling the troop of eight to attention. "Good luck. Do not tarry. Go about your business swiftly and carefully. Come home safe and sound and elvish — including you, Kringle, dear boy!"

"Hurrah!" the small band cheered.

Kringle slid his staff, which never left him, into a narrow woolen quiver on his back that Torgi had made for him. He nodded to the elves. "Let's be off, then!"

Just as they were leaving the clearing, Kringle heard a little voice calling, "Kingle! Kingle! Play!"

He turned and saw Mari on the walkway outside her house. She looked upset and jumped up and down.

Kringle waved. "I can't play now. But I'll be back —"

"Play! Play!"

He shook his head and waved some more, but the wagons kept rolling, and he had to stay with them. "Bye, Mari!"

"A fine little girl," said Gussi when Kringle had caught up. "We haven't found a home for her yet, but we will soon, I think."

"It will have to be very special," said Kringle. "The most special."

As they passed beyond the bounds of Elvenwald, the little group became immediately more quiet and watchful.

"No songs, fellows," said Vindalf. "Save our breath and double our steps. There will be mud!"

There was mud. Winter had finally passed, but spring in the north was still cold and wet. The ground was thawing in some places and clinging to snow in others.

The weather grew worse the moment they left the protection of Elvenwald. The little village soon faded away into the trees behind them. Kringle realized once again how small the enchanted elven land was. Altogether, it must have been less than a square mile in the whole of the great Black Woods.

The sheep did not hesitate for a moment. Soon, the trees

thinned out. And the rain — it had been raining off and on all night — was heavy and cold, sometimes mixed with squashy wet flakes, making the ground sodden. Progress, even for the quick elves, was slow.

A half hour after leaving, the first wagon pulled out of the forest and onto the first of the Five Plains.

The Five Plains?

Kringle found out soon enough that this was a very grand term for what was in fact no more than one vast waste of flatland with five rolling bumps to it.

As soon as they were under way on the open ground of the first plain, Gussi began to rummage in the lead wagon, peering into each of its seven sacks and checking their contents against the red book. Nodding firmly as he finished each sack, he cinched it up and went on to the next. He did this, hopping from wagon to wagon, until he had examined all twenty-one sacks in the shipment.

"Done and done well," he said finally. "Perfect work, fellows. I've checked it twice, and I think all the bare Barrowfoot feet will not be shoddily shod!"

"Ha!" cried Vindalf. "Foot feet not shoddily shod! Excellent, Gussi. There's the start of a song, I think."

Gussi chuckled and blushed. "Perhaps for later."

By the time they reached the shallow valley before the fifth and final plain, the ground was oozing with snowy mud.

The clouds were hanging low and dark overhead, and the wind off the sea was slowly turning the raindrops to ice.

"Dawn is very close," said Torgi. "Don't you think so, Kringle?"

"An hour left of dark. Possibly less. Let's hope the goblins have already gone back to their tunnels," the boy replied.

"Hope they have," grunted Holf. "Hope they have, indeed!"

In a few moments they had reached the top of the Barrow. Looking down, they saw a large, square stone wall surrounding an area of about five acres. It overlooked a narrow, rock-strewn, sandy beach and the white-topped waves of a black sea beyond. At each corner of the fort stood a watchtower like the ones Kringle had seen at Castrum. Urns blazing with flames were ranged every twenty feet or so between the towers. Ten or fifteen sentries slowly patrolled the top of the wall, crisscrossing one another back and forth. Kringle shivered when he thought that soon he and the elves would try to sneak over that wall. He wondered if Merwen might be inside, and his heart began to pound.

"Good," said Ifrid. "The sentries are wearin' hooded cloaks 'cause of the rain. The better ta not see or hear us."

"Haul yourselves some sacks, fellows and ladies," whispered Vindalf. "Load up, leave the wagons here, take your pages from the red book, and let's move out. Or rather, move down."

Because he was taller than the elves, Kringle took the

four largest and heaviest sacks and slung them over his shoulders.

"Let's see, Kringle," said Gussi. "Sacks Three through Six?" The elf leafed through his book, then slipped a single sheet of paper from it and gave it to him. "Here is the list of everyone whose shoes are in these sacks. I have One and Two, so we'll be together."

Kringle smiled. "A team. Let's go!"

In a twinkling, the seven elves zigzagged down the Barrow and across an area of flat ground that led to the wall. They did this completely unseen and in a matter of moments. Kringle, meanwhile, had barely started out from the top.

"Fine," he said to himself. "I suppose this is where it's proved that I'm not really an elf?"

"So, I'd better hurry."

"And quickly!"

He hustled carefully from rock and tree to hillock and stump as swiftly as he could in the mud. Five minutes later, he joined the others at the foot of the wall farthest from the watchtower.

"What took you so long?" asked Torgi, tapping her foot. She was smiling.

"Sorry," said Kringle. "I suppose I'm not magical."

"Ah, but you're tall!" said Vindalf, pushing him gently against the wall. "Stand still and bend your legs so!"

"What —"

Vindalf climbed up on Kringle's bent knees and — *fwit-fwit!* — he was standing on the boy's shoulders in an instant. Holf went up next, then Ifrid, Gussi, Torgi, Horsa, and finally Nar, until they formed what Vindalf called an "elven ladder" fifteen feet tall.

Reaching up, Nar peeped over the top of the wall, waited for a sentry to pass, then climbed away from Horsa and disappeared. He poked his head back over a moment later, grinned, and let down a narrow rope ladder. "Hurry before the sentry comes back!" he whispered.

"Good work, Nar!" Torgi whispered back. "Up we go!"

The elves and Kringle hauled up their sacks and were over the wall in no time. They dropped down inside just before the sentry marched back across the ramparts.

The elves knew instantly what needed to be done. Horsa ran off first, carrying two sacks over her shoulder, her long hair flying behind her. Torgi scampered just after her, with Holf and Ifrid after *her.* Vindalf and Nar (who had four sacks between them) followed the two elf women part of the way, then went off in a different direction, darting unseen just beyond the rim of firelight.

Kringle hurried behind Gussi, his staff and four heavy sacks over his shoulders. The little elf ran to the farthest side door of the first hall and slipped inside as quietly as a mouse.

He looked both ways in the dark, then nodded to Kringle. "The stairs are this way. Come. Be careful. And silent!"

"I'll be both," said Kringle. His heart pounded with excitement as he slipped down the dark hall to the stairs, then up to the floor above. He peeped in every room he could for any possible sign of Merwen. Gussi turned to him and grinned, pointing to a tiny elvish number marked above a doorway.

"Neol left that mark," he whispered. "I'd know her work anywhere. It says *five* and *one*. That means 'five pairs from Sack One.' Watch closely. This is how you do it!" Inside was a large bed that was empty at the moment, but nearby was a smaller bed in which two children were sleeping. Gussi set his sack on the floor, dug into it, and pulled out four small pairs of shoes of different sizes, tied together and tagged. He glanced at a leaf from the red book, tucked the shoes side by side underneath the small bed, and left a fifth pair under the big one. "Simple as cake!" he said.

Kringle smiled. "Thanks. I think I have it." He slipped out and down the hall and saw another tiny mark over a door. He knew it was meant to be a four followed by a three, so he entered the room. He left four pairs of shoes from Sack Three under the beds. He went into the next room and the next and the next, working as quietly as possible.

Thanks to the elves' careful planning, the entire top floor was done in a twinkling. Before Kringle was done, two of his sacks were empty. Not finding any sign of Merwen there, he and Gussi went downstairs and did the same to the lower rooms. Kringle's fourth sack was emptied shoe by shoe until there were only six pairs left.

In the final room, he turned his sack over for the last pair of shoes when something red fell out of the bottom, bounced across the floor, and rolled under the bed.

"Oh, my gosh! Mari's ball! It must have fallen in here when it struck Holf in the doorway. *That*'s what she was trying to tell me!"

He was about to reach for it when he felt a hand on his shoulder. Turning, he saw Ifrid standing there, his face white.

"What is it?" asked Kringle.

"Sounds . . . outside!"

"Sounds?" said Gussi, coming into the room now.

"Sentries," said Ifrid. "It's time for the changing of the guard. Morning is coming. We'll be seen. We must go."

"But the ball —" said Kringle. "And Merwen —"

"Come *on*!" said Gussi. "We can't be found. Outside the walls. Now!" He pushed the boy from the room and down the hall to the door. They rushed outside and ran straight for the rope ladder. They were up, over, and down to the ground in a flash.

The other elves were waiting for them. "Kringle," said Horsa breathlessly, "I found a girl awake in the rooms above the stable. I asked about Merwen, and she said, yes, she was here —"

"Here —" he gasped. He looked back at the fort.

"But she left ten days ago," Horsa said, pulling him up the Barrow after Vindalf, Ifrid, and Holf. "She was going north, trying to stay clear of the goblins, but vowing to find you."

"North," he said, "always north."

"Anything else?" asked Gussi.

Horsa shook her head. "Only that the goblins were being sighted more and more. I wanted to ask where, but the new guard was coming on. I had to leave —"

"Everyone, wait," Torgi said suddenly, stopping on the hill. "Where's Nar? Vindalf, I thought he was with you."

The old elf turned. "Nar left and went with Holf, no?"

"Not with me, neither!" grunted Holf.

Kringle paused and looked back at the fort. "He must still be inside. Maybe I can find that girl, too. I'll go."

"Kringle, no," said Gussi. "They'll see you!"

"Meet you at the wagons!" he shouted, and raced back down the Barrow before anyone could stop him.

Kringle had his hands on the ladder and was about to climb back up when he heard a sound from the beach outside the wall. "Nar? What are you doing out *there*?" Leaving the ladder, he dashed along the foot of the wall to the corner and peered around it at the water. There, barely visible in the gray air of near dawn, was a large carved bird head moving slowly up the beach. "A ship!" he said. "Pirates!"

The ship slid up the sand, stopped, and tipped to the side. Large, helmeted men with axes, swords, and spears leaped quietly onto the beach.

"Oh!" groaned a tiny voice. Kringle turned back to see Nar kneeling in the snow fifty feet up the Barrow, searching an empty sack and his tunic, muttering to himself all the while. Suddenly, he jumped up and ran back to the foot of the wall where the ladder was. "What is he doing? Nar!" said Kringle. He darted along the wall, heading for the young elf.

The raiders were moving stealthily across the beach as Kringle reached the ladder and climbed up to the top. Nar lay quivering and flat across the rampart.

"Nar, what are you up to? Pirates have landed. They're coming up the beach. There will be a battle!"

Nar sighed loudly. "Kringle, I shouldn't have done it. They'll find them!"

"Find who?"

"Not *who. What!* The rune stones!" Nar held up a small woolen pouch that was looped to his belt. He shook it upside down. Nothing came out. "I lost the gray stones. I took them for my mission, my first mission. I followed you all into the woods last night. I heard Hrothr say that runes bring luck! He said they have power. I thought . . . I thought they would give me luck."

"Oh, Nar —"

"But now the goblins will sense them. The goblins will steal them!"

"It's getting too light, Nar. Dawn is nearly here. All the goblins will have gone back to the woods by now."

"No, no. There. Look!" said the little elf. He pointed north across the coastline. From behind a ridge of rocks on the far side of the Barrow came a glint of metal in the pale moonlight. A ragged line of swords snaked silently toward the beach. At the head was a goblin riding a large, emaciated beast.

"Snegg!" said Kringle.

"Yes, and he's riding a vargul," said Nar. "Goblins sense the rune magic, Hrothr said so. Snegg will find the stones and steal them. The elven magic will be gone. We'll be doomed. And all because of Nar!"

Kringle's heart thundered in his chest. "Goblins. Pirates. This will be a night to remember. All right, where do you think you lost them?"

"I don't know. Down there. I didn't hear them when they fell from the pouch. And now I'm afraid to go back down. I'm not as fast as the others. I'll be seen. Kringle, you must help me. Here —" Nar pushed the empty pouch into the boy's hand and jumped to the ground outside the wall. Then he scurried away up the Barrow.

Kringle lay alone on the top of the wall, sputtering to himself. He watched the goblin snake weaving closer and the pirates scurrying quickly up the beach and the new sentries climbing up to take their positions. "Oh, this is fine! This is wonderful! I have to go back into the fort and find the stones before anyone sees me!"

It was impossible, and Kringle knew it. But, after all, what choice did he have? While the way was still clear, he jumped down into the shadows of the courtyard. He was never so happy it was raining than at that moment, for the sentries' hoods kept them from seeing or hearing him.

"All right, then. Which way did Nar go when we first entered the fort? Think. Think!" Kringle closed his eyes and tried to drive the patter of the rain from his mind. He concentrated as hard as he could to remember the elves' first few moments inside the wall.

Amid the silence of his thoughts, however, he found that he was hearing . . . something. Sounds? Odd sounds. They seemed little more than the air itself moving against his ears, yet soon enough the sounds began to speak like voices.

Mannaz! Uruz! Othala! Fehu!

And through the voices he began to *see* something. And the thing that he saw . . . was mud.

He opened his eyes and turned directly to the far end of the courtyard. There he saw a glimmer of wet stones scattered in the mud. His heart leaped. "Of course! If the stones had fallen on a floor, Nar would have heard them. But he wouldn't have heard them fall in the mud! And there they are. I can't believe it!"

Kringle hurried along the wall, glancing around the courtyard to be sure no one was watching. As soon as he saw his moment, he sprinted across the open ground. In a flash, he scooped up the stones and returned to the foot of the inside wall. He thought about seeking out the girl whom Horsa had spoken to in the stable, but every passing minute was more dangerous. Time was running out. He had to leave. He would learn more later.

Flying back up the wall, Kringle was down the other side and on the ground laughing before he knew it. "What luck! I can't believe the Romans didn't catch me. Maybe I'm really learning from the elves!"

It was then he remembered what Gussi had called the children: orphans-soon-to-be. How many of the children he had seen sleeping would be orphaned tonight? "The Romans have to know about the pirates. And the goblins!"

Kringle scooped up a handful of muddy snow and threw it at the nearest sentry.

"Hey!" the guard called out, whipping off his hood. But in an instant, he was on alert. "Raiders on the beach!" he cried.

Alarms jangled. All the guards raced along the wall, shouting. Torches flashed, and fresh soldiers came pouring out of the halls, strapping on their boots, yelling. They rushed up to defend the ramparts against the first wave of pirates, who were already clambering up the seaward wall.

At the same time there came a wail from the north, and the goblins charged from the shelter of the ridge, swarming the beach in the hundreds. It was the largest band Kringle had ever seen. Snegg was in the lead, waving a long, curved sword and belching commands from the back of the vargul. It truly was an ugly beast. Just imagine a large wolf that has been starved to no more than a skeleton, then add the long fangs of a serpent.

Kringle froze, stunned at the speed of the goblins. But what could he possibly do? He had to escape. The elves were waiting for him. He had their runes! He tied the pouch to his belt, dropped low, and began running. He was halfway up the Barrow when the first clash of swords made him turn. Several pirates were limping away from the fort toward their ship, while others moved past them, still attacking. One of the retreating pirates, a boy probably no older than himself, collapsed on the beach behind the others, clutching his leg. At the same time, Kringle heard Snegg howl down the beach, whipping his vargul. "Ingas, rush on, rush on! Goblins, attack the fort! I'll take the child —"

"No, no, no!" Kringle shouted. Without thinking, he unslung his staff and raced down the Barrow to the sand, arriving just as Snegg reached the boy. He jumped in front of the vargul and swung the staff, hitting the beast on its snout. It howled and tripped, throwing Snegg to the sand.

"Bearn! Hurry! To the ship!" came a shout from a swarm of pirates running back across the beach.

"Come on, boy, to your ship!" Kringle cried. He dragged the wounded boy across the sand and was nearly to the water when he smelled the stink of goblin.

Half turning, Kringle swung the staff behind him. It struck Snegg's shoulder, then slid off as the goblin ducked.

"What?" cried Snegg. "What! Boy —"

As the creature was about to lunge with his sword, a pair of huge arms wrapped around Kringle and the pirate boy and pulled them on board the ship. "Up you go!"

"No! Boy is mine!" cried Snegg. The goblin's eyes were huge and black and staring right at Kringle. But a sudden sword flashed through the air and Snegg wailed, tripping back to the sand, his hand clasped on his arm.

"Away!" shouted a gruff voice. "Quickly, away!"

"No, wait, not me!" Kringle said, falling next to a barrel filled with something foul. "I can't be here!"

But before he could act, a sudden swarm of arrows and spears launched out from the fort and landed near the ship, driving Snegg and the goblins away across the sand. Wounded pirates dropped onto the deck as their fellows pushed the ship back into the water, then leaped to the oars and began to row.

Their escape was the work of moments. No sooner had the ship sloshed into the sea than it moved away from shore, dipping and rising over the black waves. The watery *slurp* and *thwunk* of Roman spears and arrows around them ceased now, falling only upon the goblins on the beach. Soon the first streaks of dawn broke over the eastern plains, and the night creatures fled back to the ridge, their wails and shrieks echoing from the far distance.

Looking back, Kringle saw Gussi, Vindalf, and the others at the top of the Barrow. Little Nar was safely with them. They were staring out at the ship, getting smaller and smaller as it carried Kringle away from them.

PART III

IN A MATTER OF MINUTES, THICK GRAY ICE HELD THE HULL FAST.

CHAPTER EIGHT

STORMFALL

OR HOURS, THE PIRATES SAILED their ship up the western side of the mainland. Morning soon fell into afternoon, gray and freezing. When the wind died and the sail grew slack, the crew bent to their oars all the more, grunting and murmuring to one another. But if the wind slackened, the rain never did. It drove down at the ship with increasing force.

"Fine, fine," Kringle whispered to himself, huddling smaller in his cloak. "This is perfect. Out of the pot and into the fire. I should have been back with the elves now. Pirates! Invaders!"

He could tell they were heading straight north, but he wasn't sure what lay up there. Not even Merwen had been that far away from the Bottoms, and Weary-All, where she came from, was in the south, so he had no idea what was to come.

Throughout the day, the crew wrestled with their heavy oars while their captain, a big, brutish warrior with a domed helmet and a nasty-looking broadsword sheathed at his side, kept a watchful eye on the coast from his position just behind the eagle's beak.

Kringle didn't like the look of these men at all. If you or I had seen them, I doubt if we would have liked them very much, either. There were some thirty of them, all large and rough, all long-haired and bearded and dirty, most armored in battered gray iron and draped in furs and animal skins. They looked more like a tribe of helmeted bears than of men. And the dark eyes of every one of them smoldered in the pale light.

No, all in all, runes or no runes, Kringle wished he were back in Elvenwald, celebrating a good job well done.

"So much for my first mission!"

Pulling his legs up under his cloak, he felt the stones in Nar's pouch. He remembered again what Hrothr had told him — that the stones didn't like to be parted — and thought how very strange it was that they had seemed to whisper their names to him when he thought them lost.

He wondered suddenly if the pirates would also want the runes. Did they know he had them? Could they sense them, too? Did they even know what runes were? Did pirates steal magic? Kringle wasn't sure. All he could do was hide them and try to keep them safe.

But what to do next? The coast was a mile away, maybe more. "So escape is out of the question," he murmured. "I'll drown. Or I'll freeze first, then drown. Or drown first, then freeze. Either way, it's not good." The weather was a problem, too. Hadn't the wind been blowing dead against them for the last hour? Was it just hard weather? Or could it be the beginning of a goblin storm?

The pirate ship was about fifty feet long with a shallow hull made of overlapping planks. It was open to the weather except for two small decks fore and aft. A tall mast rose from its center. Rigged upon it was a giant, square sail that the pirates lowered and raised depending on the direction of the wind. Kringle huddled for warmth as best he could under the aft deck, crammed among the hoard of loot the pirates had stolen so far. There were swords and jewelry, Roman cloaks and goblets, and many, many coins in wooden caskets banded with iron. His staff had been taken from him, but he could see it propped near the captain at the prow. If he did escape, he would have to get that first. "I'm not leaving Merwen's fire stick behind!"

Merwen. The only good thing about being taken by the pirates was that they were going north and, perhaps, closer to her. "If I can escape —"

Whoosh! A sudden wave raised the ship, and the hull fell forward before being lifted aloft on another wave. The sea was getting rougher. The cold rain had now turned to colder snow. Large white flakes filled the air and dissolved into the black water.

Kringle turned to the boy next to him, who was sweating and tossing back and forth. His leg had been bandaged as soon as they had gotten him aboard, but he was still in a fever.

"How did I ever get myself into this mess?" Kringle asked himself. But, of course, he knew how. "Because I helped this boy. And how did that happen? Because the goblins attacked the Bottoms and I had to leave and then I saw the sparrow and heard the bell and went into the Black Woods and hit a tree and met the elves and heard about Merwen and came on a raid with them and tried to save the runes!"

Even if he had saved the boy from Snegg, he wasn't at all sure it was worth being captured. "Captured? Kidnapped!" he muttered. "And by pirates!"

"Keep it down!"

Kringle started. The pirate boy had propped himself up now, with his head leaning on a large iron pot. "You talk too much," he said.

"You're awake!"

"Barely," said the boy, trying to smile. "I'm Bearn. Thanks for saving me back on the beach. Of course, my father saved you, so I think we're even."

Kringle frowned. "Saved me? I don't think so. I was kidnapped. Nobody saved me —"

"Yes, he did. My father's Captain Octa. He pulled you in just as that . . . *thing* . . . was about to get us —"

"Get *you!*"

The boy laughed. "All right, get me. The goblins were going to get me. But what do you think they were going to do with you? Sing you a song and let you go?"

After a moment, Kringle laughed, too. "All right. I see what you mean."

The ship rose and fell, battling a steady gale now. It struggled to move forward over the waves.

"You're not Roman," Bearn said.

Kringle shook his head. "I come from the Bottoms."

"Queer name. I never heard of it."

"It's far away now," said Kringle.

Bearn groaned suddenly and closed his eyes, turning his head away. He didn't say any more then. Soon his head dropped. He had fallen asleep again.

"So," whispered Kringle, "that's that."

It was clear from the way the captain always kept the coast in sight that their voyage wasn't going to be a long one. Maybe Octa was looking for another Roman town to raid. Maybe he was heading for the pirate harbor, if there was one.

Wherever they were going, the pirates were afraid. They grumbled almost constantly to one another or were silent and watchful.

The rest of the first day and into the second and third they sailed north. Kringle said little to his captors, while the boy, Bearn, kept going in and out of consciousness. At least the pirates fed him — dried fish and something like spoiled cider.

When Kringle awoke on the evening of the third day, it was to the sound of grunts and muffled calls among the men. They were staring at something moving along the shore. Torches lit the black coast. One of the torches seemed to be traveling more quickly than the others. It surged ahead, then galloped back as if waiting for the others to catch up.

"Snegg," Kringle whispered.

"What's a snegg?" asked Bearn, suddenly awake again. He followed Kringle's gaze toward shore.

"A goblin," said Kringle. "The one that was trying to get us on the beach. He's not their king, but he leads their raids. He must have followed us from Barrowfoot."

"Boy?" said Octa, turning to Kringle. "Who is that following us on land? Do you know him?"

Kringle braced himself and stood up. "It's Snegg, the goblin from Barrowfoot. He must have tracked us up the coast."

"Do the goblins have ships?" asked Octa.

Kringle wondered. "I don't think so. Maybe they're waiting for you to land."

"We won't, for a while," said Octa. He turned away.

Over the rest of that night and far into the next day, they made little progress against the northern winds. And they could still see Snegg riding up the coast, disappearing into the great forest and appearing again. His torch-bearing troop of goblins kept up a swift pace on foot behind him.

"What do they want with us?" asked an oarsman finally. "Treasure? Weapons? Food? What do they think we have?"

Octa turned and gazed fiercely at Kringle. "In Barrowfoot I heard him say 'boy.' What does that mean? Why would they want Bearn? Or do they want you?"

Kringle remembered Hrothr's words about the goblins — that they sense the magic of the runes and want to possess them. "They steal children. Nobody knows why," he said. "But not usually when there are so many fighters to defend them. I think they're actually after something else." Taking a deep breath, he opened Nar's pouch and pulled a rune from it. "They want these." He stared at Octa, trying to read his expression.

The captain's face creased like old, dark leather. "So. Magic. Elf runes. I have heard about them."

Kringle was surprised that Octa knew about the runes. "The elves told me that goblins will do anything to get them. They've been trying to steal them forever —"

At once, a ribbon of light flashed out from the coast, and a sudden wind swept around the back of the ship. It battered the bow from the west, turning the ship back toward land.

"Ithgar!" said Kringle. "It's the Iron Wand, the goblin device that makes storms. Captain, they'll pull us in. Row as fast as you can away from shore. Hurry!"

The oarsmen all looked at their captain.

"You heard the boy," Octa scowled. "Row! Take us out of here!"

But the more the men tried to steer the ship out to sea, the more the wind blew it back to shore. Lightning blasted now like white-hot blades stabbing the western waters. Large black waves rose up and drove the ship eastward to the coast.

"Row!" cried Octa from the front of the ship. "Come on, you can do better than this. Row!"

The crew doubled up on the heavy oars, but another assault of lightning whipped up a wall of icy water and pushed the ship toward a narrow inlet on the coast. No matter how madly the pirates swung their oars, the ship couldn't pull away. It was driven into the inlet, where the sea narrowed up and away into the land. Waves crashed against the hull from behind, battering it forward, until suddenly the ship began to founder in the water.

"Faster! Faster!" shouted Octa. One after another, oars slapped the water hard. But the oars' splashing soon turned to cracking.

"Ice!" shouted a pirate. "The water is freezing!"

Snakes of frozen water oozed up from the river and began clutching at the hull. The waves slowed and slowed until they rocked the ship less and less and less, and the squealing, wrenching, screaming water began to still.

In a matter of minutes, thick gray ice held the hull fast.

"Chop the ice!" shouted Octa. "Try to free the hull! Oarsman, be ready for the attack. Kringle, Bearn, stay below —"

A flurry of pirates charged outside the boat and onto the ice. They began hacking away at the frozen water. Others tried to rock the boat sideways. But no sooner had the hull broken free than the water would freeze and seize the ship again. Making matters worse, the ice had begun to cover the ship itself. It slid up over the hull and down inside the planks faster than it could be cut away, catching some pirates unaware and freezing their boots to the wood.

The battle to free the vessel from the river was soon over. The ship was deadlocked in the ice, its oars stilled like so many frozen tree trunks.

"Goblin magic!" cried Octa. "All right, men. Everyone on land. Bearn, Kringle, stay together behind me." No sooner had he helped the boys down and moved in front of them, than there came the sound of hundreds of feet in the forest.

"Octa, why are you defending me?" asked Kringle. "I brought this on you."

The captain turned. "Why did you save my son? Men, be as ready as you've ever been! We'll retreat to the ship only if we need to. Remember to make your fathers proud. We are the defenders now —"

Suddenly, dark shapes flooded out between the trees as if the woods were spilling its evil out into the open air. The goblins came, their black swords raised, their eyes wild!

Kringle shrank back. There were so many of them, moving in a mass across the muddy snow toward the pirates. In ragged furs and armor they came, hundreds of them. And at their head was the goblin Kringle feared most, Snegg. He pulled the vargul's reins sharply, his eyes burning like black flame.

"This is it," said Kringle.

Bearn nodded sharply. "There's no running now —"

Rearing the vargul, Snegg shouted to his troops, "Attackkkk!"

The rush of feet across the snow was terrifying. In moments, the green horde had swarmed over the pirates, splitting the crew of thirty into two groups. Octa and his men swung their swords firmly at the first wave, but a handful of goblins slipped by and were on the two boys instantly. Bearn stumbled back as two goblins leaped at him from the side. Kringle swung his staff out sharply and caught both of them, toppling them into the snow. A quick jab of the staff's heel at the knees of a third goblin tripped him up, and now all three were down.

"Thanks," Bearn gasped as Kringle pulled him to his feet again. But five more were on them in a flash. This time, Bearn sliced the air with his short blade and the goblins jumped away, two of them wounded.

"The stones!" cried Snegg from atop the vargul, his black eyes fixed first on Kringle, then on the woolen pouch at his side. "He is the one with the stones!"

At that, some twenty more goblins charged for Kringle. "Protect the boys!" Octa yelled. Ten oarsmen struggled free of the onslaught and gathered side by side with Octa. Their shields were raised, their axes swinging. They held off the attacking goblins and even managed to push a path through the horde. But the pirates were so vastly outnumbered that it didn't last long. The goblins seemed to be everywhere at once, a wild mass of green faces and flying blades.

"Son, back to the ship!" cried the captain, wounding six more goblins with several swipes of his blade. They hissed and scrambled back, clutching their wounds.

Snegg squealed with glee to see the captain retreating to the frozen ship with the boys. Flogging Ingas mercilessly, he leaped over his own horde and landed on the deck beside them. Kringle, Bearn, and Octa were trapped.

Snegg's eyes grew wide with greed as he gazed down at the rune pouch at Kringle's side. He raised his jagged sword high over the captain's head.

"Snegg! No!" shouted Kringle. "You want the runes, take them. Take them!" He snatched the pouch from his belt and threw it as far as he could. It sailed over the heads of the goblins and struck the ground behind them. Kringle heard the stones scattering across the ice.

"Leave them! Do not touch the stones!" Snegg wailed to his troops. Stillness fell over them. Snegg tilted his large head and eyed first Octa's sword, then Kringle, huddling with Bearn behind the captain.

"Don't come another inch, you fiend!" said Octa, waving his broadsword slowly from left to right. "Or I will cut you in two!"

Snegg stared at Kringle for the longest moment. In the depths of those giant black eyes, Kringle saw hatred moving. If there was anything else, he wasn't sure he wanted to know what it was.

"So be it!" Snegg cried out. He wrenched the reins sharply, and Ingas leaped to the ice below. "Next time," he hissed. "Next time, I win against you, boy!" He grabbed up the stones one by one and stuffed them into the pouch. Then, laughing and howling, he cried, "Goblins, take everything!"

The green creatures swarmed onto the ship. They took all of its treasure and stripped the pirates of every last helmet and sword. Then whipping the vargul's head, Snegg raced away, his loot-laden horde hurrying after him. Ten minutes later, they had disappeared into the depths of the woods.

"Kringle, no!" said Bearn breathlessly. "The runes were yours!"

"They belong to the elves, but the goblins won't have them for long," Kringle said. He was trembling, but already determined to get them back. He leaped from the ship's deck to the ice below.

"You're not going to follow them?" said Bearn, looking from Kringle to his father and back again. "You can't —"

"All the way to the goblin palace, if I have to. Besides, I don't know a lot about runes, but to release their real magic I think you need all of them." Kringle pulled his hand from his cloak. In his palm lay a single gray stone.

Octa smiled. "Bold move, boy. I think the goblins will be angry when they discover your deception."

Kringle smiled, too. "I suppose they will. I'd better get on their trail."

"Wait." Bearn rummaged under the deck and wrestled something loose from the ice. He handed Kringle a small bundle. "Dried fish. Take it. It's enough for a week, if you skimp. Sorry it's frozen."

"It'll thaw in my cloak. Thanks."

"Stay far back, boy, and don't be seen," said Octa. "That's the first and last rule of following someone, and it goes double for goblins."

Kringle nodded. "I will."

"For us, then, down the coast," said Octa, looking south. "Other ships are coming."

Kringle watched the pirates make their way south from the river on foot, the wounded soldiers leaning on their fellows for support. They hugged the ragged shoreline as they went, staying as far from the woods as possible.

"Pirates," he said to himself. "Who would have thought?"

Watching them leave, he remembered the ruin of the Bottoms and the wagon leaving Castrum without him and the elves standing atop the receding Barrow. He felt as alone as he ever had in his life. But he knew he couldn't delay. Taking a deep breath, he turned to the Black Woods.

"Here I go, then. Into the heart of it." He dug Merwen's staff into the snowy mud and pushed on toward the darkness of the trees.

CHAPTER NINE

AMONG THE BLACK TREES

KRINGLE FOLLOWED THE DARK, webbed tracks right into the woods.

The goblin stink was terrible, let me tell you, even in the freezing cold. Their smell was as much a stain on the air as a blot of ink on a white cloth.

"Filthy creatures. Thieves. Murderers!" Kringle muttered. "Phew! I can't stand it!"

But of course he had to stand it, and he had to follow the smell even if it turned his stomach over and over. He breathed through his mouth whenever he could and into his cloak when he couldn't. And when he did that, he breathed in the everfainter smells of the Bottoms, and thought of Merwen and of his mother and father, and then of the goblins again, and he moved faster and more stealthily after them, thinking that perhaps their stink wasn't such a bad thing, after all.

"The smell will keep me on their trail even when I can't see them," he said, nearly laughing to realize that he might be learning some of their tricks. "Eyes aren't everything," he remarked as he entered a grove of thick fir trees where he almost lost the footprint trail. "There are ears and noses, too!"

The scent Kringle was following was fainter than it might have been, for two reasons. The first was that at some point soon after entering the woods, it was clear that the goblins had split up, with the bulk of the horde going straight north while the others, including the vargul, were heading south and east to the center of the woods. Kringle guessed from the vargul's hoofprints that Snegg was with this smaller group. The second reason was that because Kringle was traveling deeper into the woods, he was now forced to follow the goblin *snake.*

The goblin snake. Morgo invented the snake long ago, as he loved to remind anyone who forgot. For much of the time that they moved through the woods, goblins followed one another in bare eyeshot or earshot or noseshot of the one ahead and the one behind. That way, Morgo reasoned, their spying eyes covered a wide area while they themselves were as narrow as a single man abreast.

Goblins also used the snake because the forest trails were narrow, and a troop of twenty goblins could stretch itself out a quarter mile or more. Because they stepped in one another's footprints, you could never be sure exactly how many creatures there were, even if you were lucky enough to see their tracks. If you did see the tracks, however, it was almost always too late, for by then, the band was upon you.

Deeper into the woods. More tangled. And colder yet.

Kringle found himself longing for an elf cake. In fact, he longed for a dozen elf cakes, several of each kind, to ease the taste of Bearn's dried fish. But with every bite of the fish, he was reminded of his friends, recent and not so recent, and that gave him strength to go on.

Once, when the track came to a little frozen stream whose ice had been chopped up a long way down (Kringle reasoned it may have been to allow the troops or Ingas to drink), he lost both the goblins' prints and their putrid smell. "They must have crossed somewhere," he said. "Or, wait. Do they suspect someone is following them?"

He moved carefully along the near bank, trying to see where the tracks continued on the far side. But he saw nothing and went back and then beyond. Only then did he smell the leavings of the vargul. Nearly fainting, he leaped across the stream toward the stench and, if you can believe it, felt grateful to capture once again the lesser smell of the goblins. This he began to follow quickly, for he knew he had lost valuable time, when all of a sudden he found himself no more than twenty feet from Snegg himself!

Snegg! Kringle froze where he stood. The creature was hunkering alone in a copse of rotten trees, not far from where the goblins had paused to rest. Without taking a breath, Kringle slipped sideways behind a tree. From there he heard a bright clatter. Snegg was busy casting the elven runes onto a flat rock. He poked each rune tentatively, as he might an insect to see if it was dead.

Looking around and seeing that the goblin was alone, Kringle wondered whether he should pounce on him right then and there with his staff, but he was afraid. He was almost relieved when a tall, sullen-faced goblin happened by.

"Lud!" Snegg screamed, looking up from the stones. "What are you doing here?"

"Footprints!" said the goblin named Lud. "I saw footprints —"

Snegg spat loudly. "Rouse the others! We must go!" He collected the runes and stuffed them into the pouch again. He began to follow Lud, then halted. He turned around and around himself as if he were chasing his own tail (goblins do have little nubs of tail, ugly things!) and finally stopped and stared in the direction of Kringle's tree. He took a step toward it.

"Who . . . is . . . there?"

Kringle was terrified. In the moment of stillness that followed, neither he nor the goblin breathed or moved an inch. He saw Snegg's eyes grow and grow as black and as deep as pools. Kringle remembered nothing so much as that first time so many weeks before, when he had first seen Snegg at the Bottoms. In his mind's eye, he saw Merwen swinging her staff left and right at the goblins. Merwen! How very far away she seemed now, and yet as close as the staff in his hands!

Silence. Silence. Suddenly, Snegg's black eyes dwindled from the size of bowls to the size of buttons. He growled, as if he had gained then lost the sense of someone near. Turning, he raced back through the trees to his companions.

For a full five minutes Kringle dared not stir and barely breathed. He stayed behind the tree and waited and waited until the wood was completely quiet before moving again. "That," he said at last, "was very close."

The creatures did not stop often after that. Under Snegg's order, their snake collapsed to a tighter line and kept moving all night. When they rested during the daylight hours, half of the troop stayed awake and guarded their encampment. Kringle's opportunity to take back the runes never came again.

Because the forest was becoming more dense and dark (black, even, which was what had given the place its name) and the ground less thick with snow, the goblin trail became even harder to follow. The branches of the trees above him were still bare, though winter was over. But they had been so twisted by age and cold and broken by storm that scarcely any light at all penetrated the woods on even the brightest day.

The darker the woods became, the more Kringle thought he might have lost the goblins altogether, but found to his surprise that he was more or less directly on their tail. Over the next few days, as he lost and found them again and again, he discovered something that you or I might have guessed a bit sooner. Something was *keeping* Kringle on the goblin trail. The more he thought about what this could be, the more he heard the answer, for one by one, voices were calling to him through the trees in their faint, whispering chorus.

Uruz! Wunjo! Othala! Thurisaz!

At the same time he heard his own rune join the voices.

Kenaz!

It occurred to him then that Snegg might also hear the voices whispering, and that was why the goblin had been able to track them, first to Barrowfoot, then north along the coast to Octa's ship.

"No, no," he thought aloud. "The runes are good. They wouldn't allow themselves to be heard by such creatures. Or to be used by them!"

But was he sure of that? He found he wasn't, exactly, but he resolved that he could not and would not let the goblins have them for long enough to find out. He had to retrieve the runes and hold them in his hands, safe once more. "And return them to the elves —"

There was a sudden commotion in the woods ahead, and

Kringle slipped behind a rock. He peeked over it. Snegg had stopped abruptly in front of a flat, round, ice-covered boulder. Giving a shrill whistle, the goblin leaped off his vargul and tossed its reins to Lud while the others rushed together to the boulder. Kringle hung back, not daring to breathe.

Snegg unshouldered the rune pouch. "I bring a great gift for Morgo!" he growled, holding it in one hand and Ithgar in the other. "Morgo will make Snegg more powerful than ever — more than all of you!"

Snegg hissed and spat as he turned to the boulder. With his hands still raised, he bellowed, "Now — open! Open!"

Kringle was prepared for some display of goblin magic, but the boulder did not move by itself. Five goblins, including Lud, groaned, tramped sullenly over to it and seized it as best they could. With much grunting and squealing they dragged it to the side. At once, a sickly yellow light shone up from below and into the trees above their heads.

"I go to Morgo!" said Snegg. "Morgo shall be grateful —"

"No boy," Lud blurted out.

"Morgo shall still be grateful!" snapped Snegg. Kicking aside the five boulder pushers, he leaped down into the hole. One by one, the others followed.

A few minutes later, after the last had gone in, Snegg stuck his head back up and looked around. Satisfied there was no one about, he dropped away into the hole.

Just as the boulder was being dragged closed again, Kringle dashed up and glimpsed a rough earthen tunnel worming away under the ground. A moment later, the forest was black again.

The boy stood in the snow, shaking. "Morgo's palace. I've found it!" He tried to calm his pounding heart, not wanting to admit what he was thinking. He had found the goblins' filthy warren under the ground. This was it. But what if the goblins had caught Merwen again? Could she be here? Or was she still free and looking for him? And what about the children? Hadn't everyone said that the kidnapped children were brought here, too? Would he see them? What exactly *would* he find?

Kringle waited awhile, his ear pressed to the boulder. He heard nothing. So, using his staff as a lever, he slowly and carefully inched the large rock aside. His arms and back and legs ached with every motion.

As soon as the hole came into view, Kringle knelt down and gazed into it. The tunnel dropped fifteen feet straight down before flattening toward the source of the light. Once or twice, something passed in front of the light, then there was no movement for a long while.

"So, no one's there now?" he whispered to himself.

"Doesn't really seem so," he replied.

"Does that make it safe?"

"No, but you know I have to . . ."

"I know."

Slinging his staff into its quiver once more, Kringle looked around the dark woods one last time, then climbed into the goblin hole and slipped down below the frozen earth.

CHAPTER TEN

PALACE OF THE GOBLIN KING

INCH BY INCH, Kringle made his way down the hole. He tumbled behind a heap of loose tunnel rock and waited. Nothing happened for a full minute.

When he finally breathed out and back in again, he practically choked. The smell was overpowering.

"Oh . . . oh . . . ," he groaned. He waved the air in front of his face, but it did little good. All he could do was wait until his nose — his poor nose, even with his cloak held over it! — became more used to the smell.

"All right, then. Carefully, please."

He moved slowly from pile to pile and shadow to shadow as he approached the maze of tunnels that spread away from the entrance. The passages were rough-hewn and not straight, but not long after he entered them he became aware — though he wasn't sure how — that, with each step, he was moving deeper into the earth. Once or twice he thought he *saw* his way through this or that tunnel even before he came to where they split off. He wondered again if the runes were somehow leading him to them, as they seemed to have done in Barrowfoot and in the woods. Then again, as before, he wondered whether Snegg could hear the rune he himself had kept.

"Strange," he said. "But helpful. Very helpful, I think."

Crawling and scrabbling his way through one passage after another, muttering to himself, catching his breath, losing it again, he hid and waited, then charged ahead and waited and hid. He saw neither children nor Merwen, but felt they *could* be here, they *might* be here, somewhere in this vast maze. He scrambled where he had to, paused where the tunnels crisscrossed, hid time and again, then pushed forward once more.

At long last Kringle crouched just outside a great stone room lit with smoking torches and cauldrons of fire. The air was stifling. Fools! Idiots! he thought.

The goblins had apparently not mastered the concept of smoke, for there were fires all over the room, but the thick, dark smoke from them had nowhere to go. It was gathering at the ceiling into a cloud that hung lower and lower.

Kringle squirreled himself into a deep cleft in the wall between the passage and the cave. Even leaning forward, he remained hidden. But what he saw there!

In the center of the room, amid piles of garbage, heaps of dirt, and mounds of tunnel rock, was a big throne made of wooden blocks nailed haphazardly together. On it, glaring down at several hundred lesser creatures massed below him, was the largest goblin Kringle had ever seen. He was hunched over and wobbling under the weight of an enormous head with giant ears, one of which was missing its point.

"Is that . . . Morgo?" he gasped softly.

It was Morgo. King of the Goblins. His head was so much larger than that of any of his underlings, it was easy to see why he was king over them. The darkness of his green skin and the bluntness of his brow and the constant scowl across his features made him seem truly monstrous indeed, which could not help but give him power over the others.

His heart thundering wildly, Kringle could think of only one thing. "He murdered my father."

Snegg entered the cave now, followed by Lud and a third goblin, who Kringle recognized as the tail scout of the snake.

"O King!" said all three together, bowing to the floor.

"Want it! Want it!" cried Morgo, his eyes growing. "Give it to me fast! Ithgar!"

Snegg rose to his feet and held up the Iron Wand. It was the first time Kringle had seen the object up close. It was made of black iron with veins of red spiraling up the handle and ending in an ugly jagged knob at the top. When Morgo opened his hand, Kringle saw that the goblin's palm had a hideous black burn in the center.

"Forged in the Fires of the North, O King!" said Snegg. "It did good service, thy Ithgar."

"Ackk!" Morgo snatched it up and held it close. "So, so, you have brought Morgo . . . something?" His voice slithered between low gurgles and high squeals.

Snegg raised his head. "We have, O —"

"Then bring it . . . bring it! Let Morgo see. . . ."

Snegg crept forward to the throne, his head bowed again. Between his upraised hands he held a wooden chest banded with iron that Kringle recognized as one of several stolen from Octa's ship. Morgo grinned when he saw it.

"Bring it closer, my chieftain, my raider, my Snegg!"

The goblin flipped open the chest from behind. Immediately, Morgo's eyes bulged. He dug his hands into the pirate chest and came out with a long golden chain hanging with many colored stones.

"Ahhh!" said the Goblin King, draping the chain across his scalp. But the necklace was not large enough to fit over his gigantic head, and he became angry and tossed the chain to the floor. It broke, sending little jewels skittering among the piles of rock. "No good for Morgo!"

Snegg frowned and set the chest down. Turning, he called forth the third goblin, who handed Snegg a pirate broadsword in a leather scabbard.

"Much other iron has gone north, my king," said Snegg.

"Yes, yes, for Grunding," said Morgo. He snatched the

sword away, jerked it out of its sheath, and waved it in the air over his head. He jumped awkwardly up to the throne's seat, swishing the sword. "I like this! Attack! Rob! Steal! Kill! *Killlll!*" He stopped and stared down at Snegg. "And what else?"

Snegg edged forward a third time, now holding up the rune pouch. Kringle leaned closer, his blood boiling, but dared not take a step.

"What is this?" said Morgo, lowering the sword. "A pouch? Morgo has hundreds of pouches. This is nothing —"

Snegg shook it, and the faint clatter it made stopped his leader cold. "Stones," said Snegg. "Magic stones. From the elves!"

"From the elves!" Morgo cried, raising the sword again and stabbing the air. "If goblins have elf magic now, we kill the elves. All of them. Forever!" He snatched the pouch from Snegg and spilled its contents onto the seat of his throne.

Kringle gasped. He could hear the runes whisper their names — *Fehu! Hagalaz! Perthro!* — just as the single stone in his pocket whispered back: *Kenaz!*

Morgo nearly swooned over the stones, caressing them lovingly with his fingers. He seemed to be listening intently. "Magic stones," he murmured, "talk to Morgo of child. Magic stones, you say goblins will fall. But Morgo has . . . a secret. . . ." He listened for a few moments more, but as far as Kringle heard, the runes remained silent. The Goblin

King jerked upright suddenly and turned to Snegg. "And what is it that Morgo wants most to hear?"

Snegg's head nearly touched the ground. "O King, we . . . did not find the child."

Kringle's heart thumped.

"The child!" Morgo erupted. "The child! Years and years and years the words have tormented Morgo. Morgo is hateful of him. Morgo wishes death to him —" The king turned back to the runes.

"But he is close!" the lesser goblin added quickly. "We are close to the boy! All the children are being taken."

Kringle trembled. What did that mean?

"Fool! Devil!" Morgo cried suddenly. He had counted the stones, then dipped into the bag and brought out an empty hand. "Two stones are missing!"

"Two?" whispered Kringle. "No, only one."

Morgo rose up on the throne and cast a withering gaze at Snegg. "Only twenty-two stones. You stole two stones, you die —"

"No!" said Lud, speaking for the first time. "The boy! The boy! He must have. Lud go to find —"

"Snegg, go to find!" shouted Morgo derisively. "Snegg, you shall find them. You shall find the stones!"

"I will find the last of thy stones, O Great King!" said Snegg. "But there is more to tell!" He moved back, pushing Lud and several other goblins out of the way. "King Morgo, look!"

When the goblins backed up, Kringle saw for the first time a rough shape gouged into the stony floor. He didn't know what it was until Snegg grabbed a rock and slapped it onto the ground with a *clack*. "Romans gone now," the goblin said. He began laying rocks here and there around what Kringle realized must be a map. "Gone . . . gone . . . gone . . . ," Snegg repeated.

What the other goblins were thinking of Snegg's little show was unclear. They stared at his scattering of rocks for the longest time, waiting. But, let me tell you, if you had been crouching in that tunnel with Kringle, you could have seen the wheels and cogs of Morgo's giant goblin brain moving. Those gears ground, scraped, clattered, squealed, and finally spun!

The Goblin King raised his grinning face to Snegg, then to Lud, then back to the rocks on the cave floor, scanning them one after another. Finally, he sucked up a noisy breath through his mouth. Whatever muttering there was came to a dead silence then, as the Goblin King spoke. "Mor-go . . . lahhhnd! I see tower! I see many many tower! Bridge! Walls and walls, all around me. Tower! Many many tower!"

Morgo then took up a large black rock and thumped it down apart from all the rocks Snegg had put on the map. Hopping around the black rock and waving his spindly arms in the air, the king howled, "Morgoland! Morgoland!"

Soon, all the goblins chanted the word, "Morgoland!"

Morgoland. Where it actually was in relation to the Black

Woods or anything else was unclear, for the map was so crudely drawn. But Kringle knew what it meant. He slid back deeper into the tunnel, trembling with fear. The goblins want to come up, he thought. They want to come up out of the ground and spread their horrible empire over the earth!

"When Grunding is born, Morgoland shall rise!" cried the Goblin King. "The hour of Grunding comes!"

"Grunding? Grunding? He speaks in riddles!" whispered Kringle.

Morgo pawed the rune stones. "Take everything to the treasure room. Snegg, find the last stones. I will learn the elven mysteries. Go take them now. Now!"

Snegg bowed even lower, then gestured to Lud. The other goblin gathered up the wooden chest and the other jewelry. Snegg himself took the rune pouch. He slid out of the room with Lud behind him.

Kringle retreated into the tunnel until he found a depression in the cave wall that allowed him to crouch and hide. "Morgo, your day will come," he whispered. "You'll pay for killing my father. For now, I'm going to take back the runes. You won't have the elven magic!"

As soon as the tunnel was clear, he slipped away from the domed room and into one of the many dozens of tunnels snaking away from it. He followed the arguing and slapping of Snegg and Lud, who seemed to be disagreeing over which was the shortest way to the treasure room. He knew every step was bringing him deeper into the earth, and though he feared that if they went much farther he wouldn't be able to find his way out, he knew he had to follow.

Suddenly the two goblins vanished through a side crevice in the tunnel. Kringle stopped short. When they didn't re-emerge, he moved slowly to the crack and looked in. He practically turned sick to his stomach at the sight.

"This is the treasure room?"

It was.

Morgo's treasure room was nothing more than a mess of found objects, pile upon pile of what others had thrown away. All seemed to have been salvaged by the goblins and tossed in there with abandon. For every usable sword, there were a dozen broken or bent blades. A finely decorated Roman bow was cracked and useless. A raider shield was broken nearly in half. Jewels lay scattered among the rocks and debris of the tunnel, and shredded, singed paper, cloth, robes, and cloaks all lay sodden and moldering in puddles on the floor. A guttering torch lit the room dimly.

Lud dumped the pirate booty onto one pile while Snegg turned to a passage opening on the far side of the room. But when Lud tagged along behind him, Snegg stopped and pushed him away. "Don't follow me!" he growled. "Guard for intruders."

"But the stones —"

"Fool! Snegg has a mind. Snegg *knows* things! These stones will lead me to the others. I will discover their magic. Go!" With that, he spun on his heels and slipped out the opening, the rune pouch still clutched in his hand.

"You'll discover their magic, will you?" Kringle whispered. "Where are you taking them?"

Lud was left quivering amid the garbage. But he soon scowled and left the way he had come in. Kringle waited for him to leave, then moved quietly among the junk heaps to the far opening. Then, just as he passed a mound covered by a heavy gray cloth, a hand shot out, grabbed his ankle, pulled him sharply to the floor, and dragged him down under it.

"What —" he cried. "Hey —"

"Silence!" growled a voice. "Here come the Minders!"

CHAPTER ELEVEN

IN THE PASSAGES

OO TERRIFIED TO DISCOVER who or what was under the cloth with him, Kringle stared up through the weave and saw a pack of varguls lunging into the treasure room from the very opening Snegg had passed through! Each beast had a heavy chain wound around its neck. Grasping the chains were a gaggle of black-skinned goblins as thin as skeletons.

"What? What?" Kringle sputtered. "What —"

"Try being quiet!" hissed the voice behind his head.

Five beasts, six, ten in all, tramped between the heaps and piles in the room and went out the opposite tunnel, dragging the black goblins behind them.

"The Minders are one of the eastern tribes of goblins," whispered the voice. "They train varguls to kill."

Kringle trembled as the last of the beasts pulled its Minder from the room.

"They're gone now, thank the Lord," said the voice. "The varguls must just have been fed, or let me tell you, they would have fed on us!"

Kringle peered out and made certain the room was empty. Then he pulled the cloth off his head and held it up. Hiding under it was a man in a wrinkled brown robe. He was lightly bearded and nearly bald, and his skin was drawn and gray.

"*You* might want to get caught, boy," the man said, "but it wouldn't have been very good for *me*. *I'm* trying to hide!"

"Who are you?"

"I am Brother Alban," said the man, peeping his head out from under the cloth, looking around, and finally emerging. He extended his hand. "And you are?"

"Kringle."

"Hmm. Odd name. But then, you've all got strange names, you heath folk. Just a moment . . ." The man edged his way around a pile of broken wheels and ripped clothing. He rustled among the garbage, grabbed something from the floor, and tucked it under his robe. Kringle watched him turn and scurry along the wall to a third tunnel leading out of the room. The man looked back. "Well, boy. Are you coming, or do you consider that you'll be all right here in the goblins' treasure room? Varguls do regain their appetite, you know. Quite quickly, as a matter of fact. Your choice!"

Kringle frowned. "I —"

"Do come on!" Alban said sharply. He slipped into the tunnel and was gone.

"Coming!" said Kringle.

He followed Brother Alban quickly but carefully through the tunnels. Judging from the man's sunken cheeks and the way his robe hung on him, Kringle guessed that he had once been plumper but had fallen on hungry times.

Alban glanced over his shoulder, still moving ahead. "So the goblins captured you, poor child, but you got away from them? No doubt you swatted them good with that big stick of yours. Well done. But you're still trapped far, far underground. Where did they kidnap you from? Burwyn? Dimblebridge? Camblybog?"

It was the first time Kringle had really thought of explaining how he got to be there. "No, no. They didn't capture me. I came down here to find something."

The man's jaw dropped. "You didn't *have* to come, and yet you *did* come? Why would you risk this?" He suddenly paused and narrowed his eyes at Kringle. "Oh, no, no, no. They didn't send you . . . to find *me* . . . did they?"

"They? Who?" Kringle shook his head. "Sorry. No one sent me for you."

Alban blushed. A sad little smile crept over his lips as he stepped ahead in the tunnel again. "No, no, of course not.

Who even knows I'm here? And, for that matter, who would care if I went missing? Everyone's leaving the country, anyway. So, boy, what could be so valuable down here that you'd want to risk being captured by goblins?"

"The runes," he said.

"The runes. Never heard of them," said the man. "But if they are friends of yours, they'll be in the big room. Everyone's in the big room. We're going there now."

"No, no, they're not friends," said Kringle. "Runes are stones."

The man blinked. "Stones? That sounds mysterious. Do you mean jewels? Precious stones? Treasure? A lot of the good things have already gone north."

Kringle shook his head. "Little gray stones."

Alban stopped. His jaw fell again. "Little gray stones! Boy, you didn't have to come all the way down into the goblin palace for *little gray stones*! There are little gray stones everywhere in this country! You can't walk a yard without stubbing your toe on one! Why, every day I shake little gray stones out of my shoes —"

"The rune stones are magical," whispered Kringle. "The goblin called Snegg took a whole pouch of them. Runes belong to the elves. I've come to get them back —"

"Elves? Magical? Oh, pish posh!" whispered the man, shaking his head sharply. "You're talking nonsense! You're after elf stones, and the goblins have enslaved an army of children . . . hush, the Minders again!"

They ducked into a side tunnel as a different herd of varguls dragged a different troop of black goblins down the tunnel and into the lighted cave ahead. "More Minders, more varguls every day," mumbled Alban. "And they're not the only ones. Something strange is going on. Something strange and not at all good."

Kringle watched the last of the goblins pass by, and followed Alban the other way. "Well, all right," he said, "but why are *you* down in the goblin palace? You aren't from around here."

"Gracious, no!" said Alban, touching his brown robe. "I'm a priest, of course."

Kringle looked him up and down. "'Of course'? Why 'of course'? Should I have known?"

Alban stammered. "Well, unless you've never seen . . . ah . . . that is . . . well, never mind. I come from Rome. Big, wonderful, *warm* Rome. That is, I came from Rome four years and seven months ago; never mind how many days, hours, and minutes, though I could tell you, be sure of that. I was sent to teach people — you, for instance — about, well, things you may not have heard of before. The great Lord who lives in heaven, for instance."

"Where's that?"

"Where's that! Where's that?" Alban sputtered. "I would

love to tell you, but I don't think we have time for that right now, boy!"

Kringle shrugged. "You're right, anyway. I've never heard of him. What is a priest, anyway?"

Alban made a hushing sound. "Do you always talk so much?"

"Well —"

"Look, if we get out of here, I will most happily tell you what a priest is. In fact, I will tell you everything I know! But for now, my dear boy, I think we have much more important business —"

"How did you get here?"

Alban sucked in a sharp breath. "Lord! I was captured in Castrum! I was teaching a group of little children. The goblins came in a storm and we were attacked and that was nearly three months ago, now shhh!"

Three months! Had he been with the elves and the pirates that long? Had it been that long since he had seen Merwen? Three months! He remembered what Hrothr had told him the runes said: *"From the warmth of hearthfire a journey is begun. . . ."* First elves, then pirates, and now a priest. Kringle looked at the man as they carefully picked their way through the tunnels again. He had never heard of a priest before and didn't know what one was. But if a priest was taken by goblins, then a priest was a friend.

"Here is the big room," whispered Alban, moving slowly

up a very narrow passage and stopping outside a giant, firelit cavern. He motioned ahead. "And there they are. The poor souls. Kringle, look!"

The boy did look. He stared, stunned and unbelieving. "Oh, no," he said. "Oh, no, no."

CHAPTER TWELVE

THE INNOCENTS

HE CAVE MUST have been a half mile or more across and the same high, and it was full of children. Kringle guessed most of them to be about his age or younger, but all were in rags, and all chained by their ankles or wrists or both. They were huddled together in fear, surrounded by a numberless army of hissing black goblins, larger red goblins, and the usual green ones, along with dozens of growling varguls.

Kringle stared at the children's frightened faces and their sad, horrified eyes. He could barely breathe.

"They took the Roman children I used to visit," whispered Alban. "They stole the midlanders and heath folk, too — children like you, Kringle."

"I know."

"Even invader children. These poor souls are the ones who need saving. Not a silly sack of rocks!"

Several boys and a little black-haired girl clung to one

another on the far side of the cave as a snapping vargul neared them.

"There are so many, so many," said Alban, shaking his head. "I had not thought there were so many. Some lucky ones have escaped over the years. Some have even been let go. But still the goblins search, still they hunt, and still they steal. It seems they are looking for someone."

Kringle's chest ached, and his throat stung. "Did they take you to watch over the children? They took someone I love. I think they wanted her to help with the children. Is that why they took you?"

The priest swallowed several times, his chin quivering as he moved farther back into the shadows. When he finally turned his eyes to the boy, he said, "Perhaps they thought I could help because they saw me teaching the children. Or perhaps the goblins took me because of this."

Alban fished under his robe and pulled out a battered book covered with brown leather. It was what he had taken from the treasure room. When Alban opened the book, Kringle saw page after page of sketches and drawings of great buildings, bridges, walls, and towers. At once, he thought of Morgo's terrible vision of Morgoland. But they also reminded him of what Castrum might have looked like before it was abandoned and destroyed.

"I draw," said Alban. "I draw to remind me of where I came from. These are my memories of the city of Rome."

"But why would the goblins want you because of a book?"

"They think — ha, *think!* That's a strong word! — that because I draw these things, I can *build* these things! They want to build a city or something in the north. It's not quite clear to me what they're after. What *is* clear is that they are also creating some sort of giant . . . I don't even know what to call it . . . war machine. 'Forged in the Fires of the North,' I've heard them say a thousand times."

"Wait," said Kringle. "'Forged in the Fires of the North'? Snegg said all the weapons and armor were going north. I heard Morgo talking about a thing named Grunding —"

Alban's face darkened. "Grunding, yes, that's right. Grunding, I fear, is some sort of terrible weapon. I don't know where this forge is — underground, is all I know — but when I was taken there, it was already filled with thousands upon thousands of swords and helmets and armor and iron wheels and anything metal. And the largest furnace you could ever imagine. When Snegg raided Castrum, he found my drawings. He's a clever one. He took me just as I was leaving —"

"I thought you were teaching or something."

"Must you ask so many questions? I *mean* as I was leaving just after teaching the families. And the children. The goblins sent me up north to help build this horrible thing. Lord knows how, but I escaped the place. I had nearly made it back to my home when I was caught once more. This time, they brought me here. I managed to slip away again, and I've been trying to escape ever since, but each day they bring more and more children here. Look at them. There must be close to five hundred now. What do they want them for? Kringle, I tell you, I don't know what to do, but how can I leave them?"

"So you stayed here in the goblin palace . . . for them?" Kringle asked.

Alban blushed again. "I suppose I did. The children are . . . *my* runes. But now that the Romans are leaving — and leaving and leaving! — Morgo has been gathering all the goblins. The Minders and the varguls. The Borling, the red goblins. I even saw a troop of Urkens, the so-called White Biters of the west. There are perhaps as many as twenty thousand so far. Whatever Morgo is planning, whatever this Grunding thing is, it's all going to happen in the north."

Kringle stared into the room again. "North. North. Always north. Merwen was going north —"

"Merwen?" said Alban. "Did you say 'Merwen'?"

Kringle's heart nearly burst right out of his chest. "What? You saw her? Is she all right? Is she here —"

"No, no!" Alban shook his head quickly. "No, no. I saw her when I was taken the second time, near Netherbliss. She had two children in her charge. That was a little over a week ago."

"So the goblins had her again?"

Alban nodded. "I can't tell you for how long, but yes. I'm sorry. They were on their way north, too. Hush!"

A commotion of screaming erupted on the far side of the cave. Kringle watched as four Minders slacked their varguls' chains. Several children, pale and ghostlike, cried out and scrambled back in fear before the varguls were finally pulled away again. But all the while the goblins' eyes swelled with excitement, and their skin took on a darker hue.

As he watched this, desperately wanting to intervene, Kringle was struck with the idea that there might be a connection between the children's fear and the goblins. After all, hadn't Merwen always told him not to be afraid? Hadn't he seen Snegg's terrible hunger when he attacked the Bottoms so long ago? Hadn't he seen the goblin's eyes swell and swell the more he himself had feared? And could it have been why, when Kringle thought of Merwen in the forest, his fear ebbed away, and Snegg lost the scent of him?

And if this was true for Snegg and the lesser goblins, wouldn't it be a hundred times more true for their leader Morgo? Did fear, after all, give the goblins some kind of power?

"We have to go in there."

Alban frowned. "Go *in* there? Boy, what are you saying?"

Kringle shook his head slowly. "I don't know, exactly," he said, "but maybe Morgo needs the children for his plan, whatever that is. And what if there's a chance we could free them? What if together we could actually help them? Don't we have to try? How could we *not* try?"

Alban was still frowning. "All good questions, Kringle. But we aren't exactly ready for the job, you know. For one thing, there are twenty thousand goblins one shriek away. Not to mention that the tunnels of Morgo's palace writhe away mile after mile like a basket of eels! Even if we could free the children, we'd most likely get lost before we got out. You, me, everyone. Morgo's palace is vast!"

"Still, don't we have to try?"

Alban studied the boy closely. "And that's another thing. *We?* You said you don't know what a priest is, so let me tell you. A priest, Kringle, is someone who has dedicated his life to peace and love and prayer. He is not a fighter! Our Lord did not fight!"

"Who?"

Alban's mouth dropped open. He shut it again. "Never mind that just now. But what about you? You're just a boy!"

A boy. That was true enough, too. Kringle had never felt as frail and afraid as he did at that very moment, trembling in a dreadful goblin tunnel, moments away from capture or, you may imagine, something even worse. He *was* a boy. But here were children younger than himself enslaved by goblins and he was not . . . yet. He *could* help them.

He managed to look Alban straight in the eye. "I'm young. So what?"

"So what?" Alban squinted into Kringle's face. "So what! So what? Well, I'll tell you . . . I'll tell you . . ."

He paused and looked the boy up and down. Kringle's big cloak billowed around his feet, and his staff towered over his head. But whatever it was that Alban was thinking at that moment seemed, the more he looked at the boy, to alter bit by bit until the direction of his thoughts changed.

"Indeed, yes, so what?" Alban said. "Forgive me. I'm only a priest, after all. I apologize. Never mind all the 'boy' talk. What do you think we should do, Kringle?"

What do you think we should do, Kringle?

The man was actually going to *listen* to him?

"Well . . . ," he said, peering into the cave once again. He could find nothing to follow his "well," and he didn't have to. For suddenly they heard the groan of a deep horn from Morgo's throne room and a din of voices get louder and closer. The Goblin King was yelling, "Grunding!" and the other goblins were chanting back, "Grunding!"

"What's happening now?" asked Kringle.

"I don't know, but make yourself small," said Alban. "They're coming."

The man and the boy pushed even deeper into the shadows while goblins poured through the tunnels in more numbers than you could possibly imagine. Dozens. Hundreds. Thousands! Before long the children's room was filled with them. Then *he* came.

Morgo entered from the back on a platform held up by a half-dozen Borling. He waved a sword in one hand, Ithgar in the other.

"Out of the ice, out of the north, Grunding shall be born!" he cried. "And you — children — you shall see him! The world shall see him! And Morgoland will rise!"

"Grunding!" the goblins shouted, their eyes growing as they surrounded the quaking children. Even the varguls took up the chant, howling more loudly with each roar of the goblins.

"Kringle, we can't free the children now," said the priest, pulling him back even farther. "Or we'll surely be caught ourselves. If you're right, and Morgo needs the children, he won't harm them. Or Merwen. He'll need them all. And if we're free, we can better discover what he is really up to."

Kringle saw Snegg in the shadows, holding the rune pouch close to his ear as if he was listening, or trying to.

Soon the passages emptied of goblins as they pushed into the cave, and the howling grew its loudest yet.

"Now's our chance," said Alban. "The tunnel is clear. Come on, boy. Now!"

Kringle nodded reluctantly. Taking one last look at the poor little souls, he uttered an oath and rushed after Alban.

"Go left," he said at the first corner. "Another left. Straight. Right. Down. Now up." He understood less than you do how he seemed to know the way, but know it he did. Into one tunnel, out another, through this shaft, up that passage they threaded their way until at last they found themselves at a cleft in a tunnel not fifty feet from the palace entrance.

"Nice work, Kringle!" whispered the priest.

But Lud was there, leaning wearily on a pile in front of the entrance hole. He was mumbling and hissing to himself, "Snegg, Snegg, always Snegg!" The goblin's chanting echoed from the big cave. Lud glanced back through the tunnels, then dug his sword into the earth, jabbing it back and forth and making little designs.

"Careful," whispered Alban.

"I don't think we have the time," said Kringle. He tightened his cloak and gripped his staff. "Excuse me, Lud, we need to pass."

The goblin's eyes grew huge. "Hyoomuns!" he shrieked. "Boy! Hyoomuns!" Instinctively, he lunged forward with his sword.

Kringle swung hard with his heavy stick. Lud screamed and fell to his knees while the boy stumbled forward. With a second swing to the chest, he managed to knock Lud to the floor.

Alban jumped. "Kringle, that was very —"

"Up the tunnel!" the boy shouted.

But Lud sprang up to his knees, swung his sword wildly, and caught the priest in the leg. Alban fell to the ground, groaning in pain.

Kringle immediately struck back at Lud, but the goblin rolled aside and sliced up, just missing Kringle's arm, but slitting open the side of his cloak. The rune stone fell to the floor at Lud's feet with a clatter. "Ahh!" the goblin shrieked. "The magic stone! Boy! Boy!" He lunged for it.

"No!" yelled Kringle. He whipped the staff around one last time, and Lud fell behind a rock pile, moaning softly, then going still. Holding his breath, Kringle bound and gagged the goblin with rags and pulled him to a passage that was nearly hidden by a rock mound. "This may gain us some time!"

Sliding his staff into its quiver and grabbing more cloths to bind Alban's wound, he helped the priest to his feet. "Can you make it?"

"I didn't know I had a choice," growled Alban.

"You don't."

Bending for a moment, Kringle scooped up the stone and felt his pocket. To his amazement, the slit from Lud's sword had vanished. "The elvencloak," he whispered. "It healed itself —"

"Can we just go?"

Together, they burrowed up the tunnel. When they finally emerged into the forest, Alban collapsed into the mud while Kringle heaved the boulder back into place.

Judging from the blood seeping through Alban's robe from his leg wound, Kringle knew the priest was seriously hurt. But he also knew they had no choice but to get out of the forest as quickly as possible. He rebound the wound as best he could, then looked up into the trees.

"It's day already," he said. "If we're lucky, it'll be a little while before Lud comes to, and a little longer before night falls and they follow. But we still have to move quickly."

"Let's," said Alban briefly. "West?"

"West," said Kringle, "to the forest's edge."

And west they went. With every step, they heard the scurrying of feet among the trees. No, not feet, paws. The stoats, weasels, and badgers were going west, too. The whole forest was fleeing the goblin smell.

Three hours later, Kringle and Alban reached the edge of the trees, and the sounds of the forest creatures finally dispersed. Beyond the woods, the day was gray, bitter cold, and half gone.

"Kringle, this is nonsense," panted Alban, stopping. "I'm slowing you down. Leave me here. You'd best go find your elves. They're in danger, too, like the rest of us. I'm too slow. Besides, the goblins may not even want me now. It won't be long before Snegg knows you have a rune. If the goblins want them so badly, me and my book of drawings will soon be nothing more than a memory."

Kringle turned to him. The man's face was white, bloodless, his features more drawn and pale than ever. Even if he lived nearby, Alban might not make it home by himself. No, Kringle wouldn't leave him. He couldn't. Besides, wouldn't his rune help him know where Snegg was? "Alban, I'm taking you home," he said finally. "Where do you live?"

The priest wagged his head, then turned to the snow-topped mountains of the distant north. "Cragtop," he said.

Kringle nearly choked. "Cragtop? Cragtop! That's very far. I think a priest must be someone who doesn't like people very much! Cragtop is far from everything!"

Alban began to laugh softly.

"What's so funny?" asked Kringle.

"It's just that, well, Cragtop *is* far. And right now we have no food. My leg is not in the best shape. The goblins are already planning something quite horrible, but when they find out we've escaped and that you have the rune, Snegg will be after us in a heartbeat. All in all, Kringle, I'd say, we did well!"

The priest's was the first laugh Kringle had heard for some time, and it sounded good. "Alban," he said. "I'll go to the elves, I will. But if the goblin plan is to happen in the north, then that's where we need to be. And if Snegg will soon come after us, we should get there sooner rather than later. Maybe it won't be so far, after all."

Alban smiled. "One can always hope!"

Kringle gave the man his staff, slid under his shoulder, and together they began the long walk north.

PART IV

KEEPING HIS EYES FIXED ON THE BLACK CLIFFS, KRINGLE DROVE THE SLEDGE ON.

CHAPTER THIRTEEN

THE FROZEN RIVER

B Y EVENING OF THE FIRST DAY, the two escapees had put seven miles between them and the Black Woods. They were now pushing straight north, although Cragtop seemed no closer than when they had first seen it.

Darkness had fallen steadily, and Kringle feared that soon Lud would be discovered and tell his story. The goblins would certainly follow them at the first hint of night.

"We need to hurry now," he said.

"Oh, I see. Hurry *now*," said Alban, pausing to rebandage his leg. "And what exactly do you call what we've *been* doing?"

"I'm sorry. I know your wound hurts, but night will be here soon and we have to move more quickly if we can."

Alban grumbled and did the best he could. Together they hobbled over the plains, catching a piece of road when it suited their direction, but otherwise pushing through the mounds and gulleys of the open air for as long as they were able. Every now and then Kringle heard Alban whisper to himself but stop abruptly when he knew the boy was listening. His rumbling and mumbling of strange words — *deus filius . . . de caelo* — reminded Kringle of the sound of the runes, and he wondered again if Snegg could actually learn to hear them calling to one another.

When night fell, they went to earth in a small glen and waited through the dark hours. The man and the boy huddled together against the cold. They did this the next day and the next — hiding at night, traveling during the daylight hours.

At dawn on the fourth day, they went straight on until midday, then into afternoon, and finally to dusk. At nightfall, they rested at a place where two big boulders lay pitched against each other. Alban slumped to the ground between them. "Ah, rest . . . sleep . . ."

Kringle climbed up the lower of the two and looked to the to the white, frozen north. There, at the head of the endless upward plain, stood the dark shape of Cragtop, Alban's black mountain. It seemed as far as ever.

"Have we made any progress? It'll take a week, maybe longer, to cross that plain."

Alban looked up at him. "There's one good thing," he said.

"Only one?" said Kringle. "I was hoping for more."

"Don't be greedy. I was going to say that Morgo's underground palace in the woods is vast, but its tunnels don't go on forever. When the goblins move north to their forge, wherever that is, they'll have to surface. When they do, we'll see their torches from Cragtop. You can see everything from Cragtop. It is a spot very close to heaven."

Kringle looked closely at the priest. Heaven. That word again. He wanted to ask Alban about it then, but he suddenly became aware of another word. *Kenaz!* He dug his hand into his cloak pocket and took his rune from it. Closing his eyes, he emptied his mind, and the voices began. *Othala! Fehu!*

And suddenly, as he had in Barrowfoot, Kringle began to see things. He saw the goblins edging up inside the Black Woods, thirty miles behind them and gaining ground. Snegg was at their head, riding Ingas furiously. He had the rune pouch wound on his belt. Lud was riding behind on another vargul, the dark wand Ithgar raised like a sword. Behind them were some fifty others, all riding, riding.

Kringle had the terrible thought that if he could hear Snegg's runes and see him, Snegg might be able to see and hear *him*. There was something else nagging at him about Snegg and the runes, but he couldn't put it into words.

Opening his eyes, he thrust the stone back into his cloak. "Alban, no sleep just yet. They're coming!"

Leaning heavily on the staff, Alban rose as quickly as he

could. "Then let's go! The Lord doesn't help those who don't help themselves, you know!"

They hurried two more hours through the night wastes, but it became clear to Kringle that the goblins were closing the gap with every passing minute. The first faint smells of the varguls had reached the boy's nostrils, which meant that the goblins were well out of the forest and crossing the plains.

"They can't be more than three hours behind us," said Kringle, when they reached a rise in the ground. "If we're lucky."

Alban looked back over the plains. A coil of snow spun up from the land between the forest and where they stood. "If we go straight north, Snegg will catch us sooner rather than later. But" — he turned to the west — "we might gain some time by heading toward the water. Perhaps enough time for daylight to come. I overheard some Borling in the palace complaining that while the varguls are fast, they frequently need to rest."

Kringle smiled faintly. "Whereas we're slow and frequently need to rest."

"Quite," said Alban, smiling faintly. "Still . . ."

"Still," agreed Kringle. "West it is."

They went west for four straight hours across the barren land without a break until, under the dusky sky of near dawn, they came to a patch of gnarled trees on a ridge. Climbing quickly over it, Kringle staggered into a steady wind from the sea. Before and below him the land sloped down to the slithering white flatness of a frozen river and to the sea beyond. Narrowing his eyes, Kringle followed the river inland. It traveled east for a while, then straight north toward Cragtop.

Moving up next to him, Alban stumbled, his weight nearly pulling Kringle to the ground. "I really can't go on just now. A few moments, please." Kringle then saw the fresh blood staining the hem of Alban's robe and his boot beneath. The snow down the ridge behind them was printed with red footprints for the last mile. "Oh, no . . ."

"My leg wound is open," Alban said, barely above a whisper, "but I'll be all right after a short rest. We must keep going. Snegg must already have figured that we didn't go straight north."

Kringle turned and frantically searched the distance. He followed the frozen river's shape four or five miles to the sea, then back again until his eyes rested on a cluster of trees above the riverbank. Amid the black limbs was one broader than the others. It drove straight across the branches at a severe angle. A tattered gray cloth hung from it and whipped steadily in the wind. Kringle made a sound when he saw it.

"What do you see?" asked Alban, squinting.

Frozen in the shallow water some three miles from where the goblins had attacked it, half sunk, was Octa's pirate ship.

"I can't believe it," Kringle breathed. "The ship must have thawed after the goblin storm, drifted upriver, and frozen again." Looking at how the ice-topped river slipped away among the plains going north, he was suddenly seized with an idea. "Alban, if you can't walk so well, and I can't carry you, maybe we can be carried together."

The priest looked at the boy. "The river is frozen, and that boat is quite sunk, son. It's not going anywhere."

"The river *is* frozen, Brother Alban. And the ice is fast, I hope. Let's get to the ship. Lean on me. Come on."

"Fast ice? Being mysterious again? Well, carry on."

Slipping his arm under the priest's shoulder once more, Kringle practically carried the wounded man to the riverbank. He laid him carefully at the foot of a tight group of twisted trees and wrapped his elvencloak around him. "Now stay put."

"Oh, really? I was thinking of going back to Snegg. I rather miss him, you know."

"I think he'll miss us before long!" said Kringle. He hurried down to the frozen ship. Less than half of the hull's front half was visible above the ice. The eagle's head curling out from the prow was raised up to about a man's height, while the mast jutted back and away from the sunken stern.

Kringle disappeared under the small foredeck and rummaged around until he found what he was looking for. "Here we are!" He kicked at the thing again and again until it came loose. A moment later, he emerged waving a pirate broadax.

"Nice," said Alban, hunkering lower amid the trees to escape the wind. "You didn't find some food, by any chance?"

"This is better!" Kringle said as he shinnied up the mast and began to chop at the frozen rigging. Twenty minutes later, it fell away from the wood and clattered to the ice. He dragged it over the snow to Alban. The priest's head was bent, and he was whispering again.

"Brother Alban?"

The man looked up. "Sorry. I was lost in thought." He watched as Kringle strung the rigging among the trees behind him like a cobweb.

Alban smiled. "So, I'm the fly caught in the web, am I? Don't you think we should be off now? Snegg might just decide to travel in the daylight. Can you 'see' him?"

"It's a gray day, but still too bright for goblins. I think we have about five hours before nightfall. I've got to keep working." He jumped back to the ship and swung the ax down on the deck. *Whack! Whack! Chop!*

"Working?" grumbled the priest. "Looks like you are *un*working that poor boat. You're chopping it to bits!"

"My father was a woodcutter. He was very swift at his work. He even defended elves with his ax. Some people said it was magical."

"Magic, magic, always magic," said Alban. "Maybe it was just the ax of a good man?"

Kringle kept chopping. "Maybe. Can you make a fire and

thaw out that rigging? Unless you're too busy talking to yourself."

"It's called praying," the priest explained. "It's what I do when I'm worried or afraid. You might think about doing it yourself sometime. But yes. I can make a fire."

As Alban began whispering again, almost immediately lost in thought, Kringle turned his mind to a thought he himself had. From the first moment he saw the pirate ship and felt the western wind, he had seen a thing in his head. It was not a vision, nor could he have told you what it was that he saw exactly, but he knew he *could* make it from pieces of the ship, and he had to try. He hacked at its hull where the planks met the ice — *chop-chop-chop!* — while Alban prayed and made a small fire using twigs and the boards that Kringle tossed to him. Soon the rigging began to crackle and sag.

Let me tell you, for a boy who knew so little of boats, Kringle certainly knew how to take one apart! In under three hours, the front half of the hull was free of the ice and sitting upright on the surface. Then, plank by plank, using wooden dowels and thawed rivets, he fashioned and secured a back end to it. Next, he tore at the rest of the exposed hull and came away with two long staves that curved at the ends. Out of these he made two runners and hammered them securely to the bottom of the hull.

Tired, but not nearly done, Kringle crawled up to the top

of the frozen mast. Holding tight, he rocked back and forth, back and forth, until he heard a tremendous *crack* and leaped off. The mast slammed to the ice, broken clean in half.

"Excellent!" he said, breathless. "I thought that would happen."

"Oh, did you really?" said Alban.

Kringle paused to notice the sun passing across the sky. Then he mounted the mast in the middle of the hull and secured it with an assortment of planks bolted crosswise. He set a fragment of the sail on a chopped piece of yard and finally attached the thawed rigging to it. When darkness had begun to fall over them, he turned to Alban, exhausted. "I think we're ready."

The priest rose. "Ready, are we? Ready for what, exactly?"

"Exactly? I'm not sure."

"It looks something like a sledge."

Kringle laughed. "A sledge it is! We can catch the wind and take the frozen river north. It'll take us a quarter of the time to get to Cragtop!"

"What? But that will never move," said the priest. "Do you think we have enough wind?"

"We will soon!" There was a sound on the plains behind them. Kringle swiveled on his heels and saw Snegg and his band of goblins galloping over the crest of a hill not more than two miles away.

"Boy!" shrieked the goblin across the distance, waving his curved sword over his head and crying his favorite word. "Attackkkk!"

"Ithgar!" yelled Lud. He whirled the dark wand.

"Ithgar!" echoed the goblin riders.

All at once, a black wind swirled from Ithgar's jagged tip. It coiled around and around in the air until it whipped down to the river.

"Alban, get in!" Kringle said, as he helped the priest into the hull. "We need that wind!" Unfurling the canvas on the mast, he jumped behind the sledge and began to push.

Amid the shrieks of the approaching green creatures and the barking of the varguls, the goblin wind caught the sail, and the sledge lurched forward. It pulled away from the skeleton ship and skittered across the ice. Running alongside the sledge now, Kringle tugged the rigging this way and that until the sail filled with wind and the mast groaned. Suddenly, the sledge tipped and turned, gathering the wind fully in its sail, and it moved.

It moved quickly!

"Ha! I knew it!" cried Kringle. He jumped in at the last moment and hunched down beside the priest.

"You knew nothing of the sort!" said Alban, bracing himself as the sledge picked up more and more speed.

The goblins urged their beasts out onto the ice behind the sledge and tried to follow, but in their haste the first wave of varguls slipped and fell, toppling their riders. The goblins sprang up and raced after the sledge on foot.

Snegg yelled, "No! No, stop the storm!" He slid across the ice and finally slapped Lud to the ground, knocking Ithgar into the snow. "No storm!"

But as good as the goblins were at starting storms, they weren't so good at stopping them. The whirling, swirling winds launched the sledge up the river and away from the shrieking creatures.

"Ingas, attackkkk!" cried Snegg. At once, the varguls massed in a pack and charged along the riverbank after the sledge, faster now that they were without their riders. The sledge slid up the river swiftly at first, then began to slow down. Ingas, leaner and faster than the rest, closed in, howling ravenously. With a great jump forward he took a bite out of the stern.

"Kringle!" cried Alban, scrambling forward, "we're slowing down. The wind, the varguls —"

Kringle swung around quickly with his staff, catching Ingas on the ear. Even then the sledge slowed and the other varguls were nearly on them. "Begone, beasts!" he cried.

All of a sudden, a great cloud of snow blew down from the southern sky and swept into the sail, nearly tearing it from the mast. The sledge leaped away from the varguls, driving Kringle and Alban two, then three lengths ahead of their leader.

"A wind from heaven!" gasped Alban. "Thank the Lord."

"A wind from the south, I think," said Kringle.

Wherever the wind came from, the sledge shot forward on the ice, leaving the varguls and the even more distant goblins wailing in its snowy wake. In moments, the man and the boy were up the river, sliding swiftly away over the frozen water.

CHAPTER FOURTEEN

CRAGTOP

KRINGLE'S PIRATE SLEDGE flew along the icy river, faster and faster away from their pursuers. The goblins were no longer in sight when the banks began to close in and the river narrowed.

"I think we're going to crash right about there," said Alban, bracing himself against the hull. "O Lord, have mercy, there. Yes, there. The riverbank. Kringle — *right there!*"

At the very last moment, the boy pulled the sail to his left, the sledge skidded sideways on the ice, pointed north, and suddenly — *whooom!* — they bounced up the bank and soared over the top of it. When they thumped down onto a long, snowy plain — still driven by that southern wind — they were speedily sailing north to Cragtop.

"Aha!" said Kringle. "I thought it might do that."

"Stop that at once!" said Alban, mustering as much voice as he could. "You had no such thought. You had no such idea, Kringle! We just as easily could have been captured by the goblins, or eaten by varguls, or sunk through the ice, or crushed under the weight of this . . . this . . . *pirate boat!* . . . when it flipped over. And let me tell you, I believe it *will* flip over! So don't tell me you thought it might, because you had no such thought!"

"Yes, Brother," said Kringle, laughing slightly to himself. But, in fact, he *did* have such a thought. He had more and more of such thoughts. Whether they came from the runes or from somewhere else, he had no idea. But his snow sledge was just one of many ideas and visions and sounds that seemed to come to him from all around, and he was happy to have had it.

Whoosh-whoosh-whoosh! They rode over plain after frozen plain, into one snow-covered waste after another, eating up the miles before them. Each time the wind threatened to die away, Kringle pulled or slacked the ropes one way or the other and caught another wind full in the cloth. *Whoosh-whoosh-whoosh!* The sledge drove on through the night and into morning, fleeing swiftly over the snow.

The wind didn't abandon them for long. They fled quickly north, but not before the sledge drove them past a village in the east. It was teeming with heath folk and those he recognized as river dwellers and even the brown-wearing midland tribes. They carried sticks and crude swords and wooden staves sharpened into spears.

"What's all that?" he asked.

"Your people, Kringle," said the priest, watching as they sailed by. "That's the village of Triplethorn. The different tribes are gathering against the invaders, your pirate friends. I started to see this more and more before I was caught. They are gathering to defend their land. The Romans taught them a thing or two before leaving."

Kringle glimpsed some Roman armor among the men. "You mean they'll fight the invaders?"

"They may," said Alban. "They will never match the Roman might, of course. But the good thing is that the goblins may choose to stay underground for as long as they can if they know the people are armed. This is good, Kringle. Good for us." He began to pray again, and Kringle didn't disturb him. The sail soon caught another wind, and the village faded into the distance behind them.

They traveled on and on. When the afternoon came, Alban stirred enough from his prayers to say, "There." He pointed into the not-too-distant north where a range of black shapes stood high against the deepening blue of the sky. "The tallest one. That's home."

Keeping his eyes fixed on the black cliffs, Kringle drove the sledge on. It was near evening before he furled the sail and stopped the sledge at the foot of the highest mountain. It rose an almost sheer cliff above them, great black stone dotted amid the snows with even blacker crags. In the waning light, its summit was shrouded in mist.

"You live . . . up there?"

"Once. And, with the Lord's grace, I will again."

"I see," said Kringle. "So the Lord is a bird now?"

Alban scowled. "Yes, yes, laugh. It did take me a while to find the cave. But you can see everything from it. Once we get there, you'll see how fine a place it is."

"*Once* we get there? *If* we get there," said the boy.

"There's a path near the top and three pointed rocks just before the final steps I built to it," said the priest. "Then you'll know you have found it."

Kringle looked up at the ragged cliffs. "Thanks. Pointed rocks. I'll be sure to notice them."

But Alban had already drifted off again. He was breathing fitfully.

"Fine," said Kringle. He gave out as long a sigh as Alban himself might have. "Maybe I'll be surprised and things will be clearer when we get up there. Tomorrow morning."

They spent their seventh night since escaping the palace huddled in the sledge, thankful that the driving southern wind that had so fortunately come to them had now just as fortunately died away. The next morning, using energy he didn't know he had, Kringle dragged the sledge as far up the mountainside as he could, hiding it completely under the bows of a large, sturdy pine standing by itself at the very edge of the tree line. "If Snegg does follow, I don't want him finding this," the boy said to himself. "Besides, you never know when it might be useful again."

He helped Alban to his feet and started up the rocks from one ledge to the next. He wondered how long it had been, after all. It was more than three months, and possibly close to four, since he had seen Merwen. Hrothr's runes had predicted his journey from the warm hearthfire. And the gray stones' prophecy had proved true so far. He tried to remember what was next. "'Stillness, darkness, and the coldness of ice'?" he said. "It sounds like winter." But the weather had changed; he knew that much. It had been the last gasps of winter when the Bottoms was attacked so long ago. And the rain and mud at Barrowfoot — had that been spring? Far in the south, farther than he had ever been, the snows might have gone already, or they might soon be coming back. The wheel of the year was rolling on, he thought. It was rolling on, though here in the north you hardly noticed. Here in the north, it seldom stopping snowing.

Clutching Alban as best he could, and leaning on his staff, Kringle helped the old man slowly up the side of Cragtop. How long did this take? It seemed forever, but it was, all in all, only the better part of a day before they reached midway and had to stop for the night. Kringle looked out across the land below. No goblin torches. Good. Good.

By noon the next day, he knew they were close to the top

when they passed into a cloud that seemed to have got stuck at the summit. Although he knew they were nearly there, the thickness of the mist made their climb both slower and more treacherous. It was far into the afternoon before they found what the priest had called *the path*. It wasn't anything like a path. It was a vague, meandering way through the misty boulders and clefts and crags that twice led Kringle astray before he spotted a group of three short rocks pointing to the sky.

He snorted. "So they actually do exist!"

The rocks called to mind nothing so much as a trio of cloaked elves. They were some three feet tall and stood in a tight bunch like sentinels. They reminded him of Vindalf, Holf, and Gussi. He felt heavy and sad then, but brightened when he saw, twenty feet beyond them, a series of flat stones set down one after another — Alban's "steps"— leading to a narrow crack in the sheer wall of the highest cliff!

"Brother?" he said. "Brother Alban! Is this your cave?"

The man raised his eyes and smiled faintly. "Yes, dear boy. You've found it!" Then he slumped back on Kringle's shoulder with a groan.

"All right. Rest here," said the boy. "I'll take a look." Sitting the priest down among the elven stones, he made his way to the mouth of the cave and looked in.

Inside was a small, rough room. It was a natural cave,

meaning that it bore no signs of having been hewn from the rock by tools (not that Alban would have known how to do such a thing, anyway, though he might have sketched it!), but it was nevertheless an almost perfect dome. The walls rose straight up from the cave floor to a rounded ceiling. In the center at the top was a small gap in the rock that Kringle knew instantly was where the smoke from Alban's fire went out into the air. The long-cold remains of a fire sat neatly in the center of the floor. He smelled the faint furry smell of a mouse that had probably taken shelter inside the cave and had likely perished from the cold. "As I might have done," he thought aloud.

In the back stood a large wooden box. Tipping it open, Kringle found a few shriveled potatoes and apples and brown heads of lettuce that were more than half frozen. There were also parsley and nuts and a good amount of flour in a sack. "We can have a feast!" said Kringle drily.

A short, narrow bed made of logs and leather straps covered with a woolen blanket lay tucked in under the right slope of the dome. On the left was a small table and a stool made of poorly cut and hammered planks. On this table sat a very thick book.

Kringle went back to the priest. Alban was still sitting up against the stones, gazing calmly at the cave's entrance.

"Is everything as it should be?" he asked.

"It's not as big as I would like," said Kringle. "And there's a mousy smell. But if you mean is it empty, then the answer is yes."

"So, my little stone guards here have kept it safe, have they? Well done."

"Come on, Brother."

Once inside, Alban collapsed onto the rough bed and heaved a monstrous large breath. Taking snow from outside, Kringle cleaned the priest's wound and bandaged it with fresh cloths he found in the wooden bin. Alban grimaced and groaned through it all, mumbling and praying, then leaned back finally. "Thank you," he whispered. "Well, then. I'm home." He seemed to drift away for a moment, then blinked his eyes awake. "Kringle, I may sleep. I fear I will sleep, but you must watch what happens below. From Cragtop, you will be able to see everything that happens."

"When the mist clears," said Kringle.

"It will, when night falls," he said. "Soon you will see the goblins moving. You will see it beginning." With that, Alban closed his eyes and drifted to silence. In a moment his breathing calmed and slowed.

After the exertion of their escape over the last week — to say nothing at all of what had happened before — Kringle found that he could not stay awake, either. He soon fell into a deep, dreamless sleep. It was midday before he awoke, and the reason was hunger more than not having any more sleep left. As the priest was snoring heavily, he decided to venture out to search for food.

The day was gray and sunless, but the clouds were high, and he could see far. Looking around, he realized that Cragtop was indeed the giant watchtower Alban said it was. The cave was very near its summit, and the mountain itself was much the highest of several on the tip of the western land. The black sea was even visible beyond the last of them. Standing at the cluster of rocks, Kringle saw why the priest had picked the lonely spot. From a bluff in front of the opening, a sort of ledge, one could see out over a great part of the east, and all the way south across the vast dark mass of the Black Woods. And right down below, worming along from the western sea and all the way across the country to the east, was a high ridge of stone and earthwork that the Romans had built to keep out the northern invaders.

"The wall," he whispered. Seeing it now for the first time, he realized how true Merwen's stories about it had been. The wall was twelve feet high and made of great stone blocks, buttressed halfway up on the southern side by packed earth. The builders had chosen the location of their wall very well, too. While the land inclined gradually from the south to the wall, on the north it dropped off suddenly into a series of severe chasms and ravines and deep ugly wounds in the earth. Somewhere far up beyond it in the frozen stillness, in the dim and fearful mists of the north, was where the goblin forge lay. Somewhere up there was what the Goblin King wanted to call Morgoland.

"You won't," Kringle said angrily. Though to be truthful, he had no more idea than you or I might have had about how Morgo would be stopped.

Turning around, Kringle searched the clefts above the cave for anything resembling food. When all at once he spotted a creature — he thought it was a white fox — leaping about the summit, he followed it. But the fox seemed to be playing with the boy, for it led him around and around the top cliffs until he became dizzy. Tumbling to a ledge, he found himself suddenly covered with straw. A nest? A hawk's nest! He discovered roots and stalks among the straw, but no eggs. Still delighted, he stuffed whatever he could find into his cloak and brought it back to the cave. Making a small fire with the straw and some kindling (also from the big box), he stirred up a pot of something that with a very large imagination you might have called soup. But Alban slurped it up eagerly, and the boy ate it, too.

That night, he again watched the great darkness below the mountain, but saw nothing except the faint twinkle of a village far in the east.

He went out the next day and by accident discovered the fox frozen under a thin covering of new snow. Picking it up gingerly by its rear legs, he brought it back to the cave, but stopped short when he saw a small gray mouse scuttle down the rocks from a ledge high up on the cave wall and scramble toward Alban, who was again sleeping.

"You!" he said. "You're alive after all!"

The mouse jumped onto the bed, scampered across Alban's robe to his chin, and began to nibble his ear.

"What? Hey! Get away from him!"

Kringle jumped to the bed, but before he could shoo the creature away, Alban woke with a snort and a laugh. "Sasha! You're back!" he coughed. "What? Is it time to pray already? Well, then! Thank you, Sasha! Time to pray!"

"What is this? What is this?" Kringle stammered.

The mouse squeaked and ran back up to its shelf. Alban chuckled, sat up, and smiled at Kringle. "My little companion. He wakes me up when it's time to pray. Ah, you know, Kringle, I think I'm feeling better. My leg is nearly back to normal. It must be all your tending and that food you've been coming up with, though heaven knows what you're planning to do with Tiberius there. He brings me eggs from the nests, don't you know!" He nodded toward the fox, which had begun to wiggle and twist in the boy's hand.

"Ah!" Kringle let the squirming fox go, and it leaped to the floor and was out of the cave in a flash.

Still chuckling, Alban wobbled to the little desk and perched on the stool. For the first time since returning, he opened the book that lay on the desk, lowered his head, and began to whisper softly.

Kringle stared at him, amazed. "No, no, no. This can't happen. A fox that brings you food. A mouse that wakes you up. Animals don't help people that way. They can't. A priest must be a holy man!"

Alban turned abruptly from his book, his expression somewhere between anger and humility. "A holy man? Goodness, no, no, no. I certainly am not. No, no." He let out a very long sigh. "A holy man . . . holy man . . . no . . . no . . .

"But the mouse? Why did he do that?"

"Why?"

Alban was quiet for a long while, saying nothing. He did not stir from the desk, his hand still on the book, as a pained expression began to grow on his face. "I suppose," he said, "the Lord God has not hidden himself away from me the way I have hidden from him."

The boy was puzzled. "What do you mean?"

"Kringle," he said softly, "I'm so sorry."

"You're sorry? For what?"

Alban ran his hands across his face. "I fear I have lied to you. Lied, I'm afraid, about nearly everything. All lies."

"What are you talking about?"

Without closing his book, Alban rose from the desk and went back to his bed. Almost at once, a tiny fly whirled down from somewhere high in the dome, not far from where the mouse had come from. Kringle watched it circle down and then, as if it knew exactly what it was doing, settle on the page right where Alban's finger had been. It settled on the page, I tell you, exactly where Alban had left off! And it remained there unmoving, as if it had fallen asleep on the very word the priest had last read.

"What? Is that fly magical, too?"

Alban turned from the bed. "Who? Parturis? Oh, no. He simply marks my place so that I can find it again. When I leave my book, Parturis lets me know where to pick up again."

"Tiberius the fox. Sasha the mouse. Parturis the fly," said Kringle. "They . . . *work* . . . for you? You're not a holy man. You're a *wizard*!"

Alban shook his head. "Please, Kringle! It isn't *I* who want these things. . . ." He trailed off into silence for a moment. When he turned to the boy again, his eyes were wet.

"What's the matter?"

Alban smiled sadly. "So very much, Kringle, you have no idea. But let me tell you so that you'll know what kind of a man I am. I came here from the great city of Rome to be a priest in your country. In case you couldn't tell from watching me, a priest is a person who, among other things, helps people. And I did, I think, for a while. I lived in the town of Corby in the south. I celebrated Mass and taught the heath people, and the Romans who wanted to hear, about the Lord God and his holy son."

Kringle listened. "Go on."

"Two years ago the Roman legions began to be called back. They left the towns one by one. Kringle, I started to think I should never have come. I moved to another town, and then to another. Finally, I lost heart. I lost the love that made me want to be a priest. I felt alone. Then I made myself alone. I came to live here by myself. I would go below only when I needed food. I became — in another word that you might never have heard — a hermit. A hermit, Kringle, is one who hides away from the world."

"So, how *did* the goblins find you?"

The man growled softly. "Stealing potatoes and a scrawny chicken, not teaching the Lord's word, as I told you! At the end, I did try, you know. I had gone to Castrum to try to teach and preach again, but when I found that the Romans had left there, too, I knew it was the end for me. I lost faith in all of it, Kringle. I lost faith in myself to help anyone. Just my luck that the goblins attacked while I was in Castrum." He paused. "Now, I have run back to my cave again. Still, God helps me in these little ways. And not so little. You are here, after all."

God. God. Kringle had heard about gods from Merwen. The Romans had plenty of gods. In Castrum, he had seen altars built for some of them — bull gods, gods with wings on their feet, gods of grain, gods of sun and weather and sickness and health and victory, and gods of death. The goblins had destroyed the altars. He had seen small stone and clay gods in the houses at Barrowfoot, too, little figures that the children kept near their beds.

"Gods?" said Kringle.

Alban shook his head. "One God. The Lord and maker of all things."

Kringle got up and stood at the mouth of the cave. The night was rich and blue, the stars no more than silver flashes in the vast darkness of the sky. For an instant, he wondered what sort of creatures the goblins must be never to know the beauty of such a night but to use it only as a cover for their terrible deeds.

There were no torches yet. The goblins were still in their palace in the south. He thought about the poor captured children and their unimaginable fear.

Suddenly, a chill wind blew across his cheek from the north. He knew the warmer weather was losing. Cold was moving down from the dark land, as it always did. Winter was coming.

"God has done this, too," Alban said softly, standing behind him at the cave entrance, holding on to the staff. "He brings the cold weather, the warm weather, the change of seasons, time itself."

"Even the Goblin Long Night?" asked Kringle.

"Even that," said Alban. "But the coming of winter is not just a fearful time. It is a holy time. A time of wonder. A time, even, of joy."

"Merwen used to say the wheel of the year begins to slow now," said Kringle. "The year tires, becomes colder, dies after the green life leaves the world, and the nights grow long and the snow and ice cover everything."

"The wheel of the year?" said Alban. "Hmm. I suppose it is like that. It spins through all the seasons, does it? And it slows at the end of the year. Interesting. It's also when a wonderful child was sent from heaven to live among us here on earth. He is a light in our winter, a sun in our Long Night. That's quite a wonderful story, Kringle. And a mysterious one, too!"

The hermit's words reminded him of Merwen, of the stories she used to tell him during long winter evenings. For a moment, he imagined the hearth fire at the Bottoms and of cold nights spent by it with her near.

He turned back to Alban. "Tell me."

CHAPTER FIFTEEN

CAVE OF HEAVEN

ALBAN TURNED AND ENTERED the cave. He lit one candle and from it lit several more. The walls glowed with yellow light. Sitting at his little table once again, he flipped page after page of the book until he came to a picture. It blazed in the candlelight with many colors, including one that caught the flames and shone brightly.

"Is that what *gold* is like?" Kringle asked.

"It is."

The picture showed a woman and a man kneeling in a cave. Between them lay a baby in a small wooden box stuffed with straw that gleamed with streaks of gold. The child was watched by an ox and a donkey. He had one little hand raised by the side of his face, palm open, as if he were waving at whoever looked in at the scene.

Kringle's eyes were drawn up to a robed figure with large golden wings hovering in the sky above the cave. Behind it, on its right and left, were two others with similar wings. Over them all hung a big golden star with beams striking out of it like swords. Several sheep and old, bent shepherds knelt on the ground to the left of the cave. One of them reminded Kringle of Holf. On the right were three bearded men with swords and shields and crowns riding toward the cave on big, horselike animals.

Everything Kringle looked at in the picture drew his gaze back to the child lying in the box of straw.

"Who is this baby?" he asked, standing over the desk. He looked at the black words on the next page. "And what do these say? Are they like runes? Are these words magical?"

Alban gazed at the picture once more, then up at Kringle. "It's a story about a single night, long, long ago, before you and I were born. It happened even before the Romans built the northern wall. But the Romans are a part of this story, too."

"Tell me."

Alban began. "It starts quietly, with an angel. This angel had giant wings like great drifts of snow and eyes that burned like flames. It appeared to a young woman as she was praying alone one night. Her name was Mary."

Closing his eyes, Kringle could almost imagine her praying in her room, whispering as Alban always did. Mary. He thought of little Mari in Elvenwald. "Go on."

"The angel told Mary that she would bear a special child,

unlike any other. This child would be a king. But before the child could be born, Mary and her husband, a good man named Joseph, had to travel over many miles on a dangerous journey."

"Were there goblins?"

"No, no," Alban said. "No goblins, though as I said, this did happen in the dead of the year, in winter, the goblin time. When the woman and her husband finally arrived at a little town called Bethlehem that the Romans ruled, there was no place for them to stay, so they stayed in a cave where animals were housed." Alban fixed his eyes on Kringle. "A cave, I might add, not very much different from the one in which we find ourselves tonight. Think of that night, Kringle. The minutes, the hours his mother and father waited for a child, so . . . so full of wonder and worry and mystery and hope. I think time must have slowed down to nothing for those people! Then, all of a sudden, a blazing light came to them, and he was born. And all their fear was gone!"

Kringle gazed again at the little child waving at him. "What was his name?"

"Jesus," said Alban. "He's known as the Christ child. *Christ* is a word that means 'chosen one.' The night of his birth is known as Christmas."

"The chosen one," said Kringle softly.

"When he comes, we sing him songs of praise."

"Songs? Like what?"

Alban looked at Kringle. "Well . . . like this." He raised his voice in a thin song.

> *"This midnight manger cobbled by a man*
> *Beams out broad light, bearing heaven's child.*
> *Wonder comes smiling to our storm-cursed world:*
> *Storm stops, night stops, darkness takes flight!"*

Alban ceased singing as quietly as he had begun, his face aglow. "But that is not the end of the story," he said. "The shepherds who lived nearby came to worship him. And a star of great beauty rose up and stood above the baby's holy cave. Kings from faraway lands saw the star and followed it to Bethlehem to worship the Christ child. They brought him wonderful gifts. Kings, Kringle! Giving a child gifts!"

"Is this a true story?"

"It is true! Nor did Jesus hide who he was. He grew up and spent his life on earth telling us how we must love one another, and be kind above all things, and if we do, there will be peace among all people. He was the first king to ever say such things."

Smoke rose up from the candle in a frail column. It sought out the ceiling of the cave, drawn by the cold. The flame was pale and small, but the gold in Alban's book made it seem stronger.

"Was there peace?"

The priest sighed. "Alas, he was born into a dark time like ours. A powerful king feared his lowly birth and ordered all the children his age to be taken and killed. These children are known as the Holy Innocents."

A terrible thought struck Kringle then. He tried to push it away, but the hideous image of Morgo's face came to him. His mind was suddenly a welter of faces and places and aches and fears and longings, and now there was this child to add to it all. He felt himself more confused than ever.

Going out into the dark night, Kringle felt another cold wind blow by him and found that his cheeks were wet. Drying them on the sleeve of his cloak, he saw a light glimmering in the east. But it was not a star. Far below, a line of blazing torches moved on the fringes of the Black Woods.

"Alban, come here!" he called. He watched a second and third group of flames join the first, then all move in a long snake toward the darkness of the north.

"The goblins are moving!" he said.

Alban hustled out. "Oh, no, no. It's starting!"

Suddenly, the entire land below them seemed to be moving in a sea of tiny fires. Lights flickered in the south, in the depths of the woods, in the east, and below them to the west.

"They're moving north to the forge," said Kringle.

"Lord protect us, there are so many!" said the priest.

One group of torches moved faster than the rest. It seemed the beacon for all the others, leading the goblins through the

Roman wall at its center to the east. It made its way through the chasms and mist lands of the north at amazing speed.

"That must be Snegg," said Kringle. "He's riding fast!"

Flashes and twinklings of torchlight, trickles of flame, came from everywhere now. And suddenly, far down the western edge of the forest, he saw more lights gathering.

"Elvenwald!" he gasped. "The goblins are nearing Elvenwald. There are so many! I have to warn the elves."

"But how?" asked the priest. "They're many days' journey from here."

Then it came to him, what had been bothering him in the back of his mind since he first heard Morgo say it in the goblin palace. It came to Kringle now, when he needed it most. "Two were missing!"

Alban stared at him. "Indeed? Well, that explains so much. Two of what?"

What Kringle meant, of course, was that two runes were missing from the pouch that Snegg had brought to Morgo's palace. Kringle himself had one. But what if Nar had never had them all in the pouch at Barrowfoot?

What if Hrothr had kept one?

He took the rune from his cloak and held it in his hand. Almost instantly, he saw Snegg in his mind. He was at the head of a large band of mounted goblins, their varguls tearing across the miles toward the forge, already fifteen, twenty miles north of the wall.

Then Kringle turned toward Elvenwald. Holding his rune tightly, he tried to bring Hrothr's face up before him. *Kenaz!* whispered the rune. He nearly stilled his heart in the silence that followed. His breathing slowed.

Then came the single faraway reply. *Jera!*

Trembling with excitement, Kringle saw the elder elf, sitting on his stool in the main house, eyes closed.

"Hrothr —" That was all the boy said. Alban's hand was on his arm.

"Kringle, look, Snegg's turning!"

"What?" The boy looked north. Some twenty or thirty torches had split off from the northernmost riders. They were suddenly heading south.

Kringle closed his eyes again and concentrated on Snegg's runes. In his mind's eye, he saw the goblin raider riding south swiftly on Ingas, the elven pouch held to his ear, his goblin eyes swollen to monstrous size.

"Noooo!" cried Kringle. "He knows! He can hear the runes. He heard Hrothr's stone. He's going to Elvenwald!" Kringle stormed back into the cave.

"What are you doing?" Alban asked, following him.

"I didn't save the children," said the boy. "I didn't find Merwen. I didn't get the runes back. I haven't done anything!"

Alban's eyes were wide. "But, Kringle, you have —"

Anger rose in the boy as never before. He felt his face

darkening. He pulled his elf hat over his head. "Goblins! They took my mother and my father from me. They took Merwen from me. They steal children. They hate the elves. Well, *I hate the goblins!*"

"No, Kringle, not hate," Alban pleaded. "There isn't any room for that. The little child was born to save our world from hate. He brought light into our darkness. Think of that, Kringle, think of that!"

Kringle tried to think of it, I'm sure he did, but it wasn't possible. The elves kept calling him. Hrothr and Gussi and Vindalf. And his father called him, too, from that stump in the Black Woods. And the long-distant voice of his mother came like a cry to him, ringing over the years and over the miles since she first spoke his name.

Kringle!

"I have to go," he said. "I have to stop Snegg. There's no time. I've spent too long here. I have to go."

PART V

KRINGLE NEVER FELT HIS BODY SLAM AND CRUMPLE ON THE CRAG. . . .

CHAPTER SIXTEEN

AT DOOMCHASM

AND HE DID GO. When Kringle emerged from the cave, snow was beginning to fall lightly across the night. Bundling his cloak as tightly around himself as he could, he looked up into the sky. Wet flakes dropped on his cheeks.

"If you must go," said Alban, "the fastest way is down the north face, if you think you can —"

Kringle looked down the cliff side, then to the torches moving swiftly below. "I can."

"You'll reach the wall soonest that way. At each mile point is a small castle with a gate and a tower. Snegg looks to be heading for the third milecastle." He pointed to a small fort in the wall not far from the foot of the mountain. "It's his shortest way to Elvenwald, I think, and he'll likely take it and go straight south. Though God knows what you'll do if you meet Snegg."

Kringle stared into the distance, then turned. "Your wound?"

"Completely healed," said the hermit. "So, here's your staff. Happily, I don't need to use it as a crutch anymore. You saw to that." He hugged him suddenly and tightly. "May the Christ child go with you, Kringle!"

It was a strange feeling for the boy, this hug. He knew he had to leave Alban's little cave as quickly as possible, but he soon found himself adding to the embrace. When he felt a lump grow in his throat, he pulled away.

Alban fixed his eyes on Kringle. Then, smiling, he moved a finger from his own forehead to the boy's nose. "We used to be the same height. I think you've grown!"

When Kringle gripped the staff, what had been his hand's normal place on it no longer suited him. It was true. He was taller now. "I'd rather this was a sword."

"Not a sword. The King of kings never used a sword."

He never had to fight goblins, thought Kringle.

The priest made a final blessing over him. Then, when there didn't seem to be anything more to say, Kringle left. He made his way down to the first ledge and was over it and away with a small jump.

Snow fell more thickly by the minute, and he often slid his way down from crag to ledge to outcropping, saving himself more than once by jamming his staff against a rock to stop from slipping right over it and down the side.

Alban had been right. It was much faster, if much steeper, down the north face. When he finally reached the foot of the mountain, he looked back up. The little cave was lost in a swirling haze of white. "So that's that, then," he said. "Good-bye, priest."

He soon put Cragtop behind him and traveled northeast over the upland toward the Roman wall. He pushed himself for one hour, two hours, hoping that Snegg hadn't already made it through the milecastle gate, but not daring to use his rune to find out.

"He's learned to hear the voices of the stones."

"He heard Hrothr's stone. Jera."

"Maybe he'll hear my stone, too. But I can't let him know I'm so close."

"And what'll happen if I *do* see him? What did Alban say? *'God knows what you'll do if you meet Snegg'?* What did he mean by that? Never mind. I have to surprise Snegg to stop him."

An hour later, Kringle approached the third castle on the wall. It was small — more a single, squat tower than a castle — and abandoned, as all Roman things now seemed to be. It held a wide gate between the north and south, and the gate was open — probably left that way by the goblins who had already used it to get to the forge.

Moving quickly to the gate, he stopped. There, winding up from the south and through the opening, he saw a line of footprints. Among the marks were tiny pink ones. In this world of black stone and white snow, the prints were pink. They reminded him of Alban's bloody boot marks.

"Children!"

The little shoeless prints were crisscrossed and overtrodden by the awkward tracks of goblins, the ruts of wheels, and the hooves of varguls, but they were still visible. Shoeless children forced to march!

All at once, Kringle heard the muffled thudding of hooves approaching from the north. He quickly climbed the castle stairs and flattened himself on the wall as he had at Barrowfoot. The footprints wormed north from the wall, but were lost in thicker snow before the land dropped off into the ravines and chasms he had seen from Cragtop.

And now he saw *them*. Twenty, thirty, forty varguls, all galloping at top speed, goblins whipping the beasts' heads to go even faster, and Snegg in the lead. They roared out of the northern snow toward the wall and were at the gate before he could move. Snegg was through first, but pulled Ingas up short and stood by as the rest of his troop passed into the south, urging them, "To Elvenwald! They have a rune! A rune for Morgo!"

When he saw the goblins, Kringle was terrified. He couldn't breathe. He couldn't move. What was he supposed to do, after all? Leap down and fight them? He couldn't believe he had ever fought these creatures!

When the last of the goblins had raced under the wall, Snegg spurred Ingas again and rode away with them. Kringle hadn't done anything! They were leaving! The goblin he had been searching for was ten feet away, but he himself hadn't even moved!

Suddenly, Snegg twisted his reins. "Ingas! Halt!" His eyes were beginning to swell as he stared back at the wall. His troop had nearly vanished into the snows, but clutching the rune pouch, he urged the vargul slowly back.

A wave of sickness passed through Kringle as Snegg approached. The goblin could sense his presence, he was sure of it. He gripped his staff.

Closer and closer Snegg came, drawing nearer to Kringle's hiding place. All of a sudden, the goblin sprang up from the vargul with a cry and landed atop the wall. "Boy, I have found you! And your rune!"

Kringle scrambled to his feet, dragging his staff behind him. But Snegg was fast. With a fist of iron, he punched the boy and knocked him down, sending his staff skittering over the wall to the ground on the northern side.

"Boy!" the goblin yelled as if it was a war cry. "Boy!"

Kringle rolled over and was up again. "You filthy beast," he growled. "Murderer. Goblins killed my mother and father! You stole Merwen. You thief —"

The names meant nothing to Snegg, but his eyes kept growing. His jaws opened like a furnace, and he rushed at

Kringle, pouncing like a cat. The boy felt the double blow of Snegg's fists and fell on his back, then rolled free down the earthwork to the base of the wall on the southern side. He scrambled to his feet as Snegg leaped down at him, then raced through the gate to where his staff lay in the snow. He grabbed it and came up swinging when Snegg ran at him from behind. *Whoomf!* The staff slapped the goblin's knees. Snegg staggered, but did not fall. His eyes blazed like cauldrons of fire now. His foul breath smoked. "Give it to me. Give me the rune —"

"Never, you demon!"

Kringle swung at him again, but the staff slid off the goblin's shoulder and struck the ground. Snegg coughed out a laugh and leaped at Kringle, knocking him flat. They wrestled and rolled over and away from the wall a dozen times, the goblin's face pressed inches from his own, his mouth stinking of putrid animal flesh.

Kringle tried hard not to breathe, but he felt himself growing woozy at the smell. Snegg ripped at the boy's cloak again and again. Suddenly, he cried out, holding high the little gray stone. "Snegg-g-g has found it-t-t!"

Kenaz! the rune whispered.

"Noooo!" Kringle yelled. He kicked up at Snegg's right leg. The goblin howled and rolled nearly to the edge of a chasm, his eyes ablaze with fury. Kringle stumbled over to him, closing one hand over Snegg's while pressing the staff under the goblin's chin with the other. "Give me back the rune! Give it to me!"

"Ahhhh!" Snegg shrieked in frustration, then squirmed away. He sprang up behind Kringle and pushed him. The boy fell hard on the stone and began to slide over the ice toward the edge of the chasm.

Gargling a wet laugh, Snegg pelted him with snow and rocks, kicking him farther and farther down toward the edge. Finally, with the rune clutched in his fingers, he dashed the boy on the side of the face. Kringle felt the warmth of the stone against his skin even as he felt a trickle of blood down his cheek.

"No . . . no . . . ," he cried out. His head swam in pain as he tried to stop his slide down to the chasm's edge. "Alban! Gussi! Merwen!" He grabbed at passing roots and rocks with his left hand — his right was still holding fast to the staff — but could not manage to grab hold of anything.

Snegg ran after him, shouting and cursing, the rune raised high. "And now I find the last stone," he sneered. "I go to Elvenwald!" Finally, the goblin stopped his pursuit. The boy was sliding too quickly over the ice for him to keep up.

Kringle jammed his staff into the snow, trying desperately to stop himself. But it was no use. He vaulted up in the air, screamed once, then fell away from Snegg, the wall, and the staff, dropping headlong into the chasm.

CHAPTER SEVENTEEN

THE STAFF OF WEARY-ALL

KRINGLE NEVER FELT his body slam and crumple on the crag twenty feet below the chasm's edge. He struck the stone like a hammer strikes an anvil, and he was out, a snuffed candle.

How long did he lie there? He couldn't tell you.

Once, he thought he woke up and saw Snegg's menacing black eyes staring down at him, a giant rock in his hands. But as he felt nothing but a great pain in his leg, and simply drifted away again, Kringle reasoned he must have been feverish and imagined it all. Surely, if Snegg had really had the chance, he would have finished Kringle off right then and there.

Another time — was it that night or the following day? — he felt his body swimming away from the cold stone of the ledge. But glancing down into the chasm and seeing nothing but a bottomless black hole, he quickly crept back into himself, and his mind closed again.

He lay half asleep, half awake for a day and a night and another day and another night. Once, he woke and saw his left foot wedged under a jagged lip of stone on the ledge. He wondered if it hurt. Wiggling it, he quickly found that it did. Pain shot up his leg, through his side, and straight to his head before he dropped back inside himself and was nowhere again. He did this time and again; and time and again his mind went up out of itself, then right back in and back to sleep.

It occurred to him more than once that he might actually be dead, only his body hadn't realized it yet.

But no. Although snow had continued to fall, heavier and thicker with each passing hour and day, his elvencloak kept him warm. A trickle of water, clear as the streams of Cragtop, dripped from the rocks above him and onto his lips, and he stayed alive. Turning once, he found some little creature's hoard of nuts and wild berries on the ledge below him and shoveled them into his mouth. One can only imagine how mystified this animal must have been to find that no matter how often or how well he stocked his tiny pantry, it was always empty, and yet mystified or not, he kept stocking it, for Kringle kept eating.

No, the boy decided finally, he must be alive. For even in his confused state, he reasoned that if he were not alive, how could he possibly have been able to see . . . *them*?

Them.

First, there were the elves — Ifrid, Elni, Torgi, Vindalf, Nar, and the others, even Hrothr. They were busily working in the main hall at Elvenwald. "Oh," he groaned. "Flee . . . flee!"

To his own ears, his voice was no more than a frail whisper, and he knew he might not even have spoken at all.

That scene soon passed, and suddenly he saw the elves running, running, their little coats flying behind them. With them were some few children, some bundled and carried, others running alongside, all fleeing the sound of wild goblins rushing through the woods, shrieking. The names of the children came to him. How did he know them? He simply knew them one by one as they ran.

Then there was Gussi, a mass of clothes in his arms, and, peeping out of them, the little face of Mari, her golden hair a tangle. The elf rushed away quickly, his face half turned over his shoulder, when he tripped on a root and fell into Penda and Holf, and the bundle rolled and rolled. There was crying and shouting.

Then smoke covered everything. It spiraled up in big clouds and mixed with the dark sky. Smoke whirled across the black air, and wind whipped around and around it all. Elvenwald was on fire.

But this vision, too, was soon gone, and Kringle's mind wandered like a bird over the whole length and breadth of the world he had known since he was young. How was it possible? He had no rune to aid him. And yet he saw what he saw. The wild heath, the Black Woods, the frozen river, the Bottoms, the sea beyond the coast, the great sheer darkness of Cragtop, the elves' village, the hermit's cave. He saw them as if from a great height, flying over them, hovering in places like an angel.

But his heart ached as if it were being pulled out of himself, for he did not see Merwen anywhere. To search far and wide over the whole country for her and not find her reminded him of staring at the ruins of the Bottoms. He wanted to hold her and be held by her and to turn back the days and months since he had last seen her. But she was nowhere at all. No voice called to him, or spoke to him, or roused him from his painful fever.

And then he saw *them*.

Torches were moving north faster than he could imagine. An enormous mass of bodies — no longer a snake now, but a huge goblin army — was marching north across the snow. Not only could he see them, he could smell them! And somehow — how? he didn't know! — he drew closer and closer to them, so that he was flying along with them. And what was this now? Far north, very far north of the wall, the goblins were vanishing into the snow, oozing down into the earth, as if a foul black river were streaming below to its horrible underground home.

Where was this? The Fires of the North? The goblin forge?

He went down with the goblins. Down, down, down. Kringle followed the creatures into their tunnels, deep into passages, past towering heaps of trash and refuse, mounds of rusted metal, broken armor that seemed to have been torn from its owners, swords and iron wheels and spearheads and pots and pans and anything and everything iron. Until at last he was in the very center of a vast pit and there was Morgo, standing on a mountain of iron.

Morgo!

The Goblin King, fuming and bug-eyed, stood surrounded by thousands of creatures huddled and waiting, their torches blazing. The flames of a giant furnace sparked and hissed and burned high in the background. Next to it were a dozen vast pools of black water hissing and smoking. From somewhere beyond and behind the Goblin King came the cries of children, intermittent, hollow, and eerie. Kringle wondered if they were the ghosts of the children who had never survived their march through the snow, or who had never made it out of the palace. Perhaps they were the children he had not managed to save. Their cries pierced his heart.

Morgo gargled for silence, then spoke. "The people who have walked in light shall see a great darkness! Elves will die. Men will die. Goblins shall rise!" He paused while the green horde cheered, then said, "Bring forth our great son of dark-ness! Come, let us see him!"

The goblin masses turned their faces to something enter-ing from the shadows. Fifty feet tall and a hundred feet long, half rolling, half thumping, the thing shrieked and boomed into the light of the fuming furnace. It was made of giant logs and planks and slabs of metal welded together. It had the head of a dragon.

"Grunding!" howled Morgo.

"Grunding!" Kringle murmured in his fever.

Even as the iron dragon rolled in, dozens of goblins were hauling more iron plates from the cooling pools and ham-mering them onto the beast. Morgo's giddy laugher was overwhelmed by the deafening noise of iron thundering on iron.

Two giant wheels, one on either side of the dragon's long neck, began to spin. On each of these wheels were ranged several jagged blades. Grooves had been cut into each blade, making the slicing edge of each twice as long. Some blades were twisted to inflict the most damage.

Morgo jumped up and down as the blades spun faster.

"Grunding — speak!"

At once, the massive jaws of the dragon opened, and flames exploded from its mouth. They lit up the cavern even more. The goblins shrank in terror from the flames, and now

Kringle heard the sound of children screaming as if they were right there beside him.

Feeling himself fly invisibly above the War Dragon, the boy now saw dozens of goblins crawling across its huge body, fitting more armor onto it. And then he found he could peer down inside the enormous monster. It was a thing of rods and cables and spinning gears and interlocking timbers and pistons and iron cords and smoke. Pipes twisted inside its horrendous gut. And at its center, crammed together, one on top of the other, were hundreds of little souls — children! — their frail limbs working the pulleys and cords and levers of the goblin war machine. Their faces were pale, their bodies shrunken with fear. Then there was a shock as Kringle saw a face he knew. "Bearn! No, no! Bearn!"

The kind-eyed pirate boy was bound, terrified and trembling, to a fat iron lever, which he pushed and pulled and pushed and pulled as if he himself were a machine!

"Ayyyy!" screamed the Goblin King, raising the Iron Wand. "Long Night is coming. Grunding's hour is near!"

At this, the goblins roared, thrusting their torches in the air and dancing around the fiery furnace.

The horror of it was unimaginable!

Soon enough, the scene went dark. The pain of the fall and his wound from Snegg and the cold of the air and darkness flooded over Kringle again. He swooned and began to close his eyes when all of a sudden, he caught a glimpse of his staff. It stood on the edge of the chasm above him, where he had vainly plunged it into the ground to stop his fall. Its forked tip, normally black and charred, was no longer visible. Instead, blooming from the top of the staff was a bright sprig of holly leaves, bushy and green and dotted with berries the color of blood.

Old, dead wood — blossoming?

Blossoming!

How could this happen? I tremble to think how. Kringle trembled, too. His heart seized up inside him, and his breath stopped cold in his throat. He felt darkness coming on him again, but he pushed it away and awoke with a start, as if he had been dreaming for months, as if it were his first day in the world! "My staff! How . . . how . . . how . . ."

He didn't answer himself this time. His head throbbed. His leg burned with pain. His breath froze his lungs. But his heart jumped with joy and wonder, and he began to climb. To climb, I say! He pulled and pulled and lifted and lifted and managed — never mind how *long* it actually took — to loosen his foot from the rock that pinned it. Then he dragged himself up inch by inch. It was the work of hours. But this was Kringle. He was always thinking and talking and doing.

That flat rock, this foothold. "Stay away from that ice."

"Take hold of this root." "Climb, climb, climb!" In this way, ledge by ledge, cleft by cleft, he pulled himself up over the top of the chasm, flipped over, and fell on his back just as it began to snow again.

"Well, that took forever," he said. "Now I need to get to the elves!"

"How will I do that?"

"Not easily, with this leg."

"I know that!"

Kringle was back. Kringle was back! He lifted himself up on the rocks, colder and more tired than before, his leg aching with pain, wondering what to do first.

He gazed up at the blossoming staff. It stood straight and tall as if it were a tree, its crisp green leaves and red berries shining through the spinning white flakes. He grasped it, and the wood was warm. He shook the staff.

As the holly leaves quivered, the snow fell more heavily. Wind roared across the northern wastes and swept over him from the distant heights. Giant clouds of snow blew across the plains toward him, swirling in magnificent designs. He saw bulls of snow, all white and leaping, thundering at him, faster and faster, then suddenly veer away at the last moment, charge over him, and vanish down into the chasm beyond.

Startled, he remembered the strange and sudden wind that pushed his sledge free of the varguls at the river. He remembered, but only for an instant; for now whole fleets of many-sailed ships, their masts towering to the sky, sailed over him, sweeping coils of snow in their wake.

And in their wake, too, flocks of diving birds fell at him, dipping and swooping with each new wind, then soared up over the chasm and into the sky.

Through his blinking eyes, Kringle saw galloping herds of horses next. They came at him as swift and sudden as arrows, then swerved, and vanished behind him, spraying him with their hooves.

Last of all, in a sweep of flakes, came one horse alone. It bore a great silver crown upon its head as if a hundred ice-tipped branches had crashed down from above, settled on its head, and grown right up out of its brow.

Did it rush at him over the snow, or had it flown down from the distant treetops on the wings of the wind? He couldn't tell. All he knew was that when the wind blew the snow squalls away and its howling and roaring died off, the crowned horse remained, and it was moving slowly, solemnly across the white ground toward him.

Except that it wasn't a horse, either. And what Kringle thought was its crown was really a giant and unruly mass of curling, pointed bones growing out of its head.

Bones? They were antlers!

The creature — whatever it was — wore a glorious crown of silver antlers. It came to a halt not ten feet from where Kringle lay and stared unwaveringly at him.

Unwaveringly, but calmly.

Breathless, Kringle stared back, but not calmly. His heart was thumping like mad.

The creature's antlers were gigantic, magnificent, a forest of upthrust limbs. When it shook itself, snow cascaded from its fur, and its whole being shone like silver. Its flanks glinted and sparkled in the whirling snow. Stamping its hooves, it moved still closer to him and lowered its great crowned head.

Looking up at it, Kringle saw the moon framed between its silver antlers. His head throbbed and his heart thundered and his blood, first hot, then cold, raced through his veins as if he were seeing a ghost.

"What are you?" he said aloud, as if he half expected the beast to answer him.

Of course, it didn't answer him. Such creatures do not speak. They *cannot* speak! But it did have a voice, as surely as if right now I turned up from this page, looked you in the eye, and whispered some kind but mysterious word.

And that is exactly the sound this horned beast made in Kringle's mind. It was as if those ancient rune stones had come to sudden life in the whisper of a word he knew.

Arise.

CHAPTER EIGHTEEN

BONECROWN

KRINGLE BLINKED, THEN shut his eyes, then opened them again and stared, but still the animal stood before him. It was very close to him, and its gaze did not waver.

"Don't hurt me," said Kringle, afraid he wouldn't be able to run if the large creature decided to trample him. But its deep brown eyes sparkled with a kind of — he didn't even know what — wisdom? He had never seen anything like it in an animal before. He felt as if he were peering into the depths of a pool filled with life.

How it happened, I cannot say, but the moment Kringle wondered if this creature had a name — and if it *did* have a name, what it was — words seemed to sound mysteriously in his head.

I am Oliphas.

In a whisper, Kringle repeated the name. "Oliphas!"

What a name! Oliphas! It sounded of the great mysterious world beyond. It sounded ageless and yet wonderful and new. It sounded wise and powerful and friendly. It sounded like all these things and more.

"What are you doing here?" he asked.

The creature looked at him in its calm way and Kringle heard, *I am here to help you.*

The boy breathed out slowly and then, as he had done so often before, he simply "got on with it."

"Help would be very good," he said. "I have to go to Elvenwald. It's where the elves live. I have to find them."

The reindeer did not answer, or nod, or *smile,* or anything like that. Kringle knew instantly that when he chose to speak, Oliphas would not go on and on as Alban or Vindalf or even he himself might, jabbering away until they finally collapsed, exhausted. No, the reindeer — for Kringle knew that Oliphas was a reindeer — would say what needed to be said and nothing more. But that was plenty, for the creature's eyes said many things, if you knew how to listen. And apparently Kringle knew how.

Oliphas turned to the east and the Black Woods. *Come.*

Grasping the blossoming staff and climbing painfully to the top of a nearby rock, Kringle fell onto the reindeer's back and sat upright. Slinging his staff into its quiver, Kringle gripped the crown of antlers and leaned forward. "All right —"

Swooosh! In a great sweep of snow, Oliphas raced away from the chasm, galloping over the snow, faster and faster, until he gently but undeniably lifted from the ground and leaped over the Roman wall.

He lifted from the ground, I tell you, and leaped over the wall, but he did not come down again. Oliphas flew up and up in a flourish of wind-driven snow.

"Ohhhh!" Kringle gasped. "But how . . . how?"

When the boy looked down, his head swam to see the ground pull away below them. He glimpsed the deep black scar of the chasm he had fallen into and watched it recede in the distance. He gazed up and down the whole snaking length of the Roman wall before it, too, passed below them. In moments, they were soaring toward the treetops of the Black Woods, sliding this way and that on the furling and unfurling winds before them.

"Oliphas, you're . . . flying!" he cried. "This is amazing! You must be enchanted! How did you find me?"

The reindeer pumped his legs and surged forward into the snowy air. He spoke to the boy in his way. *A dead staff does not bloom in winter.*

Kringle looked back over his shoulder at the tip of the staff. Its leaves were still sharp and bright and its berries still red as blood. "You saw it?"

Oliphas leaned to the right, and they began to dip toward the western edge of the woods. *I saw it.*

"But how can you — I mean —"

How can I fly?

"Yes!"

Kringle, I am a being who lives in both worlds. The spirits of the good have found a home in me. Like them, I can fly on the wind.

"Spirits!" said Kringle. "Do you mean of the dead?"

Those with good hearts who have died before their work is done have found a voice in me and in my kind.

"'Your kind.' There are others like you?"

Together, there are twelve of us.

The words stunned him. Twelve flying reindeer! For a long while he shivered in silence as the creature swooped down toward the trees.

"What is 'a good heart'?" he asked finally.

One that watches and waits and hopes for children.

Kringle thought instantly of his mother and father.

Yes, Kringle, Halig and Elwyna are among the souls who find voice in us. In the twelve are hundreds, thousands of good souls.

Kringle's heart leaped into his throat. "But why have you come to me?"

We yearn to do good among men, to finish what was left undone by death. But alone, we cannot change the world. Alone, we cannot save the children. We live where few have seen us. But we have been watching. And waiting. We have been hoping.

"For what?" said Kringle.

For you.

"For me?"

Look now. Here is Elvenwald.

The reindeer dipped suddenly, and down they went, zig-zagging through the ice-covered trees to a small clearing. Kringle's heart hammered in his chest when they alighted. "Oh, no, no."

It was Elvenwald. Or what used to be Elvenwald.

To his horror, it was exactly as he had seen it in his fever, burned black and still smoking. Nothing was left standing. The great hall, the bridges, the ring of homes surrounding the clearing, even the little house he had called his own — all were burned black and drifted over with snow. The big twin oak trees were cracked, leaning on each other as if ready to fall. Elvenwald was no more.

Ignoring his bruised leg, Kringle leaped off the reindeer's back and ran around the clearing, calling, "Gussi! Vindalf! Hrothr! Ifrid!" But there was no answer.

"Snegg did this," the boy said, stopping at what was left of the fallen walkway. "Oliphas, I saw what happened here. After leaving me in the chasm, Snegg led his band of raiders to Elvenwald. He heard Hrothr's rune and led them here. I couldn't save them —"

"Oh, yes, gone!" said a sudden voice. "All gone. Long gone, the elves."

Turning, Kringle saw a furry-tailed creature about a foot

long scurrying among the timbers underneath the collapsed hall.

A stoat, said Oliphas. He tramped over to the remains of the hall, lowering his head.

The stoat blinked as the reindeer came near. There followed a moment of silence between the two.

Now, whether it was through the medium of Oliphas or through some other sense that he heard the stoat, Kringle wasn't sure, but hear him he did.

"Yes, yes, I saw what happened," the stoat said in a small voice. "The gobbies came one night — wait, what day is it today? Was there a full moon last week? Never mind. A few nights ago. Maybe a week. Anyway, it was very snowy. And, well, you see what they did. They didn't spare a thing. First the storm, lots of ice; then the fire, lots of that, too. They were mad, the gobbies were. They vowed to hunt down the elves until — *pfft!* — they were all gone. Oh, they were mad!"

Kringle's eyes stung. He slumped to the ground. "I wasn't able to warn them."

"Perhaps not," said the stoat, peeping under the fragment of a small door, picking it up, then letting it fall again, "but someone did."

Kringle moved closer. "Someone warned them?"

"Oh, didn't I say? The elves were gone before the gobbies ever came. 'Jingle saved us!' I heard them shouting. 'Jingle came in a dream!' Didn't sound right to me, but oh well."

"Not Jingle. *Kringle.* That's me! I tried to warn them."

The stoat turned from a smashed urn he had been licking. He looked Kringle up and down. "You? Oh, I don't think so. It sounded to me like Jingle was a boy. You're much too tall. 'Jingle! Jingle!' they said. Very strange that was."

"Tell me everything. Where did they go?"

"The elves have lots of places to go," said the stoat. "They came from all over to live here, you know. I think they headed off to different places, some here, some there. Can't go far enough to flee the gobbies!"

"But where?" Kringle asked again.

"Hold on, hold on." The stoat went quiet for a moment. "All right. Some of them went . . . where was it . . . east. The coast. Morpeck. That's it, I think."

"And Gussi? Vindalf?" asked Kringle. "Little Mari?"

The little creature shrugged. "I don't know anything about names. Except Jingle. I remember that. Jingle. That was funny."

The boy turned to the reindeer. Oliphas looked back at him in understanding. Stamping the ground, he bristled, as if he were ready.

"Thank you, stoat!" said the boy.

The little animal spied a broken plate and seized half of it in each hand when Oliphas leaped up. He stared at the enchanted reindeer and watched him fly away with Kringle on his back. "Now, that's a trick!" He shook his head, licked one side of the plate, dropped both pieces, then scurried back under the main hall. And what used to be Elvenwald fell silent again.

But you can imagine that Kringle did not. With every mile that Oliphas soared over the treetops, he knew more certainly what had to be done, and he uttered every single word of it.

"Oliphas, we'll go straight to Morpeck as fast as we can. Then we'll start bringing the elves together. There's nothing else to be done. The elves have to unite. Numbers. It's all in the numbers. Vindalf said there are a hundred elves. How can they ever be safe if they separate, a few here, a few there? There are twenty thousand goblins! So that's it, then. We have to bring the elves together and we have to hide before the goblins hunt them down and split them up for good!"

And more of the same. What Oliphas thought of it all, no one knew. Even if he had been a talker, he couldn't have gotten much more than a word in. The one word he did say, finally, was *hush*. For he had begun to slow and descend soundlessly through the treetops. He landed in a tiny pine clearing. A stump, hacked and worn, decayed and long dead, lay before them.

The boy trembled. "What is this place? We need to get to Morpeck —"

Kringle . . . Oliphas's voice was different all of a sudden. *Son* . . .

"What?"

A second reindeer made its way from the cover of the surrounding pines. It was nearly as large as Oliphas, except that its fur was glistening chestnut brown and its antlers stark white.

"Are you . . ."

I am Seraban. Your mother speaks through me.

Kringle stood, his whole body quaking. He knew it was cold, bitter even, and yet he felt strangely warm in his cloak as he watched the reindeer move together to face him. As they began to speak, first the one, then the other, he felt the urge to close his eyes.

When he did, he saw this:

Winter. Snow dropped quickly and heavily from the sky. A man — his father, Halig — stood before a tree, *this* tree, which was then still standing, and he was chopping, chopping. He worked swiftly. Night was on its way.

I was nearly done, said Oliphas, his voice even more distant than before, *when two elves ran into the clearing, one in a berry-colored cloak, the other in white. They were frantic because they were being chased by someone. It was a hideous creature. It loped into the clearing. A goblin, green of skin and black of eye. When it raised its sword against the elves, I pushed the two behind me without thinking. As they fled, I fought the creature. Finally, the goblin struck me with his blade. I fell and, falling, swung one last time. . . .*

Kringle saw the final swoop of his father's blade pin the Goblin King against the tree. Shrieking, Morgo rolled away, the tip of his right ear taken by the blade. The creature was about to crawl away from the clearing when he saw the bell around the stricken Halig's neck. Greed overtook him. Reaching for the bell, Morgo suddenly screeched and drew back his hand. It was smoking.

"I saw Morgo's hand!" said Kringle. "The bell burned him."

The bell that speaks your name, said Seraban in a voice that Kringle knew at once was his mother's. *Morgo could not steal it. It is, in its own way, a holy bell.*

Kringle was frozen where he stood. How could he take it all in? His lost mother, his lost father were speaking to him, speaking *with* him for the very first time — from beyond death! Love, wonder, desire, sorrow rose up from deep inside him, from somewhere far beneath words, and flooded his senses.

He thought of Hrothr's words predicting his long journey from the Bottoms. Where that journey would lead he didn't know. Yet here he was in a place so far from where he had begun, and yet it was as close to him as anywhere could be.

"Father," he said to Oliphas, "you wounded Morgo. You saved the elves."

But I was dying. Later, when the elf woman cast runes over me, I saw the wounded goblin's eyes still watching from beyond the pines where he had crawled. In my last moment, I heard his evil words. "I shall find the child. I shall steal all the children, until I find this 'chosen one'!" I could not hold on. Kringle . . . I died here. . . .

Oliphas' voice began to come back then. *He died here.*

When I came, Halig lay lifeless against the tree, said Seraban. *I knew the goblin was still about. I could smell him. I wrapped myself in the cloak. I took the bell. And I fled. The rest, you know.*

Kringle fell to his knees and sobbed and knew then what he had long hoped was not true.

"The goblins began to steal children . . . to find *me.*"

But Morgo did not find you, said Seraban. *Merwen took you. You escaped. And escaped and escaped.*

Because . . . you are the chosen one, said Oliphas.

Kringle buried his face in his hands, unable to move. "The chosen one? The chosen one has to defeat the goblins. How can that be me? I'm just . . . just . . ." He broke off, for all at once came a fluttering from the trees overhead. Kringle looked up and saw a small black and brown and white shape weaving in a tight circle among the snow-swept branches. It was the sparrow. His heart leaped. "Ohhh . . . wait!"

It did not wait, but as it flew away, something shiny struck the snow on the tree stump. Trembling, Kringle picked it up. Of course, it was the bell. *His* bell.

Holding it tightly in his hand now, after so long, Kringle breathed deeply, swallowed his tears, and stood. Deliberately and carefully, he twined the bell onto the staff among the holly leaves. He shook the staff, and the bell rang.

Kringle!

The boy stared at the tree stump for a long while, utterly still and silent. What thoughts moved in his mind, what emotions seized his heart just then remained unspoken. He simply nodded once and turned to the waiting reindeer. "Oliphas, Seraban, let's go to Morpeck. To the elves. Now."

Oliphas and Kringle galloped faster than the wind across the sky, with Seraban beside them. They passed high over the trees once more, weaving east across the vastness of the forest, until they came over flat white plains that sloped gently to the coast. Below, and with an unbroken view of the sea, stood a great earthen mound, and nearby an ancient circle of standing stones. An assortment of small white tents stood in the center of the stone ring, nearly invisible in the snow.

"There?" asked Kringle.

There, said Seraban. *Morpeck.*

Gliding downward finally, the reindeer circled the ring of stones. It was after dusk when they touched down.

First to see them was Holf, who with his sheep stood aghast when Oliphas and Seraban galloped down from the sky. "Can't do that, can you, Blendl?" he grumbled. Then his gaze fell on Kringle, and his eyes widened in disbelief. "Elves, look here!" he cried.

As soon as they saw Kringle, the elves came running, hooting and cheering. First Gussi came, then Vindalf, then Elni, Nar, and finally Ifrid.

"I'm so glad to see you all!" Kringle said, hugging them. "Is this everyone?"

"Kringle, it was horrible," said Elni. "The goblins tore at everything, burned everything. Thanks to your warning we had already fled into the woods, but we watched. Snegg cursed us and vowed to hunt us down wherever we went. We have been on the run ever since."

"I haven't seen Torgi for weeks," said Gussi, not holding back his tears. "She may have escaped to Timtamblybush, maybe, if she's still . . . well . . . she's there, I think."

"And the children?" asked Kringle. "There were children with you?"

Gussi hung his head. "Taken. Even our little Mari."

"The Goblin King is mad in the head!" said Vindalf.

The boy's chest first heaved with sorrow, then with anger. "And he'll keep hunting you down until he finds you. I don't know everything, but I know one thing. The elves must unite. It's the only way to save yourselves —"

"We've called all the elves!" said Ifrid. "From Sunderby and Pernbury and Frippenith and Hydepool and everywhere! Or, rather, Hrothr did."

"Hrothr!" said Kringle. "I must see him. It was the runes

that helped me warn you. I rather think he planned the whole thing."

"He did!" said Nar. "He told me to bring them to Barrowfoot. I was to lose them, Hrothr said, and you were to find them. It was a test. Hrothr said —" Nar broke off.

There was a sudden moment of silence among the elves. Then Vindalf sighed heavily. His face was grim and his eyes moist when he looked at Kringle. "Hrothr has asked for you, boy. He is . . . he is . . ."

The look on Vindalf's face told Kringle in an instant: The elder elf was dying.

The boy followed the elves to the base of the giant snow-covered mound. It towered over a wide white plain that sloped a long way down to the eastern sea.

"The cairn," said Gussi, his voice weak.

Kringle didn't know if "cairn" was the name for a giant dome of earth or some long-ago forgotten house that the ground had covered over, but right now it seemed like nothing less than a tomb. A dark opening the size of a man stood in front.

Amid the soft crying of the elves, he went in.

CHAPTER NINETEEN

TOMB OF EARTH

IGHT HAD FALLEN by the time Kringle entered the mound. Inside, he was surprised to find not walls of earth but enormous slabs of stone laid side by side to form a passage. It looked like the work of giants. Roman cities like Castrum were dwarfed by the cairn's size and grandeur.

The passage ended in a round room whose walls were made of massive stones that sloped up to a high ceiling. Tiny Hrothr sat leaning against one giant slab, cross-legged, silent, his ancient eyes staring at the flames of a single candle he held out before him. He looked older and frailer than the last time Kringle had seen him.

"Hrothr," he whispered.

The elf moved slightly, as if woken from a trance, and flicked his eyes up at the boy. "Kringle. You came. I hoped to see you one last time. I never doubted it."

The words troubled Kringle. "The elves are being hunted," he said. "We have to leave this place."

"Sit there, please."

Kringle sat down, facing the elf.

"Do you see those?" Hrothr asked, pointing up.

Directly above Kringle were several openings in the very top of the dome. Through them he saw stars twinkling.

"Are they for smoke?"

"No. For this." Hrothr lowered the candle to the cairn floor, revealing a dazzling white stone some ten feet across. It lay nearly completely buried in the ground and was so old and open to the air that rain and ice and snow and time had worn its surface nearly smooth. Visible on it, however, were the coiling lines of a great double spiral set upon what looked like the spokes of a giant wheel. The wheel's hub stood in the very center of the chamber.

When Kringle followed the spiral from the outside to the center, he found his eyes were drawn back out to the rim. Its end was its beginning. "What is this a picture of?" he asked.

"Yule," Hrothr whispered. "*Yule* is an elvish word meaning the 'Wheel of the Year.'"

"'The Wheel of the Year,'" Kringle repeated. "The wheel's turning that is the year's turning? Merwen told me about this."

The elf nodded. "At the very end of the year, the wheel slows, night lengthens, darkness reigns longer —"

"The Goblin Long Night," said Kringle, remembering that Alban's story happened on Long Night, too.

"Long Night," the elf whispered. "This cairn was built by your people very long ago. Through its openings, one can mark the sunrise on the shortest day of the year. This wheel also marks the movement of the moon on the longest night of the year. Now, Kringle, do you know why the goblins cherish Long Night?"

He thought about that. "Because people are afraid that the sun won't come back? And the goblins like fear? And they like the darkness."

Hrothr smiled slightly. "Fear and darkness, Kringle. Darkness is not simply the lack of light, you know. It is its own powerful force. We have all felt it. Stand in a forest clearing at dawn, and you are happy above all things. Stand in the same spot after nightfall, and you will feel the darkness close in around you. You will feel fear. The goblins know this. When the light is gone, souls begin to fear — children fear most of all. From that fear, from that darkness, the goblin gains power."

"I saw that happen in the goblin palace," said Kringle.

Hrothr paused for a moment, gazing intently at the boy. "As trees, flowers, birds, men, and elves take life from light and thrive in it and in the hope of new dawns, goblins hunger and thirst for darkness. Sunlight starves them, parches them. Their need for darkness has kept them in the wintry north, has kept their deeds confined to nighttime only. But, Kringle, there is one who, if given the chance, can vanquish light altogether. It is the ancient beast of darkness, a shadow by the name of Grunding."

"Grunding?"

"Since time began in our world, Grunding has lived as a powerful shadow-being under the earth. He is a fearful thing whose strength waxes and wanes. But he is strongest, most powerful, and most dangerous on the night of greatest darkness."

"Long Night," said Kringle.

Hrothr nodded. "Twelve years ago, Morgo, King of the Goblins, discovered the beast's lair in the north. It was Grunding who told Morgo to create the Iron Wand, and the Goblin King was seduced by its power. Now the shadow has commanded him, 'Give me shape! If darkness rules over the land, goblins shall own the earth!' Kringle, the Goblin King is building a shape and a form for Grunding —"

"The War Dragon!" said Kringle, horrified.

"If Morgo succeeds in giving Grunding a shape in our world, there will be no return of the sun. Only knowledge, Kringle, can defeat fear and darkness."

"Knowledge of what?"

"Ah," the elf said, his old impish smile returning. "For that, we wait. We wait." The elf closed his eyes and went silent.

As you can imagine, Kringle had several thousand questions to ask Hrothr. But the elf seemed to pull himself so far away from the moment that the boy felt alone in the stone tomb. Kringle and the elder elf sat in silence for a long, long time. Finally, at the third hour, the elf's eyes popped open. They were glowing and mischievous.

"Kringle, watch now, up there. Look. It comes!"

As they watched, the orb of the moon moved over one of the openings in the ceiling. It cast a slender shaft of silver light onto the spiral and the wheel.

Suddenly, the candle's flame lengthened to a point as if it were a spear of beaten gold, and it appeared to slow and slow until it almost stopped moving.

"Look at that!" said Kringle. "What's happening?"

Hrothr stretched out his closed hand before Kringle until it was directly above the center of the wheel. He turned his hand over, then opened it. A small gray rune stone spun slowly from his palm toward the ground. But it did not strike the floor. It slowed and it slowed its fall. Gradually, its spinning came so near to stopping that it hung almost motionless in a circle of its own golden light, a light that bathed the faces of the elf and the boy and the stone wheel below.

Kringle gasped, his voice now as hoarse as the elf's. "How are you doing that?"

"Not I," said Hrothr. "It is Yule. The Wheel of the Year has nearly stopped its turning. It is the very dead of night, so close to the end of the year, and Yule turns now so slowly, slowly that the hours stretch and nearly stop. Through this rune, I have merely asked the wheel to pause."

"That rune . . . is it your favorite?"

"The one I kept," said the elf. "It is Jera, the rune of the wheel. Having it allowed me to hear you across the miles." Hrothr's voice grew softer then. "Kringle, with this rune and this knowledge, you can use time. You can make the great wheel stop before it begins again. Three nights from now is Long Night. Grunding will rise and take the shape that Morgo has made for him. He will use fear. He will use darkness. Kringle, Grunding will enter our world and evil — true evil — will win. The Romans have left our land. The southern invaders may be strong enough to overcome the heath folk and the hill men, but not the vast goblin horde. On midnight of the third night from now, the year slows to its actual end. That night is the longest of the year —"

"Hrothr," said Kringle suddenly. "Morgo is using children to power his War Dragon. I saw it in my vision. Freya's prophecy terrified him. He began to steal children . . . in hopes of finding me. And now he's using them to help Grunding rise!"

The elf closed his eyes. When he opened them again, they were wet. "That's why, Kringle, you must be the one to stop him. Now, every place in this country has a name. Find out where Morgo's forge is. I give this rune to you. Unless you use it, Grunding will rise, the goblins will win, and our world will fall. Stop the wheel and defeat Morgo. Kringle, stop the wheel!"

This is where we must draw away from the story for a moment. We must draw away because no one knows exactly what happened next. Not me. Not the elves. No one. Hrothr, as the great and magical elven elder, knew perhaps, but he did not tell.

All anyone can say is that as Kringle stared at the hovering stone, and stared and stared, all the things that had ever happened to him, all that he had ever thought, and all that he had ever felt came together like the spokes of Yule itself, and he *knew*. And what he knew was how it all worked. He understood as never before how the great wheel turned through every day and night from the beginning of the year to its end, until it grew finally tired and slow, and winter loomed, and the nights grew longer and longer, until one night the wheel stopped.

His whole being trembled. The more he watched the light, the more he felt his body lean into it, and the more he knew that the very big mystery of Yule was somehow connected to the very big mystery of the child of heaven. For it was in that time between when the wheel stopped and when it started again that the child came down to earth to be born among us.

Was it the most dangerous time? It was. Was it the holiest time? It was that, too. Kringle knew this as, I suppose you could say, it was foretold from the beginning that he would.

The child shall know.

All at once, wind whooshed across the opening in the ceiling, snow fell into the cairn, and the candle flickered. At the same time, the elf's rune stone dropped with a sharp *clack*.

"And now, Kringle, you know this, too!" said Hrothr. With that, he ceased speaking. Staring at the boy, his lips set in a gentle smile, the old elf passed away with a single breath — *hooo* — and the moonlight moved across the floor, and time went on.

"Hrothr!" Kringle cried, but truly, he knew that the old elf wasn't really there anymore. Slowly, the boy reached for the small stone. In its two interlocking angles he saw the image of a turning wheel. *Jera!*

When Kringle finally emerged from the cairn and laid the tiny body of Hrothr in the center of the ring of stones, the elves clustered around. They mourned and sang dirges and sent fires of scented smoke coiling high up to the snowy heavens. Kringle mourned, too, for the passing of the great elf. He wept and sang with the others and prayed and wept again.

Solemnly and with great reverence the elves buried their beloved old Hrothr, weeping anew as they laid his body in the earth at the center of the ring of stones. Then they crowned Vindalf the new elven elder.

He nodded sadly. "I shall not take the white cloak just yet," he said, his eyes downcast. "Our world, friends, the world of the elves, is collapsing around us."

"Falling apart," added Holf, trembling.

Ifrid sighed. "So, are the great days of the elves coming to an end?"

Kringle turned toward Oliphas and Seraban, who stood together beyond the stone circle, facing north. He imagined he heard again the voices of his father and mother speaking through them. *You are the chosen one.*

All of a sudden, he heard other voices.

"Maybe not," he said. "Look."

Everyone turned to the south. A tiny caravan of wagons led by seven fat sheep was stomping toward them through the heavy snow. Spotting Torgi in the first wagon, Gussi made a small sound and jumped, then ran as fast as his legs could carry him. "Torgi! My love!" He swung the little elf off the wagon and hugged her, twirling her around and around. When he told her quietly that the old elf was gone, Torgi wept, then said, "Hrothr's last act was to call the elves back. And they are coming. They're all coming!"

Even as she said this, two more wagons rolled over the hill from the south, then another four from the west. They came and came until before long the elven family numbered nearly seventy strong.

Now, I've told you that Kringle's mind was always moving,

always questioning, always wondering. Even as he watched the ranks of the elves grow ever greater, he began to form a plan. It wasn't all in place, but it was coming together. I might say that Alban's words suddenly came back to him at this point, but I like to think that there was no "suddenly" about it. What the hermit had said had never really left his mind. He heard the old voice as if Alban were as close to him as I am now to you. "This little child did not hide, Kringle. He came into the dark world, and each year he comes again on that one night to save us. Think of it, Kringle, think of it!"

And this time, he did think of it.

"Elves!" he called out. "We can't hide! We have to march against Morgo. We must defeat the goblins! And we can do it. Hrothr showed me how. Three days is all we have to find the goblin forge. On Long Night, the beast Grunding will rise. We have to stop the goblins then, or it will be too late."

Everyone looked at everyone else.

"Will there be war?" asked Nar, his tiny face trembling.

Kringle knelt to the little elf. "Nar, there will be war. And I can't read the future like Hrothr could. I don't know everything that will happen. But look around you. The elves are here."

Nar smiled then. "And Kringle is here!"

"And together," said Vindalf, "there may just be nothing we can't do!"

At that, Kringle turned to the silver reindeer. "Oliphas?"

At once, the wind roared across the field and into the trees around the cairn, blowing great clouds of snow up from it. The air was filled with silver powder sparkling in the light of the bright-faced moon, rushing back and forth in little white squalls, rising like whirlwinds, swooping like downdrafts, until all at once three reindeer galloped down through the trees.

Kringle knew for certain then that it had been the reindeer who had saved Alban and him on the river. He turned to Oliphas, and between them passed an unspoken word.

But more came! Some stormed out of the woods now and joined the first. Still others took shape from the spin and flash of silver flakes beyond the cairn. One spun out of the snow amid the standing stones, and Kringle knew that the spirit of Hrothr had now joined the multitude of souls who spoke through the twelve.

More came and more until, in one great sweeping fall of snow, the wind ceased and the trees stilled and there stood a dozen majestic reindeer. Each one bore a great crown of antlers, silver or white or black, sparkling in the moonlight.

Kringle tried to pierce the huffing and breathing that came next and could not. But when the reindeer turned toward him and bowed as one, he heard their words clearly enough.

We will fly for you.

PART
VI

ALL WERE WEAPONED, SHIELDED, SWORDED, DAGGERED,
AND SPITTING AND HOWLING ABOVE THE ROAR OF THE STORM.

CHAPTER TWENTY

A GATHERING OF SOULS

RINGLE'S PLAN WASN'T entirely put together, but there was no doubt in his mind about what had to be done first, for he leaped straightaway onto Oliphas's back, nodded quickly to Vindalf, and turned west. "First things first," he said.

Vindalf laughed. "Elven ladders, friends. It looks like we're going for a ride!"

It was the work of moments for the elves to clamber onto one another's shoulders and onto the backs of the reindeer, and only moments more for the reindeer to fly right up into the sky. Oh, the whoops and shrieks the little passengers made then!

"First things first?" said Gussi, holding tight to Kringle, his little cloak billowing up behind him. "Why are we flying west? Is there time? There can't be time. The three days will soon be two and a half days. We must go straight north. How can there be time?"

"If Kringle says there's time," said Torgi, popping her head over his shoulder, "then there's time — oh, oh, ohhh!"

Oliphas swooped suddenly toward the ground, and Kringle and the two elves held tight. The reindeer's silver head weaved left and right, its icicled antlers bearing firmly into the wind.

"There's time for this," said Kringle. "We must find my dear friend Alban. We'll need him, I think!" Glancing back, he saw the eleven other reindeer flying in formation behind them, their elf riders clutching their antlers and each other for dear life.

Down below, less visible by the moment, was a flock of sheep with Blendl in the vanguard, a soft, woolen army making its way north as Holf had told them to do.

An hour later, Kringle's heart raced nervously when Oliphas rounded the dark cliffs of Cragtop and set his hooves gently on the snow-covered path before the cave. He slid off the deer's back even before it stopped, and rushed to the opening.

"Alban! Alban!" he whispered. "If only you're still here. You have to be with us now. We can't do any of this without you —" He stopped. The cave was empty and dark. It was cold. Even the mousy smell was gone.

Gussi padded up behind him. "I'm sorry, Kringle. Perhaps he left with the last of the Romans. He was friends with them, wasn't he?"

"Or," said Vindalf, peeping in, "was it the goblins who finally found him?"

"Stole his cave clean!" grunted Holf, gazing past them and shaking his head sadly.

Kringle entered the cave in disbelief. Every stick of furniture, clothes, books, bed — everything was gone. His heart sank. "Alban . . . I can't believe you're not here."

For a few long minutes he stood rooted to the spot, staring at the place where the priest had told him about the child born to save the world. The silent chamber stared right back at him.

At last, Kringle turned to go. "Elves, I thought to bring my friend with us. But we'll have to make our way into the north without him. We can't waste any more time. We'll have to stop the goblins alone —"

Slap-slap!

Kringle and the others hushed. There was a noise from the far side of the cave. It was the sound of feet sloshing quietly, tremulously through the snow. Raising his staff, and careful not to make the bell ring, Kringle mouthed a single word at the elves: *Snegg!*

Then, thrusting his staff ahead of him, Kringle tore around the side of the cave, yelling, "Ahhhh!"

The response was loud and clear and sudden.

"Will you attack an old man with his own crutch?"

Kringle stopped. Alban stopped. Then they both rushed

to each other and hugged there on the ledge for a long, long moment.

"Ah, my boy!" said the hermit finally.

"I thought you were gone!" said Kringle. "There was no light, the cave was empty —"

Alban laughed. "Silly boy. It was empty because I have packed it all. And one doesn't leave an empty cave lit when one is not going to return to the cave for some time. *Quite* some time, *if ever*, I might add! Besides, there are, in case you haven't heard, creatures called *goblins* about. It doesn't do to let them see you. I thought you'd learned that lesson the hard way. I doused the light because I planned to come with you. And I *am* coming with you, like it or not!"

Through his tears, Kringle nodded his head wildly. "And I came to ask you to come with us!"

"It's settled then!" said Alban.

When Kringle introduced Alban to the elves, they all bowed and said their names. "Pleased finally to meet you all," he said. Then looking up at Kringle, he added, "You know, boy, the three inches between us has become six, and not because I have shrunk any. Kringle, you have grown!"

The boy had grown, and he knew it. His father's cloak was not long on him now. His hands didn't hide in the sleeves anymore, and the frayed bottom edge no longer snagged the ground. The cloak's tattered hem strings hung freely. Maybe he had, as Hrothr had suggested so long ago, grown into it.

"It happens," he said.

Then, when Alban saw the staff's bright leaves and plump red berries clearly for the first time, he gasped abruptly. "Hold on. It's . . . blooming! How is it possible? How ever did you do that?"

"Not me!" said Kringle, looking the staff up and down. "Merwen brought it from where she used to live. More than that, I don't know —"

Alban trembled and clutched the staff to keep from falling. "Only once have I heard of dead wood blooming. And that wood was holy."

"I've been saved many times by this staff," said Kringle.

Alban released it, still trembling. He smiled. "Perhaps we'll all be saved by it before long. To the north, then?"

"To the north!"

"And to help our travel," said Alban, "we must take your wonderful pirate sledge. It took me nearly the past month to pack it all up! Follow me!" He tramped down the path, and down and down, and everyone followed. When they finally came to the tree line, Alban tore away a large cloth and scattered snow everywhere, revealing Kringle's pirate sledge. It was packed stem to stern with every stitch of the priest's belongings.

Kringle's eyes lit up at the sight of his old wooden sledge. "Thinking of doing some traveling, were you?"

"I shall be its driver," said Vindalf. "Or shall I not?"

"You shall," said Ifrid. "After me —"

Suddenly, Oliphas galloped above the tree line, then stamped his hooves on the ground. Everyone turned to the valley below. There was a short goblin snake weaving its way north over the plains toward a deserted milecastle on the Roman wall. Kringle's heart raced. He looked into the east. Dawn was no more than a few minutes away.

"So," he said, "in every plan, there comes a little luck. We have the elves. We have the reindeer. We have Alban. We even have the sledge. And now I think we've just found who can tell us where the goblin forge is. They won't want to, but perhaps we can persuade them."

"I'll persuade 'em!" said Ifrid, rubbing his hands together. "I'll do't, by golly!"

Kringle leaped onto Oliphas's back. "Quickly now, before the goblins hide to escape the sun. Penda, Nar, Seraban, to the middle of the wall —"

We shall bring the sledge.

"Thank you!" he said. "Everyone else, follow me!"

You should have seen Kringle then. In a berry-brown elvencloak that no longer scraped the ground, taller than ever, his bushy staff pointing the way, he leaped off the mountain on the back of a flying reindeer, with a troop of seventy elves and one priest flying behind him!

The whole thing was done in a second. There was no attempt to be clever or sneaky about it. Kringle had had quite enough of lurking in passages and hiding in caves. On his command, the reindeer swooped down toward the mile-castle. The elves jumped off as soon as they touched ground and charged the goblins. Vindalf was in the lead, swinging his clubs. Together he and ten little elves jumped on seven goblins before they knew what hit them and knocked them all into the snow.

"Elves!" the surprised creatures yelled. "Elves!"

Yes, elves! They swarmed over the goblins as the goblins had swarmed over the pirates. *Fwit-fwit-fwit!* Kringle let fly with his staff and caught the leader of the snake, who turned out to be none other than Lud. The goblin was heaved up from the ground, flipped over, and landed with a sharp *thud* onto three of his fellows. When he sprang back at Kringle, his dagger drawn, Ifrid was there with a club.

Lud flew into a rage. "You boy!" he shouted. "Snegg say you are dead!"

"Not just yet!" said Kringle. Together, he and Lud fell to the snow, rolling and fighting furiously.

A black, vargul-less Minder bolted across the snow and away, while another ran at Alban with his sword drawn. The priest lurched aside, and Oliphas knocked the sword to the ground.

Gussi and Torgi pelted the fleeing goblin with snow, while the rest of the reindeer cornered the others.

In a last desperate move, Lud cursed and jumped at Kringle, but the boy stood firm, knocked him down, and pinned him under the neck with his staff. The goblin roared and begged Kringle to free him, but the boy wouldn't loosen his grip.

"Armies are marching on the goblins' stronghold even now, Lud!" he declared. "The Fires of the North will burn away to nothing, but not before they burn you!"

"Kkkkk!" gargled Lud. "Goblins. Flee to the tunnels! Run to Dragon's Nest! Tell Morgo. Hurry!"

"Dragon's Nest!" boomed Vindalf. "I know it, the ugly place!"

"Fool!" one of the other goblins snarled at Lud. "Now they know!"

"Ha!" said Kringle. "We do know where the goblin forge is! Elves, let's tie them up and find a dark place for them to spend their daylight hours. They've been so helpful, we wouldn't want them to suffer."

"Not much, at least," said Holf.

It was accomplished in moments. Using stout elven twine and the goblins' own chains, the elves bound Lud and his companions and locked them in the Roman gate tower.

"Good work, fellows," said Kringle. "Now, everyone, let's fly!"

As dawn broke palely across the plains, Kringle and the elves hurried back to the reindeer and with a word were aloft once more.

CHAPTER TWENTY-ONE

ARMIES OF
THE NIGHT

J UST AS KRINGLE, Alban, and the other elves landed at the summit of the Roman wall, Penda and Nar barreled across the plains in the sledge pulled by Seraban.

In no time, Kringle had leaped off Oliphas and was pacing up and down the wall, looking into the cold, bleak north. The old straight tracks of Roman roads soon dwindled to seldom-used footpaths, then finally to untrodden wilderness.

"Vindalf, tell me what you know," said Kringle.

The big elf breathed in loudly. "Dragon's Nest is a fiend-ish, dark crater, an unholy place. It's some thirty miles north of here and is five miles from side to side. Dragon's Nest is the most horrific pit of evil in all the north! It has long been forbidden, but I was there once in my youth."

"Of course. Where else would a goblin forge be?" said Kringle, still pacing. He fingered the single rune in his cloak pocket. It was as warm as Hrothr's hand. "It could only be in a horrific pit that Grunding would be born. It's where the forge is, where the War Dragon is, and where the children are. It's where we have to go."

"Ah, yes, about that," said Alban, standing next to him and scanning the bleak northlands. "You said there were armies coming? What armies? And from where, precisely?"

Kringle smiled. "Forgive me, Brother. That was a little lie, though I hope to make it true. I've been thinking of a plan for some time now —"

"I'll just bet you have," said the priest.

"The first part of it is that you and I have to persuade the invaders and the native folk to march on Dragon's Nest. They must take on the goblins, engage them in the crater. Otherwise, the elves, though they be the best fighters I could possibly imagine, would be overrun in an instant. Even with elves returning each hour, there are still only a few over seventy of us. What are we against twenty thousand goblins?"

The priest narrowed his eyes at the boy. "Excuse me, Kringle, but you should know that there aren't twenty thousand goblins anymore. While you've been resting in chasms and flying all about, I've been watching from my cave. There are more like *fifty* thousand goblins now."

Kringle felt his hope sink, but he tried not to show it. "All the more reason to bring as many warriors we can. Brother Alban, let Seraban take you to the heath tribes. We saw them in Triplethorn on the way to Cragtop. Marshal them as best you can. Tell them their world is at stake, as, in fact, it is. Do everything you can to persuade them to march to Dragon's Nest and to be there in two nights."

"On Long Night," said Gussi.

Kringle turned. "On Long Night. I'll go with Oliphas to the invaders and tell them the same. And whatever you do, tell them not to fight the War Dragon. The children are inside."

Alban crossed his chest with his fingers. "Bless those poor innocents. And may the Lord bless our work, too."

"We have little time," said Kringle, leaping onto the reindeer's back. "In two nights this must be done or we fail. Elves, we must meet —"

"At the Bones," said Vindalf, gazing nervously into the northern mists. "It's an old cluster of boulders south and west of Dragon's Nest. I have no doubt Oliphas will find it. It will make a good meeting place."

Kringle nodded. "The Bones, then, tonight. And pray this works! Everyone — go!"

As Alban scrambled atop Seraban's back, and the reindeer galloped into the eastern sky, Oliphas swooped with Kringle up from the ground and into the south. Together they soared high over the coast, mile after mile, until they saw the Five Plains ranged beneath them, snow covered and barren.

"I know this place, Oliphas. It's not far from where I last saw the invaders. Go west to the water." Before long, they spotted the fort at Barrowfoot. Only now it was surrounded by tents, and campfires were piled up the Barrow to its top. From the fort waved the dull red banner of the invaders. "The Romans must have left here, too," said Kringle. All up and down the coast, for a mile or two beyond the fort, were close to a hundred ships, smaller ones like Octa's as well as wider, longer warships.

"The invader army has grown," said Kringle. "For us, now, this is good. Down, Oliphas, and wish us luck."

The reindeer descended swiftly, but Kringle urged him to make several passes over the camp until he found what he was looking for. They landed finally in a swirl of snow behind the top of the Barrow. "Wait for me here."

Keeping low, Kringle peered down to the campgrounds. He spotted a large, bearded man in battle armor moving among the tents. It was Octa. The boy's heart pounded when he thought of Bearn. He crept over the top and hurried down toward the captain.

"You, there!" someone shouted. "Hold! A spy —"

An arrow whizzed past Kringle's shoulder, and he flattened to the ground. "Stop, stop —"

"Arms down!" cried the deep voice of the captain. "I know that cloak. He's a friend. Kringle!" Octa approached him at the head of a troop of warriors. His face was darker and showed more worry than the boy had remembered.

"Kringle," he said, embracing the boy. "It's good to see you." He stopped. "Bearn was taken. I fear . . ."

The boy shook his head. "Bearn is alive. The goblins have him, but he is alive —"

The captain grabbed him by the shoulders. "Have you seen him? Tell me!"

Kringle told him as best he could what he knew to be true. "The goblins are massing in a crater called Dragon's Nest. It's thirty miles north of the Roman wall. Octa, there are fifty thousand goblins ready to rise up and swarm over the land. With the Romans gone, there is no one to stop them."

"Bearn is with them?"

"He is, with hundreds of other children."

"What can we do?" asked the captain.

"Only small forces exist in the north now, little tribes who are not ready for a huge war. Even your army can't hold back the goblins with the numbers they have. Your only chance, *our* only chance, is for you to attack them while they are still in the crater. Octa, you have to attack them first."

"Attack the goblins?" said one of Octa's men. "That's nonsense —"

"Face Morgo now," said Kringle, "or it will be too late. In two nights, I promise you, if you march on the goblins, we can defeat them once and for all. If not, there will be no stopping them. They have a power, a force of darkness far greater than anyone can withstand."

"'*We*' can defeat them?" said Octa, scowling under his heavy brow. "You mean you and a hundred elves?"

Kringle had to be honest. "Seventy-seven elves," he said, "and twelve . . ." He was going to tell him about the reindeer, then decided against it. ". . . well, yes, seventy-seven elves, but some of them have fought the goblins of old. My friend Alban is talking to the heath men and the other native tribes now. The Romans armed them before they left, and they've been massing to repel you. If Alban can convince them, I think there will be enough of us. But the elves can't do it alone. March to Dragon's Nest now, strike at the goblins at moonrise two nights hence, and we can stop Morgo."

"Moonrise?" said Octa. "Just what are you planning, boy?"

Kringle hesitated. "There are fifty thousand goblins in the crater. I need the cover of battle to get past them and enter the pit. March to the crater, Octa, or the children will suffer. Bearn will suffer. The goblins will win. And you'll never live in this land."

Octa turned and surveyed the armies ranged up and down the Barrow below him. "Kringle, if I did this, if I loosed my troops and persuaded the other captains to listen, they *may* fight the goblins. But after that, we *will* fight your countrymen. We will have this land. It will happen. There's no stopping it now. If we don't take this land tomorrow, we will soon. The tide is already turning. It will happen. *Time* . . . will happen."

Kringle breathed out slowly. "Time may happen, but the goblins must be driven down by moonrise in two nights or it will be too late, even for you."

The invader chief looked Kringle in the eye. "You talk like a warrior now," he said, the faint glimmer of a smile on his lips. "I'll speak to my men. We have no love for goblins, after all."

"That's all I ask," said Kringle. "Bearn will come back to you. And leave the goblin War Dragon to me."

Octa snorted a laugh. "Gladly."

Kringle hurried back to Oliphas. Together they leaped into the wind and soared high over Barrowfoot.

It was near dawn when they reached the Bones. It was as Vindalf had told him, an outcropping of boulders seven miles southwest of the goblin crater.

When he jumped from Oliphas's back, the elves rushed to him. So did Alban, huffing and out of breath.

"I don't know if it worked," the priest said. "The heath tribes are constantly fighting among themselves. Not to mention their squabbles with the river folk and hill dwellers. And there's something about who actually owns a handful of mangy horses. But if they have a leader, it would be a heath-man named Brigo. When I told him the children are in the crater, and that our leader, one of his kind — you, Kringle! — has a plan, I think I may have moved him. You do have a plan, don't you?"

Kringle touched the rune in his pocket and smiled. "I do. Let's hope we did our work well and in time. For now . . . we wait."

Dawn came and morning wore on to midday and midday to evening. The elves took turns standing guard in threes and fours from the uppermost boulder, spying for any signs of movement. All was quiet. There was nothing but silence from the north, for the goblins were deep in their vast underworld.

Kringle paced alone around his sledge in a wide circle of his own tracks. He asked himself questions and answered them quickly. He had really no doubt about what they had to do. His only doubt was whether there would be a force of ten or fifteen thousand against the goblins, or a mere seventy-odd elves, a priest, and a handful of flying reindeer.

He slept in his sledge, or tried to, under the warmth of his cloak, but his mind would not rest. He ran over and over what Hrothr had shown him and told him.

At midnight, he felt the darkness growing stronger, and he knew Grunding was stirring. Then, suddenly, a flicker appeared in the north. He stood in the sledge and watched it. Soon the flicker rose into a flame, then finally into a conflagration. "The Fires of the North," he breathed. The flames vanished as quickly as they had appeared, and Kringle felt more afraid than he had ever felt before.

"Grunding is coming," he said. "With fifty thousand goblins."

He trembled to think what such a battle would be like. He sat in the sledge alone. He knelt on the ground alone. He paced and paced alone. Finally, hearing in the dark quiet of early morning the soft gulp and splash of a stream, he took off his cloak and hung it over the sledge, propping the staff against it. Then he walked out past the last lights of the elves stationed on the boulders.

The night was still silent and cold and he felt it surrounding him as he made his way to the black stream. Bending, Kringle cupped his hands together and drew out a handful of freezing water. He splashed it on his face. It both chilled and refreshed him for the battle he knew was coming soon. Standing, he saw now that it had begun to snow again.

"Lord," he whispered. "Hrothr. Help us now."

All at once, two breathless elves ran down from the highest boulder, shouting, "Armies! Armies!"

"One from the west —"

"Another from the south —"

"They're coming north and both are within ten miles of Dragon's Nest!"

Kringle breathed out a long breath and shivered. *Thank you!* He ran back to the camp, his heart thundering, and was met by a rousing cheer.

"Friends!" he shouted back, climbing to the top of the boulder, as seventy-seven elves, twelve reindeer, and one priest gathered below. "Long Night comes tonight. The time is now! We march on Morgo!"

"Seventy-seven elves are with you!" boomed Vindalf, his chestful of medals clinking and clanging noisily. "Let's march on Morgo!"

"And here is something for Kringle to march in!" cried Gussi suddenly. He and Torgi rushed out from behind one of the boulders. Between them, they carried Kringle's berry-colored cloak. Only it was different now. The two elves had stitched a thick band of white fleece to its bottom.

"What is this?" asked Kringle.

"A little something to hide the frayed hem," said Gussi, beaming. "And because you are getting so tall. Maybe taller even than the elvencloak can be!"

"Plus a hat to match," said Torgi. "Which I ought to have made much sooner!"

Kringle leaped to the ground and slipped the cloak on. It hung full length, nearly to the ground. The hat, berry-brown and fleecy, too, matched perfectly. He felt his heart heave with emotion. Kneeling, he hugged both elves. "Thank you. Thank you. It's perfect. I'll be close to invincible wearing this."

"The scary part," said Alban, "is that you might need it. In fact, I think we could all use something like that!"

"Ha! Me? I'm ready," Vindalf grunted, making his way slowly among the elves, clapping his hands on his breastplate of elven armor and pulling his two short battle clubs from his belt. "I've always been ready for a battle. It's what we older elves are known for, you know. I was called Vindalf Twinclub in my day. And let it be known: Vindalf Twinclub likes a loud time!"

Kringle beamed. If ever the elves actually had formed an army — and among some people, there is still some doubt about that — this mass of elves under his lead was the mightiest army ever created.

"Follow Kringle!" shouted Gussi.

"Follow Kringle!" roared the little army.

And they did follow him. While Kringle pushed forward into the thickening snow, his heart pounding, his eyes narrowing, his mind thinking, that tiny band was right behind him, driving straight north to the crater called Dragon's Nest.

CHAPTER TWENTY-TWO

DRAGON'S NEST

EVERYTHING HAD A name in this country — sometimes several names, depending on who you were talking to — and from each name you could learn something about each place. Sometimes, you could learn more than you wanted to.

Dragon's Nest was also known as the Wild Place and Thornpool, and by some as Demon Pit. Rumors had long associated it with bad doings, strange black fires, and ominous noises. It was a steep-sloped crater, a tangle of thorns and briars, uprooted stumps and broken rocks, hidden dens, earth gashes, pits, holes, pools, frozen rivers, bottomless drops, and all of it covered with mud or snow or ice. The whole northland was pitted and gouged with such craters, ravaged by the goblins for their iron, and this was the largest, the deepest, and the worst. It was as if all the refuse of the country had slithered down into its sinister hollows, pooled there, and turned to ice.

By the time the twelve reindeer slowed at the crater's crest, the two armies, invaders and native folk, were less than two miles away and closing in.

Octa's troops were a dark mass pouring north across the white land. Some were on horse, most on foot, all armored and weaponed with swords, spears, axes, shields. The captain was one of a dozen riders who fronted the men. On any other day, such an enormous army would have struck terror into Kringle's heart. But tonight, he welcomed them and wished they were a force ten times as large.

Coming straight up from the wastes to the east were the native armies. They were a dense rabble of common-folk-turned-fighters, armored by the Romans or brandishing makeshift blades and sticks and farm axes. Their leader, Brigo, rode at their head, his spear held high.

"The battle will come soon now," said Alban.

Kringle breathed out heavily. "It will."

When he climbed up the rocks at the summit and looked down for the first time, his hope nearly vanished. The crater seemed to draw light into it and swallow it up. It was a place of death, a rotten place, a place the goblins knew well. And at the very bottom of its awesome pit stood the deep black maw of the earth, a vast misshapen mouth of stone, flickering red and smoking black from its untold depths.

"The forge," said Kringle. "That's where we need to go."

"We're ready," said Vindalf, clacking his two short clubs

together. "We'll follow you everywhere, Kringle. In good times or bad."

"This will be bad," said Alban, staring down into the pit as a low, dark mist moved slowly across the frozen pool at the bottom. "I don't suppose we have the element of surprise?"

Kringle closed his eyes. Because he had Hrothr's rune and Snegg still carried the others, he could see into the depths of the crater. The moment he saw Lud and the other goblins they had surprised three days before, panting and gesticulating, Kringle realized it no longer mattered that the goblins knew he had a rune. Lud had gotten free, and Morgo knew they were coming. And soon enough, there was the Goblin King himself, perched on a rock high above a vast sea of green bodies, their dark iron weapons flashing and glinting in the light of innumerable torches.

Morgo raised the Iron Wand high over his head and shrieked a goblin curse that echoed in the darkness.

"They seek to attack our stronghold before Grunding's hour is come!" he cried. "We shall destroy them first. Ithgar shall send a storm upon their puny armies that will rip them apart. They shall never reach Dragon's Nest! The armies of men shall perish, Grunding shall rise, and victory shall be ours!"

Kringle gasped, opening his eyes. "Quickly, Nar, Elni, take the reindeer, fly to Octa and Brigo. Tell them to rush to the crater. Tell them to keep the storm at their backs. Do not delay. We need them here!"

Even as Nar flew off in one direction and Elni in the other with news of the storm, whatever light was in the crater now fled. The sky blackened and a dark streak appeared, a gathering ribbon of gloom, coiling up from the depths of the frozen pool. It swept in a wide circle around the countryside, flashing with lightning. But Nar and Elni had acted swiftly, for both armies were already rushing ahead of the storm. They climbed to the crest of the crater and charged down into the pit without a pause.

"It has begun!" said Kringle. "Oliphas, stay on the crest with the reindeer. We'll need you to fly in later. Vindalf, everyone, forward!"

Kringle's plan was to lead the elves to the bottom of the pit, make his way to the forge, and get to the War Dragon before Grunding was let loose into the world. From there . . . from there . . . well, he had faith from there on.

Under the boy's lead, the elves began their mad scramble down the slopes. From rock to rock they stumbled, trying to make their way along a narrow winding pass between the two armies. The elves quickly found they couldn't zigzag down the slopes as Kringle had hoped. Brambles and slithering roots crisscrossed every downward and crossward path, and the little band was forced to double back three times before they could move forward.

"The evil of the place is too great for us," said Gussi. "Our elven powers of swiftness are useless here!"

"Fine," said Kringle, moving down as best he could. "A little band of elves, led by a boy into a goblin crater called Dragon's Nest!"

"It could have been worse, you know!" growled Alban, plunging up to his waist in snow.

"Oh? How?" asked Kringle.

"*I* could be leading these poor fellows!"

Kringle smiled. "A joke even now? Good, Alban. Come on. We're making progress. Keep going —"

"Anywhere!" said Vindalf, clacking his clubs. "Let's go!"

Meanwhile, more and more troops were pressing down the crest and into the crater, followed right behind by the swirling storm itself. Octa's burly rabble pushed down the west side of the crater. On the opposite crest were the ranks of the native tribes. A call went up from their leader, Brigo, and they moved downward slowly, lifting their shields up over the deepening drifts.

Snow fell harder and harder. The black clouds were streaked with lightning. Kringle didn't want to be caught in the middle of the two armies, but that was exactly where he and the elves were putting themselves. They struggled down through the rocks to a small outcropping with a natural wall in front of it and paused there. The air was thicker and whiter every minute, and moving five different ways at once. Looking behind them, Kringle saw that not only had the storm closed off the little pass they'd just come through, it had already sealed off the two great armies from any sort of escape.

"Keep going, fellows!" he called.

But before they could move, a dull, low groan came from the pit. It sounded like the earth itself wailing in pain.

"Morgo's horn!" cried Alban. "It means —"

He didn't have to say anything more. For at once, the goblins began to emerge. The horrible army sprang, tumbled, leaped up from a hundred holes all across the frozen pit floor. From innumerable dens and caverns and holes and chasms came tens, hundreds, thousands of them. All were weaponed, shielded, sworded, daggered, and spitting and howling above the roar of the storm.

Isolated shrieks came from the ranks of both armies as they descended to engage the goblins. But the terrain slowed them down, even as the goblins poured up the slopes at the warriors.

The first of the green forces met Octa's men halfway up the western slope, jabbing with their spears and hacking with their swords and whipping with their whips. Brigo's heathmen clashed in confusion near the top of the eastern ridge. The horrible sounds of battle — metal clanging, screams, cries — filled the air even as the storm pushed down over the crater top. Its swirling black wind drove both armies faster into the goblin mass. All the while, snow fell harder.

Then Kringle saw the varguls. Thirty or more emerged

from one tunnel not far away, growling and howling up the snow-covered rocks toward the elves. Nar screamed and turned to run back, but there was a sudden flash of silver and Oliphas was there, charging past the elves, his antlers lowered. Seraban and the other reindeer swooped after him and met the varguls, driving them yelping away from the elves.

Kringle hurried downward. "This way. To the pit opening. The way is clear —"

But Snegg was suddenly there now, and Lud, too, with a band of fifty goblins behind them, rushing from the great mouth of the pit.

"Boy!" yelled Snegg. "Now we fight, and now you *don't* live!"

Leaping over rocks, he and ten others pounced on Kringle before he could move. The boy fell back under the quick assault, and his staff clattered to the ground. A dozen other goblins were on him in an instant. But Alban pushed through the snow, grabbed the staff, and shook it.

Kringle! it rang out.

"Save him!" shouted Alban.

Then all of the elves raced after the priest, scurrying down the rocks to the boy, battling goblins every inch of the way. Vindalf's clubs were a blur of motion. Gussi was beside him, his little dagger thrusting forward. Torgi was there, too, her elven dagger out.

Snegg yelped when Alban swung the staff at him. It struck his shoulder, then smacked his head. Snegg dropped his sword and sank to his knees.

All at once, the reindeer, fresh from their rout of the varguls, rushed in, dispersing the goblins in confusion.

The elves surrounded Kringle and pulled him up. He grasped his staff. "Forward!" he yelled. And forward they went. Inch by inch, yard by yard, the little band struggled the rest of the way down the massive crater until they stood at the mouth of the giant pit itself.

The storm winds hurled and roared, then paused for a moment. It was only for a moment, but during it Kringle listened above the shriek of goblins and the thunderous cries of warriors and heard the tiniest sound emerging from the depths of the pit. *Errr, errr,* went the sound. And he knew what it was.

The squeak of an iron wheel.

CHAPTER TWENTY-THREE

THE WAR DRAGON

KRINGLE TURNED HIS head. His eyes scanned the black hole of the pit ahead of them. He heard the sound again, louder this time.

Errr. ERRR!

Then there came a creak, and a cranking, and then a rumbling and a scraping. And finally there was the shriek of wood on iron and rope on wood and it was the twisting, thumping, roaring, booming of the War Dragon itself as it rolled its way out of the pit's opening and onto the crater floor!

The elves withdrew in terror. Nar cried and clutched at Vindalf's cloak. The machine was monstrous.

As terrifying as the iron dragon had been in Kringle's vision, the goblins had labored on it since. It was seventy feet tall now, and nearly twice as long from head to tail. The great log-hewn dragon's head was horned and helmeted. It

269

was mounted with iron fangs below and spikes above, all of which turned slowly. Its body of black wooden planks was bolted all over with thick jutting rivets and plated with heavy sheets of iron. It lumbered along the ground, sliding, shuddering, *crawling* at a slow, steady pace.

But that wasn't the worst thing. A frightening shadow lingered in the darkness of the pit. Kringle knew — he *knew* — that the spirit of Grunding would soon leave the goblin pit to inhabit the beast with its evil.

"Grunding! Arise! Arise!" came the shouts of a hundred goblins.

What Kringle felt then was the ancient darkness itself. Grunding, old king of the night, rose up from the black hole of the earth like the shadow of a storm. It had no voice, no shape, no sound, until it came over the War Dragon, and then it had *its* shape, its sound, and it breathed flames.

"Long Night is here!" wailed the voice of Morgo. "Grunding is — alive!"

And now there rose up from within the dragon itself a throne of black iron. Sitting in it was the Goblin King. As frightening as he had appeared before, he was darker and larger now, as if the shadow of Grunding had possessed him, too. Kringle quaked through and through to see the awful change in him.

Below, on the ground next to the moving dragon, were

Snegg and Lud. Snegg wore the rune pouch around his neck, and Lud brandished two twisted longswords.

Morgo glared down at Kringle from his throne. While the goblins still roared up the crater at the attacking armies, the War Dragon rolled to a stop.

Morgo spoke. "Grunding lives, boy! The goblins shall win. And you, boy! You have every time got in my way. I will finish you — now!"

Not stepping back, not budging, Kringle stood firm. His right hand whipped his cloak aside, and from its inside pocket he pulled the rune stone that had fallen from Hrothr's hand.

Jera!

Now, some might say that little stone held knowledge, wisdom, mystery, and magic older than all of us. Some might say it was Kringle himself who somehow possessed those things. For me, what happened next — *what Kringle did next* — must simply be believed. Without belief, there is no going on with the story.

When Morgo stared down at the boy with his enormous, bulging black eyes, Kringle braced his feet in the ice, spun the stone in the air, and that little stone began to glow.

It glowed, I tell you, in front of Kringle like a miniature sun. A whirling wheel of light came swimming out of the rune, and all of them — the boy, the elves, the priest, and the reindeer — were bathed in its radiance.

"Sahhhh!" Morgo growled. He leaped up from his throne. Raising the Iron Wand, he hissed some inscrutable words, and — *flick-flick-flick!* — three ugly blades emerged from the wand. "The child shall know? The child shall die!"

Then Morgo leaped at Kringle.

More or less.

The Goblin King dived down from his throne. But his leap slowed and slowed and slowed until he finally hung in midair, his face frozen in a gnashing, twisted, menacing scowl of fury.

The snow slowed and slowed and slowed, too.

Kringle turned completely around. Gussi looked up at him. Torgi was standing next to the elf, Vindalf next to her, eyes wide, clubs waving back and forth in anticipation of something. All seventy-seven elves were next to them. Alban and Oliphas and all the reindeer were there, too. They stood together within the circle of light, while everything around them wound slower and slower and slower until it all came to a stop.

Nothing moved. Snowflakes stood still in the air.

The armies were stilled. The goblins did not stir. Not a sword cut, not an ax swung, not a spear flew. The whole dark crater, lit only with the blaze of unmoving torches and the flame of hovering arrows and the glowing rune stone itself, was stilled.

"Dear Heaven!" gasped Alban. "Kringle, how have you done this?"

The boy moved his palm, and the stone stayed where it was, flat in the air, showering them in bright light.

"Not me. Yule," he said. "The year is over. Tonight is the longest night, when the great Wheel of the Year slows to its end. I just . . . well . . . asked it to stop." Looking then in Alban's eyes and smiling, he added, "It's the holy moment of the child's birth, too, you know."

"Dear Lord, it is!" said Alban, bowing his head and crossing his chest.

"Everyone!" Kringle called. "Open the War Dragon. Free the children! No child should fear this holy night!" With these words, Kringle took up a gnarled goblin ax and began to chop through the outer shell of the dragon.

"Yes! Yes!" boomed Vindalf. "Oh, have I waited for this day!" He walloped the dragon's armor at its seams, double walloped it with his twin clubs!

Soon all the elves leaped upon the thing, prying, hammering, thumping, cracking.

Kringle broke open the dragon's hinges one by one with the goblin ax. Then, using all his might, he wedged his staff into a crack and pulled. Slowly but steadily, the belly of the enormous beast fell open. Everyone drew breath and stopped. Inside, as on a giant galley ship, were row upon row of benches stretching the entire length of the dragon. On the benches were the shriveled, huddled, frightened children, the lost ones. From four or five years old to twelve or thirteen, they were crammed next to one another in a frozen mass.

"Oh, oh!" moaned Alban.

Kringle looked around in an instant. "No Mari." Then he shook himself, as if waking, and said in a voice choked with sorrow and anger, "But here is Bearn! Free them. Free them!"

He led the elves in among the children, using the ax to break their chains and cut the leather straps binding them to the benches. Winding his staff into a thick chain that connected the dragon's head with the engine, he began to twist and twist so tightly that it seemed as if the staff would snap in half. But it did not break. With one final twist, the chain burst right out of the timber. It slipped away from the children, and the light of Kringle's rune stone fell over them. They stirred, they moved, and as they did, a vast black shadow moaned and wailed, and a freezing wind blew across Kringle's face. It hovered in the dark air for a moment, then flew back down into the earth, its cries echoing into the hollows until there was only silence.

"It's Grunding, fleeing the light!" said Alban, staring at Kringle in amazement. "The wind of fear has left the children!"

It was a moment never to be forgotten. It was, some might say, a holy moment.

Kringle whispered to the children, a sob in his throat. "It's all right, now. You're free. Follow the elves." And the elves, for their part, hurried the children out of the dragon to the crater floor.

Kringle rushed to embrace Bearn, who was dazed. But the boy recognized his friend and wept. "Kringle!"

"It's all right. Your father's waiting. Go with the others."

As Kringle took the children's hands one by one, he saw in each of their faces the little child from Alban's book. He thought of their mothers and fathers, of his mother and his father, and of Hrothr and Merwen and Mari and of all of the lost everywhere. If you had seen him then, with all the children crowded around him, bathed in light, you would have said that Kringle himself was the sun that came so surprisingly to that dark world. Certainly, when the rune's golden light came over them, all the children's fear was gone.

In a matter of moments, Torgi, Gussi, Vindalf, and all the elves had brought the children lovingly, gently, one by one away from the War Dragon and up out of the pit.

"They're free," Alban said, blessing the children as they passed. "After all these years!"

Kringle put his arm around Alban's shoulder. "We're not done yet, Brother," he said softly. "There's a bit more work to do. And I think you'll like this part. After all, you like to build, don't you?"

The priest wiped his eyes and began to smile. "Apparently, it's what I'm famous for."

With the children safely away from the pit behind a wall of reindeer, and the goblins, all of them, frozen where they stood, the elves quickly pulled out their hammers (which elves always have with them) and set right to work.

And they worked ferociously, making a din that reminded Kringle of nothing so much as the good old hammering in Elvenwald's big house. *Tap-a-tap-tap! Blam! Blam! Blam!*

Torgi guided Nar's delicate fingers underneath the bladed wheels, first the right, then the left. Ifrid, Elni, Horsa, and Penda urged one another up into the arched tail of the dragon, where there was a dreadful repeating crossbow.

Climbing to the top of the silent head, Kringle found a wide pipe that curved down from the dragon's neck to a furnace in the beast's belly, a furnace that was stoked by the children with shovels full of coal from the goblin mines. He chopped the pipe in two.

For thirty minutes, fifty minutes, an hour, if you had been there you would have heard a deafening noise of *clinks* and *clunks,* of *whirrs* and *blams.* It was as loud as the terrible tunnels of the goblin palace, of Dragon's Nest itself! And all the while, the goblins and the two armies stood frozen in battle on the slopes of the dark valley.

Soon, the elves' building noises stopped — first here, then there, and finally everywhere.

After the reindeer flew the children up the sides of the valley to the safety of the crater's rim, Alban glanced all around. "Are we done, then?" he asked.

"Not quite," said Torgi. She and Nar were crouching on the ground, pulling something from around Snegg's neck. When they came back up again, Nar was holding the elven pouch. He bowed and handed it to Kringle.

"All runes accounted for, sir!" he said.

"You hold on to them for now," said Kringle. "I know I can trust you." Then he smiled. "*Now* we're done!"

"We are!" yelled Vindalf. He gave the dragon one last double thrump with his clubs. "And let me say — that was both loud *and* fun!"

Kringle returned to where the rune stone hovered. Looking around at everyone and everything, he nodded once, then simply closed his hand over the stone.

The golden light vanished, night came back, and the snow began to fall and fall and fall around them.

CHAPTER TWENTY-FOUR

YULE,
WHEEL OF TIME

HE FIRST THING they heard was the terrible noise of battle coming back — a clashing and a clanging and a yelling and a wailing — all up and down the slopes inside the crater. The second thing was Morgo's feet slapping the ground in front of Kringle, Ithgar raised high and flashing, and the groan of his lungs as he spat out a nasty howl. "Goblins!"

In an instant, the valley floor was filled with goblins thirty feet deep around the little group.

Morgo grinned. "Outnumbered, are you, boy?"

In response, Kringle shook his staff lightly. When the Goblin King heard the little bell he had tried to steal thirteen years earlier, his eyes became huge with anger. But before he could move, before he could utter a single command, there came a tiny sound — *ping-ping-ping!* — and something struck the ice at Kringle's feet. He picked it up.

It was a rivet from the dragon's head. He held it out to Morgo. "Yours?"

"Eh?" the goblin said.

The War Dragon made a sudden mortal moan. *Oooorrrrrraaahhh!* All at once, it wobbled; the head dropped and swung suddenly from side to side, hanging by ropes and cords. With a shrieking sound, the cords raveled away, and the head plummeted to the ground with a tremendous crash.

Morgo froze to the spot, quivering like a leaf, as the War Dragon's giant body first tilted, then swayed, then buckled in two. There followed a terrific second crash, when the great iron beast drove itself down to the icy ground, splattering and scattering about in a crazy tumble of black lumber and mangled iron plates.

Snow and flames flew up. Great, sudden, white, twinkling waves of spray showered Morgo where he stood, and fire ignited the oil from the dragon's fire drums. The whole creation burst into flames with a thunderous roar.

Morgo gave out a blood-freezing yell as if he were being pulled inside out. "Grunding! *Grundinnnngggg!*"

"Not here no more!" shouted Ifrid.

The Goblin King shrieked a curse from the darkest part of his being. He rushed at Kringle with the Iron Wand.

The boy raised his staff and swung hard. When Morgo's

powerful stroke met his staff, the wand exploded into a thousand pieces that ripped across the goblins and sent them leaping away in agony.

Snegg tore suddenly at his neck for the rune pouch, crying, "Magic!"

But Nar stepped forward, dangling the pouch from his hand. "Looking for these?"

When the goblins saw that Ithgar, the runes, and Grunding were no more, they sent up a horrific cry that reached to the heavens. Morgo staggered to his knees, and the two armies of men took this as a sign to begin attacking the goblins all the more. Instantly the elves were upon the goblins, too, wielding clubs and swords and daggers, throwing ice and snowballs, driving the green creatures in a full retreat into the pit.

"Ingas!" cried Snegg, and from the darkness leaped the giant black vargul at the head of a pack of ten or more growling beasts. The varguls' jaws opened ravenously, but they were met by a sudden flurry of antlers, ripping at their heads and sending them howling. It was a fierce but short rout, and the varguls fled down into the forge for good.

Meanwhile, Kringle whirled and twirled the staff, knocking Morgo in the knees, and in the arm, and about his big green head — *thwack-thwack-thwack!* With each stroke, the tiny bell seemed to speak: *Kringle! Kringle! Kringle!*

"*Eeeee!* No, no!" cried the king, shielding his face. "Kringle shall not kill Morgo!"

"What I *can* do and what I *will* do are known to me alone!" the boy snapped, pushing the green king closer to the entrance of the pit. "The magic of the cairn and the love of the child together have defeated you, Morgo. But if there's no room for hate in our world, neither is there room for you. If the little child banished darkness, then I banish you to the earth forever —"

"Forever?" cried Morgo. "Noooo!" As the Goblin King hovered at the entrance to the pit, he uttered a horrific parting vow. "Goblins will come, Kringle!" he hissed. "Goblins will come back! This is our world, too! From the earth's black heart, I will return. Goblins will live under the earth, but we will return and battle Kringle again and again, until one time, we shall win the earth forever! Long Night we shall come. Long Night we shall return, each year more full of power than before. We will come for the children. Fear will grow. Darkness will grow. Grunding will live! When the great wheel winds down —"

"By Heaven," said Kringle, his hands white as they clutched the staff. "Let Long Night be our battleground! When the great Wheel of the Year rolls to its end, I will drive you back to earth again! Hear me, Morgo! I will do this every year! The children shall be free. If it takes forever, I'll come forever. I'll find you and I'll fight you!"

"So be it!" cried Morgo.

At that, Kringle raised his staff high and said what may have been no more than sounds to the goblins, but to Alban and the others they were words that will ring in their memories forever. "By Heaven, the angels, the sun, the moon, and stars — no goblin will ever again darken this holy night!"

Then a sudden invisible wind blew out from the holly leaves of Kringle's staff and thrust the goblins roughly into the shadowy earth. They shrieked and howled, they wailed and screeched, but the wind drove them down and down and down!

The massive dark mouth of the pit closed up behind the Goblin King. Ice oozed over the stone, and Dragon's Nest was sealed.

Silence fell over the crater.

The goblins were gone.

Everyone stared at the place where the pit's opening had been, struck silent. Even Alban and Vindalf, though they sputtered quite a bit, were speechless.

Kringle turned and there was Gussi, his large eyes looking up at the boy. The elf's face was smudged and bloody. He was breathless, but smiling.

Beyond the elves stood the children now. Their faces were dirty, but full of moonlight. The armies stood beyond them, ranged up the slopes, the great armored men, looking at one another and wondering. And Kringle knew. Octa had been right: Time *would* happen. He couldn't stop it forever.

The pirate captain made his way down the crater. So did the dark-haired, helmeted leader of the heathmen. Octa wrapped his son Bearn in his arms as if he never intended to let him go.

Then he turned to Kringle. "How did it ever come to this? Our children taken by . . . those creatures. Never again. Never."

Kringle embraced them both. Alban blessed them all one more time.

The two armies took the hundreds of children between them, bundled them, and went away to their villages and camps to fight another day. Soon only Kringle, Alban, Oliphas, the reindeer, and the elves remained.

"I don't know how you did what you did, Kringle," said Alban. "If I had a thousand years I don't know if I could understand the mystery of what has just happened here. But, my dear boy, the big and small of it is, you defeated the King of the Goblins!"

The elves cheered with all their might. "Kringle!"

The boy blushed and smiled. "Morgo will be true to his word, though. We can't ever think he won't be. He'll come back on this night every year, when the goblins are strongest. Long Night has been the goblin time forever and it will be so forever. But it is also a holy time. The time of the child's birth. That's forever, too."

Alban turned away, trying to hide his tears, but Kringle must have seen them, for he put his hand on the priest's arm. "All in all," he said, "I'd say we did well."

"At least you know *when* the goblins will come," said Gussi.

"True!" said Vindalf, slapping the twin clubs back in his belt. "And we shall be back on Long Night! Shall we not?"

Kringle laughed then. "I think we shall, my friend. But maybe not until then."

Alban frowned. "Another mystery, Kringle? What do you mean by that?"

The boy looked to the north. "Now that the goblins are gone, maybe it's time for us to leave this world, too. The magic time has ended. The world should be left for the people."

Vindalf cleared his throat. "Perhaps you're right, boy. I feel it in my bones. Maybe time does belong to the world of men now. Perhaps we *should* leave it to them."

"But what about helping people?" asked Gussi. "What about the giving? We have to give. That's what elves do!"

Kringle smiled. "Of course, Gussi. That'll never end. Hrothr said we have a choice: to give, to take, or to do nothing. The elves have always been givers, and that will always be so. In fact, the time has come for us to be about the real important business: the children. I think we'll give as we've never given before. And we'll do it all on one night."

"One night," said Torgi. "You mean . . . Long Night."

Kringle took a deep, frosty breath. "When darkness is at its longest, and the goblins come back, that's when we'll be there to brighten the darkness — with gifts!"

"Shoes?" said Nar.

"And more," said Kringle, thinking of little Mari. "Toys. So that the children can play and not be afraid." He looked at Alban. "A long time ago, some wise and wonderful kings traveled halfway around the world with gifts for a tiny baby. I think we can try to do the same."

"Yes!" cried the elves with one voice. "Yes, yes, yes!"

"Kringle," said Alban, "what about Merwen?"

The boy drew a slow breath. "I can only hope that we'll be together again someday. Maybe soon. She's not with the goblins, so she must be out there somewhere. But if she taught me anything, it's that my duty is to the children now. I know hers would be."

With that, Kringle turned to the reindeer. "And what do you think, Oliphas?"

The creature looked at Kringle, its eyes as deep and dark and gleaming as the midnight sky itself. *We will never leave you.*

Alban coughed. "If I can tell by your expression, Kringle, that Oliphas said he would come with you, then I think that makes it complete. For, although it's likely to be farther north than I really want to go, I am certainly going with you!"

Kringle laughed and hugged him as he had twice before.

All at once, Holf turned to the southern crest of the crater just as a woolly head poked up over the top. "Blendl," he said. "Right on time." With the sheep was a flock of fifty others. They made their way slowly down the crater toward the elves. A single tear came to Holf's face, and he added, "Good. All here then. Fine to go."

At that, Kringle turned north. "Friends, I see great halls and towers and kitchens and stables. Our new home has everything. It even has a name. Frostholm — 'Home of the Frost.' With Alban's help, and the elves' handiwork, I think we can make it happen."

"Sounds good," said Holf. "Like it already."

"Collect yourselves and your boots, people," said Vindalf. "Count off by twos and follow the leader. We're going on a trip!"

"That calls for a traveling song!" said Gussi. With that, the elves broke into a new song, made up just for the occasion:

"We journey to the northland! We go to find a place,
Though very-very deep-deep snows
keep flying in our face.
We'll find a frosty home that's snug
and make the little gifts
That keep good children happiest,
no buts or ands or ifs!"

Roaring and singing, the happy family of elves, with Kringle and Alban and Oliphas, the other reindeer, and the sheep, began their long journey, farther north than you or I would ever care to go, into the land of the deep snows.

PART
VII

THE SOUND OF ITS BELLS CRACKLED IN THE FROSTY AIR.

CHAPTER TWENTY-FIVE

FROSTHOLM

UNDLE CLOSER NOW; we're nearly at the end.

Wind blew on that journey north! Oh, it did. Ice hardened, and snow thickened, but everyone knew it was just the weather this time. Thanks to Kringle, the Iron Wand was destroyed, and goblin storms would never menace our world again.

Up over the ice mountains, down into the snow valleys, across vast wind-blasted plains, Kringle trekked, and his little band of voyagers trekked with him. Gussi, Torgi, Vindalf, and all the elves looked longingly at each amber-lit cabin and house and town they passed, but the lights faded soon into the darkness behind them, and the world turned blue and black and white, and still they journeyed on.

Did Kringle know where they were going? He certainly felt it was better to make everyone think he did. Each night as the little troop rested, he climbed up on something high and made a show of scanning the horizon. Giving a big nod, he said, "All right, then. We're doing fine. Getting closer!"

Closer to what? He didn't say.

"Eh, Kringle," asked Alban on their tenth morning of heavy snow, "I suppose you've imagined it in one of your visions, but will we actually know this Frostholm when we see it? I mean, no one has ever been this far north, you know, and certainly not you, no matter how far you've traveled since we were last together. Besides, who would live in this cold? It's really not very likely that we'll find anything at all."

"Just what I'm hoping for," the boy said with a smile.

"Thank you," muttered Alban. "That really clears things up!"

After the first month, the elves were weary, but they didn't complain. They could tell in Kringle's eyes that he would know the place when he saw it, and they would not question him before.

Then one gray morning, no less than six snowy weeks after what the elves had come to call the Great Goblin Defeat, the reindeer pulled the sledge up a rise in the land and stopped. Far in the distance were two giant crags of ice that thrust up from the ground like twin signal towers.

"Oliphas . . . ," was all that Kringle said. The great reindeer and his fellows pulled the sledge straight to the towers. Kringle hopped out and walked a short way, stood between the towers, and looked into the distance. All the others stayed back, muttering to themselves.

"Is this it?" he whispered. He tilted his head, clamped his eyes shut for an instant, and found himself smiling. Then he knew.

"Everyone, we're home!"

Home! When Alban, the elves, the sheep, and the reindeer rushed to him, they found nothing there. And by *nothing*, I mean to say that what Kringle was looking at was not very much at all. Beyond the twin towers of ice lay a ring of ice hills forming a massive valley of ice scooped gently out of the frozen earth. Thousands of trees were felled from the center of the valley outward as if, in fact, some great thing had dropped there from heaven and blasted the earth out every which way.

"Lumber," said Vindalf.

"Lumber, indeed," said Kringle. "And there's where we'll build." He pointed toward the center of the valley. Of the handful of trees still standing among the fallen was a single giant fir. It was two hundred feet tall if it was a foot.

"Home, is it?" Alban asked.

Kringle smiled. "It will be. What do you think?"

"What do I think? I think there's a lot of ice down there, and I'm cold."

Kringle laughed. "I mean your drawings. Do you think you could help us build a new home for ourselves?"

Alban frowned down into the valley. "Really? A home? And I could draw it? Hmm. Well, then, hmm. Really, you know . . . I rather think so!"

"We're agreed then," Kringle said.

Taking his blossoming staff, he strode between the ice towers in snow up to his knees and laughed all the while. "Ho, ho! This is it! Frostholm, we've found you!" He pushed his way through the drifts and led the elves and reindeer and sheep one by one between the towers.

It took them quite some time to work their way down to the valley floor, but right away Oliphas and his herd and Holf's sheep began to move the fallen trees and rocks and the blocks of ice that covered the valley. Together, they formed a wall five miles long that circled the valley floor. I say "circled," but the wall was not circular in any way. One of Kringle's first requests was that only trees that had been felled by time or storm could be used in the building of Frostholm. All others should be preserved to grow as they would. This is why the great wall of Frostholm loops inside or outside each and every standing tree in the valley.

And what a wall! It was ten feet thick and thirty feet high from base to rampart. Even before the wall was quite finished, as huge a mansion as man or woman or elf or beast had ever seen began to rise up inside it. And not only a mansion. Day by day, week by week, month by month (it wasn't built in a day, you know!), Frostholm itself grew.

Pillars, columns, arches, and bridges were hewn and carved out of timber and stone and ice. Walls and ceilings, vaults and cellars went up and down the whole length and width of the city. Frostholm rose up and out, a frozen fortress, a city of elves, a castle of ice, a refuge, a workshop, a home at the very tip of the world.

The mansion, or main house, was like the great hall in Elvenwald, which the elves described to Alban in every detail. Only here it was ten times larger. Two tall fir trees flanked the front door.

"We need the space," said Kringle. "We'll be making lots and lots of toys. And we'll do it all year long."

The elves cheered. "Toys!"

So the big hall went up. And up and up! It had five vast levels, with wide, open staircases looping from one to the next, all the way to the top. And the most remarkable thing was that the hall grew around the giant tree that Kringle had first seen from the valley's crest. *Grew around the tree!* Its branches spread seventy feet wide at the base. A gallery on each level of the hall looked out over the tree, whose fragrance filled the rooms day and night. The uppermost level of the house was divided into a hundred little rooms, each with a grand view. These became the living and sleeping quarters for Kringle, Alban, and the elves.

Each of the other four levels was divided into three giant workshops connected to one another by large archways. In one of the workshops on the first level the elves built an iron-works, including a furnace, and a smithy. The furnace kept all five levels warm and snug the whole year round. Of course, it backed upon the enormous kitchen and fed the house's ten large ovens and fifty hearths.

At the very summit of the house, Kringle built himself a cupola, which allowed him a complete view of everything in Frostholm, the valley beyond, and the sky above, so that he could track the movement of the sun, moon, and stars. He called his special room, quite plainly, "the Top."

The moment the hall was finished, the sheep and reindeer stables were quickly begun. These comprised four long, low buildings, with twenty spacious stalls each, two on one side of the main house and two on the other.

Alban told everyone how the Romans had used pipes to heat buildings, so hot water was piped from the furnace up to each floor of the main house and into each of the four stable wings.

Then the outbuildings began. There were any number of these. A hall for indoor sports was first to be built. Then a theater, a music hall, a library, a row of shops (including a bakery), and a second row of shops (including a second bakery) — all of these were built faster than you can imagine. Streets and alleyways went down between these buildings, and streetlights went up, then areas for the parking of carts and bordered paths for the sheep to travel.

Last but not least, a stone chapel was erected on a little rise near the main house. This was Alban's idea. It had a steeply peaked roof and an altar raised above the floor at one end, with rows of benches facing it. The chapel looked east, because, Alban said, that is where the child was born.

This pleasant stone house was a place for everyone to celebrate (in the oldest meaning of that word) and for Alban a place to teach, which is what he decided he liked to do best. It gave a wonderful warm sound to any singing that was done inside its walls, and you can be sure that when the elves were in there (which was often), there was quite a lot of singing.

"So," said Kringle, when the first phase of the building was nearing completion. "I think we've done well, after all."

Alban looked over the newborn city. "Happy are they who dwell in this place, Kringle."

As winter neared, the boy spent more nights in the Top, watching the stars and moon move. On these occasions, he began the next morning by plunging his head out the window and running his staff along the eaves. The musical clatter of icicles down the sides of the house and onto the crusted snow below was a signal to the elves that the day had begun.

The elves!

They chattered from the moment they woke and didn't stop until their work was done, which was often late into the night.

Over the first few months, some elves that had rushed off from the fire at Elvenwald made their way to Frostholm. The first group was led by Plifi and his wife, Unga, who brought with them, if you can believe it, twenty-two more sheep, each one a fat bundle of ice-covered wool. Kringle welcomed them heartily, and the entire tribe of eighteen elves set right to work with their fellows.

"How ever did you find us?" asked Torgi.

"A little bird kept showing us the way," said Unga. "Whenever we got lost, it was there to guide us."

Everyone marveled at this — Kringle most of all. His thoughts turned again to Merwen, although truly she had never been far from his mind. The last he had heard was that she was moving north to see him, but that was nearly a year ago now. There had been no word since.

A little while after those elves arrived, others from the eastern shire woods found the valley. They had been pushed out by the constant fighting of warriors of every description and origin. They, too, were led by a sparrow, and eagerly joined their friends at the workshop tables, happy to have found a home once again.

One evening not long after that, when the nights were growing longer still, Elni and Hensa burst into the great hall at second dessert, all a-twitter. Someone had been seen from the ice towers.

"Not an elf," said Hensa.

"And certainly not a goblin!" added Elni.

Kringle shared a quizzical look with Alban. "I think we'd better have a look."

"I think so, too!"

Together, they rode on Oliphas and Seraban to the towers. There they could see, struggling through the snow, a cloaked figure. It wandered back and forth in the snow, as if it were searching for something but not quite knowing where it was.

All at once, Kringle's heart seemed to burst inside of him. No. It couldn't be. It was impossible.

Was it?

It wasn't her. It couldn't be her.

Was it her?

He moved closer.

"Merwen?" he whispered. He rode out beyond the towers. "Merwen? Merwen . . . Merwen!"

It was her!

He leaped off Oliphas and ran to her, his arms open wide. "Merwen —"

"Kringle!" she cried.

He swept his arms around her tighter than he had ever held anyone in his life. Merwen, dear Merwen — older, more frail, smaller than she had ever seemed, and yet it was her, her face, her arms grasping at him, clutching him, embracing him as if to never let him go!

"It's been forever!" she wept into his cloak. And indeed it had been! When a little cry came out of her ragged robes, she pulled away. "Ah, yes, then, Kringle, there's . . . *her*, too."

Kringle blinked. "Her?"

Unslinging a large bundle from under her robe, she knelt in the snow and uncovered a small child — the tiniest thing!

"Mari!" cried Kringle, weeping with joy at the sight. "Mari!"

It was Mari. She was still small, though now nearly four winters old, her fair hair golder than ever and her beaming eyes as blue as the morning sky. Dozens of elves rushed out (they had followed Kringle and Alban; of course, they had!) and crowded around the little child. Not the least of them was Retta, the old elf who had first taken care of Mari in Elvenwald so very long ago. The elves swept the little girl up through the towers and cheered and wept and sang all the way back to the main house, where they settled Mari and Merwen before the giant hearth near the tree. And while some asked a thousand questions (Were the goblins back? No. Did you see any Romans? They're all gone now. Are there wars? Yes. Are you hungry? Famished! And more like this . . .), others rushed in with platters of food and armfuls of blankets. Vindalf and Holf and Retta fawned over Mari and fed her and gave her toys, and she played with all of them simultaneously while stuffing her mouth dangerously full of elf cakes. All this happened before you could blink an eye, and you couldn't have stopped it if you'd wanted to!

Later, by the still-blazing fire and over their second dinner in as many hours, Kringle told Merwen about everything that had happened. She cried and hugged him at each new part of the story.

"Kringle," she said. "I should have known when that bird jangled that bell so long ago that it wasn't the last story to be told about you! Kringle and the elves. Kringle and the goblins. Kringle and the pirates. Kringle and the sledge. Kringle and the reindeer! I'm glad to have found you before any more stories came about and I wasn't in them!"

"You taught me the first lesson of all," he said quietly. "If you care for the children, you care for everyone."

Merwen laughed and wept at once. "It worked for you!"

Alban, who had been waiting patiently through all of this, finally touched her on the arm. "Merwen, please," he said, "tell me about the staff. How did you come by it?"

She looked over at her old fire stick, standing against the front door of the hall, blooming as gaily as ever. "I can't explain the blossoms, sir. But in my younger days, I nursed an old man on his deathbed. Outside his window stood a big old tree. He loved to watch it gather with birds and to listen to the wind sing in its branches. He died one winter's morn. That's all I know, sir. My old fire stick is a branch that fell from that tree."

Alban rose, as perplexed as ever. "I suppose we shall never know. But, tell me, what sort of birds used to visit the tree?"

"Why, plain old sparrows, sir!"

"Ah . . ."

Everyone was quiet with their thoughts for a while. Finally, Merwen spoke to them in hushed tones about the horror of her and Mari's time with the goblins, but it was over now, she said, and the goblins had not been seen for nearly a year.

"Nearly a year," said Kringle, rising from the hearth fire. "Which means they will soon be back. We have so much to do."

So Merwen joined him, helped him, and never once left his side from that day forward. She was back, and Kringle was happy. And every day, they made more toys.

Tap-tap! Squeak-squeak! Alban likened the sound to that made by Christ's father when he fashioned little toys for the baby to play with.

"I like that story," said Gussi. "Tell it again!"

Alban did tell it many times, in the workshop and in the chapel, and the elves could never get enough of it.

"I like the king part," said Vindalf. "And the camels!"

"Like the shepherds!" added Holf. "Think there might have been one named Holf. Don't mind that at all."

When the nights began to get very long, Kringle, Alban, and Merwen went out into the valley's forest and came back with green pine boughs to brighten the house. A giant wreath was hung on the massive door of the hall, while a garland of holly was looped around inside. It was jeweled with bright red berries like the ever-blooming holly on Kringle's staff. Clusters of pine trees stood plump and fat and full of snow outside the hall.

The giant fir tree that stood at the end of the main room was decorated then with candles and bells and silver garlands and red and gold glass balls. And the elves sang all the time around it, odd little elf carols that added a kind of sparkle to Alban's heavy poems, for all elf songs are happy ones. Their tunes are simple, rising, falling, rising again, then finally drifting into silence. But when a song ended, if anyone had given the slightest hint, the elves would start it up again, more rousing than before.

Frostholm! Oh, it was a merry place from its first day on. It is a merry place still!

CHAPTER TWENTY-SIX

O HOLY NIGHT!

UT THE COLD deepened as it always does, winter approached, and Kringle thought and planned. He drew maps and charts and made up lists, penning in the names of the children he knew from the visions he had (he remembered all of their faces, too), and the names and locations of every town and city and country. He made maps of the goblin world, too. It would soon be time for him to go back against them, for the holy night approached.

What a solemn, tender place Frostholm became as that night drew near. The days grew short, the nights long. The sun barely peeked over the horizon. And yet the elves took on a glow.

"The special night is coming!" you heard in the streets and snow-trodden alleys, in the library, the bakeries, and in the market shops.

"The baby comes again!" was murmured in the bustling stable stalls. "Time for the songs!"

In the deep of night, Kringle would often leave his cupola in the main house and spend long hours in the stables with Oliphas and Seraban. He could hear wonderful things in their silent words — as few as they were — and knew his parents were with him often.

"Can I really do this thing?" he asked them one night.

"Yes," came the voice of his mother.

"You are Kringle," said his father.

"Yes," he said with a brief but firm nod of his head.

Kringle looked constantly at the sky, checking the day, the hour, against his calculations until late one bitter afternoon, after the sun had been absent from the sky for weeks, he flung open the door of the chapel and strode in. "Alban. Alban. The night the Lord was born . . ."

"One week. Seven nights away," said the priest.

Kringle nodded gently. "I knew it. Long Night is near."

From that moment on, the elves redoubled their work. And the collecting and labeling of gifts began. Some elves hustled among the tables and darted along the walls, checking the great long lists they had made up from their old red book of boot owners. They rechecked their names against Kringle's list. Poor Gussi had a time keeping the two up to date. So many more names had to be added by the elves who had come from different parts of the country.

Some workers collected bundles of finished toys and stacked them in huge piles inside the hall door. Others' arms were piled high with boxes and bags or draped with golden and purple and green ribbons, and all of them singing old elvish songs or making up new elvish songs — some five or six tunes going on at once! — and not one of the elves ever happier than at that very moment.

Oh, it was a harmonious factory! It was a hall of joy!

"Four days now," said Kringle early one morning when he came down to find the workshops still bustling from the night before. He was dressed in his dark berry-brown cloak trimmed with even more fleece now, along with twin rows of tiny bells that jangled and plinked as he paced back and forth between the busy tables.

"We know," said Gussi, looking up from a wagon and spinning its little wheels. "It was five days yesterday."

"But will there be enough toys?" he asked.

Amid the tapping of tiny hammers, Vindalf, stern captain of the elves, gave the happy answer: "Always enough, Just Sir Kringle!"

The boy seemed to grow an inch or two or three as he strode among the tables, greeting every elf by name. "Very good, Neol, excellent, Penda."

Then one night, just after supper, Kringle left the hall

and set his eyes to the twin ice towers in the south. He knew.

Alban and Merwen joined him. Together they stood in front of the main hall looking out at the black world.

"The goblins are gathering," said Alban. "They're moving in the tunnels. Even I can feel it."

"I can feel it, too," added Merwen, rubbing her hands. "Kringle, I'm afraid."

"Ho, ho, yes! But Morgo is so much weaker now!" growled Vindalf, who had come out, too. "I think even I could take him. Old One-and-a-Half-Cabbage-Ears! Shall I this year, Kringle? Shall I thump him a good one or two and send him burrowing into his stinky hole again?" Vindalf was waving his arms in a fiery manner now. "Oooh, shall I do it?"

Kringle chuckled. "Thank you, Vin," he said. "But no. We have the only weapon we'll need." He held up Hrothr's rune stone. "Besides, elvish arms and hands aren't really made for fighting, you know —"

"Whose are?" asked Merwen.

Kringle looked at her and bowed his head. "None," he said finally. "Maybe soon, everyone will know that."

There was a quiet moment when he looked around and saw all the elves behind him. In every face he saw a little bit of Hrothr. And a bit of the child's face, too.

"So, are we ready?" he asked.

"We're ready!" said Torgi.

Oh, what happened then!

You've heard how innumerable fishes and heaps of bread were collected after a crowd had fed on just five loaves and two fishes? Or maybe you recall the bottomless magic bag? The poor man pulls more and more coins from it until he has a mountain of silver that could not possibly fit in that bag?

Imagine then how legions of elves, one after another — even laughing little Nar — emptied the bulging workshop and filled the sledge. Alban and Merwen stood back as the elves formed a line from the open door of the hall right to the door of the sledge — yes, Kringle put a door on it to keep the sides as high as possible — heaving packages wrapped in bright paper from one to another, all the way down the short path from the hall to the sledge, in a busy garland of chirping workers.

"Hold on, hold on . . . all right, then, hurry again!" Gussi said, standing on the sledge's vast seat, checking things off in the ever-bigger red book. One after another, the packages came. One after another, they found a home in Kringle's sledge. That old pirate boat — its mast and sail gone to make room for more gifts — was loaded in a twinkling, crammed from hull to stem to stern with the entire contents of the workshop. And everything fit! Everything found a place!

When the sledge was full and ready, Gussi attached two stout woolen loops to the sledge with Kringle looking on.

"Is this what you wanted?" asked the elf, standing back.

Kringle propped his staff upright next to the seat, its holly-blossomed head sticking up like a prickly wreath. He shook it. It was firm, but the bell jingled, too. "Perfect," he said. "Well done."

Then he marched right up to the main hall, poked his head in, and called out to the high desk in the corner that was draped with a garland of red-berried holly sprigs.

"Alban! Stop that writing, and come bless our journey —"

At that moment, a fly came whizzing down from the molding at the ceiling, crossed the room over the last few workers' heads, and circling, circling, settled down into the margin of the page, as close to you this moment as it was right then to me.

CHAPTER TWENTY-SEVEN

THE WINTER GIVER

OMING, KRINGLE!"

I'm sure you've guessed it after all, long before I hopped down from that desk and hustled past the elves' tables and out to Kringle, leaving the work I had been writing — this very work you are reading now!

Parturis settled right there on that page, his tiny shape barely making a shadow in the candlelight: *zzzt-zzzt!*

"Yes, yes!" I rushed past the tables where some elves were just finishing up their last bits of work. "Now, hurry along with that," I said. "Kringle doesn't have all night, you know!"

This brought a round of chuckles from the elves, because, of course, it was a little joke of mine. They jumped up after me, and we all hurried outside to where Oliphas and his eleven fellows were hitched to the sledge, stamping and stomping and awaiting the final packages.

"Alban," said Kringle, turning slowly, nodding to the out-rageously packed sledge. "Not bad, eh? Over ten thousand gifts."

"And all for the children," said Merwen.

Kringle smiled. "I can see each of their faces, every one a little light in the darkness."

"Indeed!" said Vindalf. "Look at it, Brother Alban. More gifts than we had all thought possible! And still not up to capacity. I call that good work well done and a very good first year!"

"An excellent first year," I said. Then I closed my eyes and uttered a prayer. "Dear Lord, watch over Kringle's danger-ous journey as you did the kings' journey so long ago. Bless all the children of the world and give them peace and joy in their hearts and homes, wherever they may be. Free the world from the goblin menace once more!"

I blessed the sledge and Oliphas and his fellows one by one, and the three elves that were traveling with them and all the gifts, and Kringle most of all.

"May God go with you every inch of the way."

"Thank you," he said, towering over me by several inches now. He bowed his head firmly, then wrapped me in his arms in a hug he must have learned from the polar bears that sometimes haunt our valley.

"Yes, yes, well, well," I mumbled. "Off you go."

One thing I will tell you is that I never felt so completely safe as I did when Kringle was near. If it's not too strong a thing to say, I rather imagine the friends of the Lord must have felt like this when they were near him. That is the effect Kringle had on people — still has on people. Wherever he was, everyone around him knew that they were safe and sound and just where they should be. He was, in his own way, the center of a world.

I won't use the word here that is so often used when talking of a very *good* person. You know it. It begins with the letter S, or in the rune language **Ϩ**. For all my belief — and it grows stronger all the time — I won't say it. Kringle is a friend of the world and of its children, and that is quite enough to say. Others will take the story forward when I have done. And I suppose I'll be done pretty soon.

But soft. Here comes a sound from out on the snow.

"Ready now!" yelled Gussi, squeezing the last gift into the sledge and plopping himself between Vindalf and Torgi. Kringle took the reins just behind the eagle's prow. He touched them lightly. At once, Oliphas and his fellows drew the sledge easily down and away to the center of the valley, to where a track of ice had been smoothed and readied.

And that is when something so very remarkable happened that none of us could speak. For out of the wind, from the black depths of the sky, came the tiny sparrow that began this story, the poor lost soul who was never lost at all. It came with the speed and lightness and beauty of an angel from heaven. It flitted by Kringle's staff, and the tip of its wing struck the bell hanging there.

Kringle!

As we all watched dumbfounded, it soared up to the top of the Top and sat on its peak. Kringle's eyes did not leave the little bird for an instant.

"The sparrow has found a home," I whispered.

It was amazing! It was astonishing! It was impossible! And yet, I must believe it happened, for I saw it. It happened that first year, and has happened every year since. You must believe it, too, or I've not told the story right.

Kringle raised his blossoming staff, shook its bell again and again, and sang out to Oliphas, "Go, friend. Fly up into the world! Away, away!"

In that simple command was everything he needed to say, for away they went. The sledge jerked forward, jangling the bells on the harness that Penda and Horsa had draped on the reindeer. The sound of its bells crackled in the frosty air.

The sledge roared along the surface of the snow now, its contents heaped neatly and snugly, a city of gifts towering over Kringle's head. It whooshed along at amazing speed, its twin runners sliding and jumping over the ice as Oliphas and his fellow reindeer galloped faster, faster, until at once they leaped into the frosty sky.

"We're up!" shouted Gussi, waving down to the others below. His face was beaming. Torgi, next to him, loved it, too, above all things. Vindalf held on for dear life, and yet he was laughing, too.

Oh, how that sledge flew!

Whoosh-whoosh! Kringle swooped it around the chapel, laughing; he circled the main hall, with all of the elves on its front lawn waving and cheering, then weaved around our heads, as you might imagine him doing over *your* heads, coiling around and around, until he soared up and away over the ice mountains, trailing a vast ribbon of twinkling frost behind him.

Then he was gone. We stood staring, all of us, for a long moment, and I could just imagine every second of his journey.

Whoosh! Whooooosh!

The sledge would fly high over the world, dipping and rising on the whirling winds, when suddenly Kringle, Vindalf, Torgi, and Gussi, scanning the countryside below, would see something moving on the ground that was not quite right. The hair on the back of Kringle's neck would stand on end, and he would know.

"Goblins!"

"Aye, there they are," said Vindalf, clutching his clubs. "A dark darker than darkness!"

Oliphas understood it, too, and the gift-laden sledge swooped down through the sky and landed. Kringle jumped into deep snow, raising his hand to the elves to stay on board. He slid his staff from its support and moved ahead carefully. Soon he heard a rustling and a crackling, and the smell came, and there was Morgo, leaping out from the darkness, hissing and spitting with the vilest curses you ever heard. He was at the head of a great snake of goblins rushing through the night toward a tiny village.

"Kringle! Kringle! Yes, boy! It is Long Night. We have come again!"

Snegg and Lud came crawling out of the darkness, too, wielding frightful weapons. They were armored hideously and helmeted with great spiked masks.

"Grunding rises once more!" they chanted. "We steal the children. Their fear makes him grow —"

"Darkness will never advance on this holy night!" said Kringle, holding up the rune stone. "On this Long Night, joy will vanquish fear. All that is good and holy commands you down below!"

The goblins howled and shrieked, but when Kringle spun the stone and let it fall, it began to glow and slowed itself in the air until it went still. And the goblins froze where they stood. Everything everywhere halted across the world, and wherever the goblin tunnels opened out, in the frozen north, in the east, west, and south, the creatures were stopped in their tracks. The whole world stopped in its tracks.

"And now," said Gussi, looking fearfully at the frozen goblins, but warm in the glow that came from Kringle himself, "to the real important business?"

"The children," said Kringle.

"Aye!" said Vindalf. "Every last one of them!"

At once, Oliphas and the reindeer flew them high across the countryside.

"A house," Kringle would say. "I know that one. Little Durin and Elda and Arthr live there. Oliphas —"

No sooner had he said the reindeer's name than the whole herd would swing down to the house and light on the roof, and Kringle would leap from the sledge. If there was a chimney, he'd slide down and leave a toy at the foot of the bed, in a shoe, or sitting on a table. Once he left the gifts behind, he would be back in the sledge in a moment.

If there was a door and only a door, or a window, Kringle used them, but he much preferred unusual entrances, like stovepipes and chimneys and cellars. Once, he slid into a house sideways through the eaves. "It's more fun that way!" he told me.

And he had fun the whole long night through.

At last all the gifts were given, and he returned to Morgo, still frozen in rage in the dark valley where Kringle had found him. Closing his palm around the rune stone, he charged at

Morgo with his staff raised, crying, "To earth, you fiend, your Long Night is over! The child of light has come!"

The goblins shrieked and wailed, but had to obey the word and vow of Kringle. Morgo uttered the same earth-ringing promise to return as he had the first time, and all the goblins were thrown back into their tunnels by the rushing wind from Kringle's staff. He thrust them, toppled them, crammed them, *blew* them back into the earth. The varguls whimpered and cowered, their tails between their legs, their snouts low, their eyes downcast, but they were driven down, too.

The goblins were gone once more.

That is how it would happen, how it did happen, and how it happens still.

"Haven't seen any cabbage ears now these many long years," said Holf, squinting up at the sledge until it became so small, he couldn't see it anymore.

The jangling bells echoed for a moment across the sky. Then they, too, faded into the frosty air.

"Nor have I," I said. "Not a lobe, not a point, not a single one."

Nor, I guess, have any of you!

Which means only one thing.

That Kringle has been doing his job.

And now, after all these years, these *very* long years, I have finally done mine.

But, if you please, a solemn moment.

Kringle, you know, has never stopped. He is filled with the spirit, the love, and the wonder of that baby born so long ago on that dark night in Bethlehem. And each year when the time comes for us to remember that mysterious and glorious moment, and the great wheel of time winds down to the end of its year — slowing, slowing, slowing to the point of stopping — and the dead of winter is on us, and darkness comes down like a heavy dome of lead, well, then, Kringle's happy adventure happens again.

Wonder comes smiling to our storm-cursed world:
Storm stops, night stops, darkness takes flight!

And it keeps on happening! Of all things, that is the one we can count on, you and I, when everything else changes or ages or hurts a little more in the morning.

Time *does* happen, for the rest of us, though slower here that anywhere else, I think. Being near Kringle has made all the difference in that.

But through it all, he is there, nearly ageless, fit and joyful and jolly and solemn and happy and proud and wise and kind.

Kringle is the child who *knew*.

And that is why I have stayed.

Over the many years that have passed since those first nights, wiser minds than yours or mine have moved the date of the baby's birth, a night here, a night there. But Kringle's power, like that of the child of Bethlehem, is not affected by such things. The miracle of Yule happens every winter as it has for centuries and centuries notwithstanding.

So then, time's up.

Off you go, now, all of you, to bed. Shoo!

Dream, if you like, of the time when goblins roamed the earth, winter was bleak, frost was cruel, and the earth as hard as iron. Dream, too, of a child who was born in a storm and fought the goblins so that now you can be free.

Dream, if you like, of the sound of a bell jingling — *kringling!* — in the night, for it is mainly in dreams that you might hear that sound.

For me, I lay down my pen now and say no more about the boy. Boy? Oh, yes. Though he is quite a man now, bearded and cloaked, he'll always possess the wonder of a child.

For that is the mystery of Kringle.

There then. I'm done. Good night.

I F THERE WERE not so many authors and sources and people to acknowledge and thank for their help in creating this book, I would almost hesitate to speak at all, for the real inspiration here (and ultimately blame) is profoundly personal and, like all innermost impulses, neither public nor pulled down from any shelf. *Kringle* comes from far away and deep inside and is the product of my own half-century of Christmases, winters, and longing.

And yet . . . there are some things I feel I should say. After decades of taking the magical and miraculous elements of the Winter Gift Giver's story for granted — the flying reindeer, the children-inspired mission, the journey across the world in a single night, the Nativity, the elves! — I was suddenly startled to find them shaping themselves into nothing less than an epic fantasy. Why this happened, I can't say, but these elements immediately began to intertwine in new and potent ways, like the strange intricacies of an Anglo-Saxon coiling pattern. The more I imagined, the more I realized I didn't know, and the more I felt impelled to restore the central figure in this story from the commercial character he has become to the mythic and cosmic hero he is.

I have always felt that an uncrossable chasm exists between the fourth-century bishop known as St. Nicholas of Bari, about whom we know so very little, and the legendary figure of the Gift Giver; so Nicholas's story was set aside and played no part in my reimagining. I wanted instead to trace backward from the modern character to a more fully imagined source, much in the way one reconstructs an ancient civilization from the shards of its remains. By doing so, I hoped to breathe new life into the mystery. I quickly found that this became a very personal mission.

Of all the dozens of names by which this figure is called around the world (Father Christmas, Sinterklass, Grandfather Frost, Pere Noel, and Father Star, or even the stranger Belznickle, Mikulas, and Julemand), "Kringle" was the one that would sustain the history I knew was there to be discovered. The name whispered itself to me, as all great characters' names do — *Kringle!*

There were other voices, too. Elves have always played a part in this story. There is a tremendous amount of literature regarding elves, all of it fascinating, from *The Saga of the Volsungs* to *The Lord of the Rings*. It was a particular delight for me to align the Grimm Brothers' notion of shoe-mending elves with Kringle's assistants. Delving into their story, however, I began to hear, and to smell, goblins afoot. Traditionally earth dwellers and nighttime raiders, goblins are as old as history, and scurry about in countless legends as the enemies of elves, so they became part of this story, too.

From the first moment of digging away at these elements to find the story of Kringle, I "discovered" that it took place against the very real end of the Roman occupation of Britain around the year 410 A.D.

The abandonment of the Roman legions, the existence of invaders, as well as the presence of priests, hermits, and missionaries sent from Rome is well documented. My reading included *The Age of Bede* edited by J. F. Webb, Eleanor Duckett's *The Wandering Saints of the Early Middle Ages*, and Henry Mayr-Harting's *The Coming of Christianity to Anglo-Saxon England*. Recent research may have shed doubt on some of the conclusions of works of a certain age (as Leslie Alcock graciously allows in his classic *Arthur's Britain*), but as springboards to the imagination, they were invaluable.

In Bede's *A History of the English Church and People*, readers will find the famous sparrow story, in which a bird flits unknowingly through a lighted house in the midst of a night storm, a symbol of the soul's brief time in this world: oblivion before, a startling moment of consciousness, and oblivion after. The stark beauty and profundity of this tale are at the heart of the inspiration for this book.

My inclusion of "pirates" is also based on fact. Saxons were by many accounts raiding the British coast as early as the fourth century. I have, however, taken Brother Alban's "a little to the left" literally, and given the pirates routine access to the western coast of the island. In reality, the southeastern coast of England is commonly referred to as "the Saxon Shore."

The geography of *Kringle* is very roughly that of northwest England, mostly south and then north (and finally *very* north) of Hadrian's Wall, though I have invented a handful of basalt mountains at the western end of the island near Solway Firth. Peter Hunter Blair's succinct and readable *Roman Britain and Early England, 55 B.C.–A.D. 871* is an excellent source for information on the wall as well as on just about every aspect of the late-Roman period. Regarding the exact location of the Fires of the North, I offer here my deepest apologies to Scotland.

For the general texture of the time and the soul of its people, I owe a debt to *The Earliest English Poems* by Michael Alexander, which I first read in college and have kept by me for the last thirty-odd years. It is from his translation of "The Ruin" that the title of Chapter Three is taken. He is also author of a superb version of *Beowulf.* Regarding the latter poem, it was Seamus Heaney's translation that most drove me into the dark past. To the eye and (in its audio version) to the ear, his *Beowulf* is as stirring as it must have seemed to its original Old English hearers.

Kevin Crossley-Holland's handy anthology *The Anglo Saxon World* is a solid overview of texts. Among its many felicities are the so-called "Advent Lyrics," number II of which was the initial (though now very distant) inspiration for Alban's nativity song.

True runic scholars will probably find themselves put off by my liberal interpretation of the power inherent in the "little gray stones." Nevertheless, with its interlocking angles, the rune Jera is considered to represent the cyclical aspect of nature, moving time, the solar year, and the great wheel. It was for me a short step to bind its magic to the magic of time itself.

Finally, bringing all my reading back home, as it were, I wanted to tell Kringle's tale in a way that would honor the classic stories I grew up with, specifically *The Wind in the Willows* and *A Christmas Carol*, to which I thank my mother and father respectively for exposing me.

Acknowledgment and gratitude must go to my wonderful editors, Beth Dunfey and Shannon Penney, for their enthusiasm, good nature, intelligence, and critical guidance throughout the writing of *Kringle*; in that, they made an exacting schedule a writer's delight. About Craig Walker there is no afterword long enough to describe the inspiration he provides with a look and a laugh and a phrase. Without his constant spirit in these pages, *Kringle* would have been a wholly different and, for me, not nearly as satisfying work.

To my agent, George Nicholson, who has never flagged in his confidence and support of me, and who has urged me since the beginning to write something big, I say, with affection: here.

Finally, I cannot leave this book without thanking my wife, Dolores; I share with her all the devotion and love I have for our two daughters, to whom this work is dedicated.